Alternative Theologies

Parables for a Modern World

Alternative Theologies

Parables for a Modern World

Edited by
Phyllis Irene Radford and Bob Brown

Cover Design
Sara Codair

Published by

B Cubed Press
Kiona, WA

Copyright

Editors' Introduction

We did not know what to expect when we put out the call for this volume. We knew we had ground rules. Hate was not welcome. Christians are not evil. The stories we received made any such rules un-needed.

We found ourselves taken on a journey of beliefs and ideals that truly restored our appreciation of what it is to believe. This volume is filled with the personal love many of these writers feel for their faith, and at times, the anger they feel for those who would corrupt those tenants of their faith.

In all, we've never seen such an uplifting set of work. We wanted to change the title to Chicken Soup for the Atheist soul. However you believe, whomever you revere, you will find a defense of yourself in this volume.

There is, of course, an alternative. If you are embedded in the concept of religion as a means of suppressing, then, you might find the book slightly disturbing. No quarter is given to those who would suppress the tender souls of those who find comfort in faith, or only give credence to the faith of greed, pain, absolute control, or as a shield for the abuse of children.

We invite you to sit back, read, and contemplate, and maybe let our writers inspire you to find your own path and figure out what *you* believe, then carry forward living your faith, be it in God, Man, or Yourself.

Phyllis Irene Radford and Bob Brown
Editors, B Cubed Press

Dedication and Acknowledgements

First of all let us thank our proofreader, Ben Howels and our E-Book formatter, Vonda N. McIntyre. They make the words these writers wrote look good. And looking good is important, because a share of the book's sales goes to the ACLU of Washington.

And to all of the writers who trusted us with these stories. The level of trust is humbling and we hope that this work does justice not only to their individual works, but to their collective efforts as presented in this volume.

And last, with respect and admiration to my Uncle Jim Featherston and Francis Mays. Two people I knew and loved, both of whom preached the gospel to me as a youth. Each in their own way, and I can say if all of the persons of faith in the world put the tender and caring side of their faith forward as these two did, the world would be a better place. They left a legacy of respect and that is a testament to their lives.

Table of Contents

Foreword

Jim Wright

Theology.

Now, there's a topic for you.

The legendary writer Robert Heinlein once said, "One man's theology is another man's belly laugh." In 20 years of military service, much of it spent in the so-called Holy Land, and in the many years since that I've been writing professionally about politics and religion (and really, it's often difficult to tell the two apart), I've found Heinlein's observation to be particularly pithy.

One man's religion is another man's belly laugh.

And truthfully, how could it be any different?

Those things about religion that some of us find so utterly ridiculous, others often take with deadly seriousness. And vice versa. Wars have been fought over such disagreements, over mirth at religion's expense. And nowadays any conversation on social media regarding theology has to be moderated with an iron fist or it quickly dissolves into holy war.

But, it seems to me that the problem, at least in large part, is that "theology"—that is: the study of the nature of God and religious belief—describes the impossible.

By definition, mere human minds can never know the nature of any god. And attempting to quantify belief, well, you'd likely be more successful getting Twitter to agree on a single definition of "sandwich". Or God, for that matter.

Thus, theology by its very nature can never answer any of the questions asked of it, only nibble a bit around the edges.

Think about it. Religion often describes its deity as omniscient and omnipotent. All knowing. All powerful.

Perfect. Immortal. Many may regard this supposed god as worthy of worship and heap upon it accolades and hosannas in hopes of a boon or in fear of its wrath. Others might regard such a being the way a lab rat regards the scientist in charge of their maze, thanks for the food-pellet, Poindexter, but I'm going over the wall at the first opportunity. Who's right? I certainly don't know. But I have to wonder: what would *that* creature, that god, be like? By definition, the god of most religions isn't limited to the few paltry dimensions of human perception. No, *that* God simultaneously occupies the past, the present, and the future all at once, across the unimaginable vastness of space and time. He (for God is almost always male is he not and why? What need has God of crude biological sex? What does he *do* with it?) is the creator of suns and planets, light, gravity, time, and the very forces that bind atoms together or tear them apart in nuclear fire. He holds the power to make life itself from lifeless dirt (again, He makes life from nothing, why would such a being be a *He*? But, again, I digress).

Now, imagine that. Imagine *that* consciousness, *that* awareness.

Imagine it.

But that's the thing, isn't it?

You can't.

You can't imagine it. It's impossible. How can the human brain, a few kilograms of soft meat that dimly perceives the universe through a handful of crude senses, fathom such a vast intellect?

How can a small human mind wrap itself around such limitless potential?

It can't.

It simply cannot.

No. Humanity can no more fathom the mind of God than an ant can imagine a quantum computer.

But that doesn't keep us from trying, does it?

And that's where the belly laughs come in.

You see, we imagine this God as the consciousness who created the heavens and the earth, who separated light and darkness, who made all the birds who fly in the sky and all the fish that swim in the sea and all the beasts that walk upon the land, and *then*, well, then we imagine *that* vast power cares if you trim your sideburns or eat meat on Fridays.

It seems ridiculous to me, but what if the adherents of that religion are right? I allow for the possibility that my mirth is misplaced. The universe is vast indeed and there is room enough in it for nearly anything—including a god who doesn't want me to mix fabrics, eat shellfish, or have sex with another dude.

You can't imagine God.

You can only imagine what *you* would be like with such power.

Which is why we always imagine God as some boundless intellect and then hobble him with our own human pettiness and frailty.

Don't get me wrong. Theology, like philosophy, like science, is the history of mankind and our endless struggle to understand ourselves and the bottomless terrible, terrifying universe that surrounds us.

And it is terrifying.

It is.

Step outside on any clear night, look up. Vastness. The limitless unknown. Possibilities without end. Room for *anything*, gods, angels, demons, endless heavens and endless hells. Against that, we are less than a single grain of sand on an infinite beach.

It is terrifying.

It's also exhilarating.

But, more terrifying, more stimulating, is the idea that some vast cool boundless intellect made it all up from nothingness. Because against *that*, we are indeed less than ants dreaming of quantum computers.

The truth—if that word has any meaning here—is that we can never know the mind of God or plumb the depths of

3

the universe. We school like minnows in the shadow of immense creatures swimming in some wine-dark sea. Will we be ignored or nurtured? Crushed by accident or indifference? Scooped up in jaws the size of worlds as food for giants? Or perhaps, just perhaps, one day we minnows will grow into whales ourselves.

The universe is so vast, that literally anything is possible. And if you can't laugh in the face of *that*, well, my friends, then you'll never stop screaming.

Poetry, prayer, story, song, and most of all, laughter, these things are how we puny humans shrink that vastness down into something our small gibbering monkey minds can hold. This is how we spit into the eye of God and shake our fists in defiance—or in supplication.

That's why we give our deities human frailty, why we make them ridiculous and small.

Because otherwise we would go mad—and have.

That's what you hold in your hands now.

This book of alternative theologies. It is a volume of prayers and poems, of virgin births, of prophets and preachers, soldiers and scientists, of righteous justice and terrible injustice, of mighty gods and fiery angels and poor mortal men. The stories contained herein were written by old pros and newbie authors, believers and nonbelievers alike. Some will make you laugh. Some might make you cry. Some will certainly make you angry. And some, well, some might make you wonder about the nature of this world.

You'll find no answers here.

Theology offers no answers, no truths, no lies. Only possibilities, *alternatives*, attempts to describe the unknowable and impossible and to both rail at the heavens and beseech the gods as we puny humans have always done.

Read.

Enjoy, or not, as your nature may be.

And when you are finished, step outside and look up, past the affairs of men and gods, past the worlds and past the stars, at the endless, terrible vastness. Laugh at the staggering hubris of imagining that you can ever understand the magnificent wonder of it all and know that in this regard you are not alone.

Jim Wright

Counting Sunrises

Heather Truett

It's early. I like to watch the sun rise. Strange how, as a kid, I took the sun for granted. It would always be there, and I would always be here, and that was just how things were. Now I'm counting down the sunrises.

"365," I say.

"I know, and it's beautiful isn't it? Maybe more beautiful than yesterday's."

"No, yesterday's had purple. I don't see any purple today."

He knows how I love purple.

"Purple," he says.

I gasp. We've been together for eighteen years now, and I'm still startled by him, by what he can do.

I sigh. "Each one is more beautiful than the last because there is now one less."

We're quiet for a while. The sun burns, but I don't want to go inside, not yet, not while the purple is still in the sky.

A handful of neighborhood boys walk past. There was a time when children were kept safe inside their homes at night, but most run free now. What does it matter, anyway? That's what some of these people think. Most couples don't have babies anymore. Why bother?

The little boy at the head of the pack points in my direction. I can hear the other kids sniggering.

"Every morning?" One of them asks, his voice too loud for the quiet street.

"Yup. Every morning, with that empty chair beside her. She even talks to it, like someone's really there."

"Crazy," the loud kid says.

I sigh. "Why can't they see you?"

"Oh, they'll see me soon enough. I'm not here for them right now."

This is always his answer.

"Won't you miss this?" I ask.

"I don't have to miss anything," he says. He is patient. I often repeat myself, make him repeat these answers. Over and over, as though something could change. Nothing will change, and tomorrow I will count 364 sunrises left before the end.

"Your concept of time is an illusion, Emmy. You have only 364 sunrises left, but I have all of the sunrises, all of the sunsets, every noonday from behind and before you. All of them are now."

"I like it when you talk that way," I tell him. "I like thinking that then is now and tomorrow is now and there is no ending after all. Why don't you stop it?"

"Because earth's time has come."

This is always his answer.

Once the sun is high over the horizon, we walk into the house, the tiny two-bedroom mill house where I was born, where my parents lived and cared for me until the day I turned ten years old.

"Happy birthday, Emmy. The world is ending. You're on your own now."

Maybe that isn't exactly how they said it, but events unfolded that way, regardless. One day, I was a happy nine-year-old girl, planning a sleepover with my best friend, Lillian. The next day, Lillian and her family disappeared completely and my own parents weren't far behind. I could have gone with them. They wanted to take me to the hills, to the bunkers being stocked and fortified in the bowels of the earth.

I cried. I didn't want to go. I liked my pink bedroom and my dark wood bookshelves and my pretty white dollhouse. I wouldn't go.

"Just leave her," my dad said. "There's only so much room."

My dad wasn't a nice man, but he wasn't evil either. He was just scared and selfish. And Mom never had disobeyed him, never, so why would she start then, with the world set to crumble at her feet? What did any of it matter anyway?

"I'll take care of her," the man said. He hadn't been there before, but suddenly he was. He was standing beside me on the front porch, one hand on the splintered rail and one hand on my shoulder.

My mom didn't look at him. She only looked at me. Dad had to force her into the car, and she was screaming, but I had quit crying. I wasn't scared anymore.

"Who are you?" I asked, when my parents' car disappeared over a distant hill.

"My name is Jesus. Your grandmother told me all about her sweet girl, Emmy, and I've been waiting for the chance to meet you."

My grandmother had passed away just the month before. My mom's mom, she was, and Dad said she spoiled me. She didn't like my dad, but there wasn't much she could do.

I pray for you all the time, she said once. *I pray that Jesus will take care of you when I am gone.*

I nodded. "Gram told me about you too."

While the world was going crazy outside my doors and windows, Jesus taught me how to play chess and checkers. I read to him from my favorite books, stories of a girl named Anne who always got into trouble and a land called Oz where fairies really lived and evil witches got melted in the end. He told me stories too, stories about rainbows and a garden where every kind of food grew, and people were happy.

I didn't leave the little house for a year. I never wondered where Jesus got our food. He made me eggs for breakfast every day, and he pulled loaves of fresh bread from the oven. The fruit bowl on the kitchen table was always overflowing with apples and bananas and grapes and even some exotic fruits I'd never seen before. I remember my first slice of kiwi and how I marveled when he showed me star fruit.

After the first year, things calmed down around us. Some of the neighbors came back to their homes. Many of the houses had been burned or burglarized. I took a walk with Jesus. Sometimes, we stopped so he could wrap his arms around a crying lady or kiss the cheeks of a newborn.

"Life always wants to go on," he tells me, when I comment on the babies still being born.

On our block, my house was the only house untouched. Neighbors marveled. How had I stayed safe? Where was I getting food? How come no one broke into my little house?

"Jesus takes care of me," I explained, but that only made them shake their heads. By the time I turned eighteen, the neighborhood was full again, but people were never the same, and my own parents never returned.

No one spoke to me, save an elderly woman who lived across the street. She used to come over with a cup of coffee in the mornings. That was before I started watching the sunrises. Actually, she was the person who suggested we mark the days that way. Sort of like the paper chains I used to make before Christmas. Each day, I ripped off one construction paper link, until all of them were gone and Santa Claus had come at last.

The sunrises are different. I love each beautiful day, but I mourn it too. I know they will not ever come again. When I was small, there was always another year; another paper chain, another Christmas, but this won't be like that.

oOo

300 sunrises left. I break the chain link in my mind. Jesus pours me another cup of coffee. I give him the paper to read while I scramble eggs on the stove. I still never go to a grocery store, but now I know enough to marvel at the presence of food in my home.

I hear the doorknob turn, and then there's Liza, an adorable blonde child who lives three blocks away. She comes to see me every morning now. I have her place set and I scoop the eggs onto her plate. Jesus passes her the still-warm bread. I used to worry about Liza walking here by herself. After all, that pack of boys roams the streets at all hours, and a few of them have been known to accost young women.

"Aren't you scared to walk all that way?" I asked when she'd been coming for a week or so.

"No, I'm not scared. Why would I be scared?"

"When I was a little girl, walking by myself like that would have scared me," I told her.

"But, Emmy," she exclaimed. "I don't walk here by myself."

"You don't?"

"No silly," she laughed. "Jesus walks with me every morning."

Maybe someone else would point out that Jesus was in my little house during the time Liza walked three blocks, but I didn't. Actually, having lived with Jesus for eighteen years, it's sad I didn't realize he was with Liza the same as he was with me.

"Do you stay with Liza a lot?" I asked Jesus after she had gone home on the day of 300 sunrises.

"Not as much as I've been with you. Liza's mom takes very good care of her. I just go with her when she walks. She likes people, our Liza does. She loves them with my own whole heart."

I know what he means. I've seen Liza sneak some bread into her bag before she leaves my house. I know she takes it down the road to Mrs. McAllister. In the afternoons, Jesus and I take lunch to the very same woman. She's old, was old even eighteen years ago, and she can't get around real well. Her husband died last year, and she says she's missing him, ready for these last months to pass so she can be with him again.

After visiting Mrs. McAllister, we walk to the old church a few miles into town. It's an orphanage now. The women who work there smile to see me coming. They don't notice

Jesus is with me, but when I tell them he is, they always seem happy to know it.

"You are his hands and his feet, Miss Emmy," one of the women said to me a year ago.

"I'm not your hands and feet," I told Jesus as we were walking home.

"You are though," he replied. "They can't see me standing here, but they see me when you give them food, when you walk all this way to tell stories to the children. You are all they see of me."

oOo

"1," I say. "Just one day left."

"Are you ready?" He asks.

"No," I tell him. "I don't want to leave the babies or Liza or Mrs. McAllister."

"You won't be leaving them," Jesus sips his first cup of coffee. He likes a spoonful of sugar, no cream. "They'll come too."

"Is it going to hurt?"

"Perhaps. But it will be over fast, and I'll be right here beside you."

"What will become of this place?" I've wanted to ask that question for a long time. He knows, but he's been waiting on me to get the courage. He doesn't do things for me, Jesus. He gave me a brain and expects me to use it.

"Do you remember the awful fires that broke out years ago? The big ones that came after The Announcement?"

That's what everybody calls it, "The Announcement." They mean when political leaders around the world stood side by side and explained what was going to happen, how hopeless the situation was, that everyone would die. There was nothing they could do.

"It would take an act of God," our President told the American people. My dad was already packing. Mom was watching the TV screen, wailing in despair.

"They didn't have much use for God yesterday," My Gram would have said. "But they expect him to save them today."

"I remember the fires," I say.

"What happened when they finally burned out?"

"Nothing, at first," I answer. "But then, things grew. Photos were on the news. People thought it was a sign of hope."

"And so it was. Still is."

"How so?"

"Earth's time has come, Emmy, but there will be other times, and a green blossomed earth will spin anew. There will be hope."

"One," I say again.

"It's a beautiful one isn't it?"

I smirk. "I think it needs more purple."

And Jesus laughs.

The Pale Thin God

Mike Resnick

He stood quietly before us, the pale thin god who had invaded our land, and waited to hear the charges.

The first of us to speak was Mulungu, the god of the Yao people.

"There was a time, many eons ago, when I lived happily upon the earth with my animals. But then men appeared. They made fire and set the land ablaze. They found my animals and began killing them. They devised weapons and went to war with each other. I could not tolerate such behavior, so I had a spider spin a thread up to heaven, and I ascended it, never to return. And yet *you* have sacrificed yourself for these very same creatures."

Mulungu pointed a long forefinger at the pale thin god. "I accuse you of the crime of Love."

He sat down, and immediately Nyambe, the god of the Koko people, arose.

"I once lived among men," he said, "and there was no such thing as death in the world, because I had given them a magic tree. When men grew old and wrinkled, they went and lived under the tree for nine days, and it made them young again. But as the years went by men began taking me for granted, and stopped worshiping me and making sacrifices to me, so I uprooted my tree and carried it up to heaven with me, and without its magic, men finally began to die."

He stared balefully at the pale thin god. "And now you have taught men that they may triumph over death. I charge you with the crime of Life."

Next Ogun, the god of the Yoruba people, stepped forward.

"When the gods lived on Earth, they found their way barred by impenetrable thorn bushes. I created a *panga* and cleared the way for them, and this *panga* I turned over to men, who use it not only for breaking trails but for the glory of war. And yet you, who claim to be a god, tell your worshipers to disdain weapons and never to raise a hand in anger. I accuse you of the crime of Peace."

As Ogun sat down, Muluku, god of the Zambesi, rose to his feet.

"I made the earth," he said. "I dug two holes, and from one came a man, and from the other a woman. I gave them land and tools and seeds and clay pots, and told them to plant the seeds, to build a house, and to cook their food in the pots. But the man and the woman ate the raw seeds, broke the pots, and left the tools by the side of a trail. Therefore, I summoned two monkeys, and made the same gifts to them. The two monkeys dug the earth, built a house, harvested their grain, and cooked it in their pots." He paused. "So I cut off the monkeys' tails and stuck them on the two men, decreeing that from that day forth they would be monkeys and the monkeys would be men."

He pointed at the pale thin god. "And yet, far from punishing men, you forgive them their mistakes. I charge you with the crime of Compassion."

En-kai, the god of the Maasai, spoke next.

"I created the first warrior, Le-eyo, and gave him a magic chant to recite over dead children that would bring them back to life and make them immortal. But Le-eyo did not utter the chant until his own son had died. I told him that it was too late, that the chant would no longer work, and that because of his selfishness, Death will always have power over men. He begged me to relent, but because I am a god and a god cannot be wrong, I did not do so."

He paused for a moment, then stared coldly at the pale thin god. "You would allow men to live again, even if only in heaven. I accuse you of the crime of Mercy."

Finally Huveane, god of the Basuto people, arose.

"I, too, lived among men in eons past. But their pettiness offended me, and so I hammered some pegs into the sky and climbed up to heaven, where men would never see me again." He faced the pale thin god. "And now, belatedly, you have come to our land, and you teach that men may ascend to heaven, that they may even sit at your right hand. I charge you with the crime of Hope."

The six fearsome gods turned to me.

"We have spoken," they said. "It is your turn now, Anubis. Of what crime do you charge him?"

"I do not make accusations, only judgments," I replied.

"And how do you judge him?" they demanded.

"I will hear him speak, and then I will tell you," I said. I turned to the pale thin god. "You have been accused of the crimes of Peace, Life, Mercy, Compassion, Love, and Hope. What have you to say in your defense?"

The pale thin god looked at us, his accusers.

"I have been accused of Peace," he said, never raising his voice, "and yet more Holy Wars have been fought in my name than in the names of all other gods combined. The earth has turned red with the blood of those who died for my Peace.

"I have been accused of Life," he continued, "yet in my name, the Spaniards have baptized Aztec infants and dashed out their brains against rocks so they might ascend to heaven without living to become warriors.

"I have been accused of Mercy, but the Inquisition was held in my name, and the number of men who were tortured to death is beyond calculation.

"I have been accused of Compassion, yet not a single man who worships me has ever lived a life without pain, without fear, and without misery.

"I have been accused of Love, yet I have not ended suffering, or disease, or death, and he who leads the most blameless and saintly life will be visited by all of my grim horsemen just as surely as he who rejects me.

"Finally, I have been accused of Hope," he said, and now the stigmata on his hands and feet and neck began to glow a brilliant red, "and yet since I have come to your land, I have brought famine to the north, genocide to the west, drought to the south, and disease to the east. And everywhere, where there was Hope, there is only poverty and ignorance and war and death.

"So it has been wherever I have gone, so shall it always be.

"Thus do I answer your charges."

They turned to me, the six great and terrible deities, to ask for my judgment. But I had already dropped to my knees before the greatest god of us all.

Devine Justice

Philip Brian Hall

"Silence in court!" The usher's voice is a deep, booming bass, each sonorous syllable tolling like a death knell.

Further away, other bells join in, all the churches of The Square Mile contributing their peals to one great rolling clangor. Can it be noon already? Somewhere above my head The Old Bailey's own bells chime—*When will you pay me?*

I smile inwardly. You'll have to get up earlier in the morning to catch Horatio St. John Devine. A near thing though.

Frankie Arkwright, my client, has of course committed the murder of which he's accused. The prosecutor knows it; the judge knows it; I know it. The newspapers have condemned Frankie already. That's not the point. He's innocent until *proven* guilty. I've as usual sowed the necessary reasonable doubt in the minds of the jurors. This skill is why I'm paid the highest fees in any of the Inns of Court.

But my imperious closing address to the jury is rudely interrupted—*Crack! Crack!*

What were the odds against the victim's widow smuggling a pistol into the courtroom, hey? Then drawing it out, aiming and hitting Frankie in the head with her first shot across the crowded floor?

Some people appreciate neither the laws of the land nor the laws of probability.

Terrified screaming. Spectators in the public gallery fighting to reach the exit. Smoke drifting down into the body of the court and mingling its caustic sharpness with the panicked, sweaty smell of the great unwashed. The venerable old oak benches clearing faster than a lawyers' wine bar when I walk in.

Lord Justice Featherstonehaugh ducks behind the oak-paneled facade of his seat of justice without regard for the dignity of his office, his full-bottomed wig flapping like the ears of a startled spaniel.

I'm dizzy. Number One Court reels like a cross-Channel ferry. Fog wreathes about me as I struggle to regain my balance. Reaching out blindly through the murk, I touch a wooden surface and cling to it. My desk. I'm still in court then, not carried out on a stretcher.

"Prisoner at the bar!" the usher calls.

From the look of Frankie's face with a neat, round hole in his forehead, the usher will have to shout a lot louder to get him to hear. Why's the court still in session? The widow's action constitutes a *de facto* adjournment in my book.

That lady's certainly going to need a good defense counsel. Step forward Horatio St. John Devine QC. If there's anyone within the fellowship of the criminal bar who can get off someone caught in the act, holding a smoking gun, in front of a hundred witnesses, then I am that man. I thrive on notoriety and there can hardly be better publicity.

"Prisoner at the bar!" the usher cries again.

I have to hand it to the man; he doesn't give up easily.

"Prisoner at the bar!" he calls for the third time. "You will stand to hear the charges against you."

The fog begins to thin. The floor's ceased to misbehave. I discern familiar but somehow subtly altered surroundings. Surely the walls should be beige, not white? When did someone repaint the cherubim around the ceiling? They look remarkably lifelike today. I get up and look around to see if Frankie's body's been taken away.

What on Earth? I'm no longer in my accustomed place. I'm in *the dock*.

"Horatio St. John Devine!" cries the usher. "You are allegedly a great sinner."

What's that? I'm the accused?

"On the first count, you are charged with 763 instances of perverting the course of justice by securing the acquittal of the guilty.

"On the second count, you are charged with 8,213 instances of responsibility for crimes committed subsequently by the said wrongly-acquitted offenders.

"On the third count, you are charged with breaking God's Law, observance of which is obligatory on all men.

"On the fourth count, you are charged with lack of the proper humility befitting a creature of God."

Can I believe my ears? Religious crimes? Stuff and nonsense! Medieval relics, not modern law. Nevertheless, he's certainly talking to me.

Perhaps I'm delirious? Knocked cold in the disorder, I'm even now in a hospital bed with worried friends clustered around.

No, not at all probable. I've no friends. Envy; that's one of the penalties of success.

Well then, the bed's surrounded by prosecution lawyers dancing jigs?

No. I can't imagine any of them calling for silence amid the general rejoicing.

Can I really be dead? Nonsense! Religion's just a human invention designed to give power to priests; there's no afterlife. Yet I must be *somewhere*. Well, if there's life after death and it's anything like The Bailey then I, Horatio St. John Devine, must be in my own personal Heaven.

"Prisoner at the bar, how do you plead?" demands the usher. The court's obviously awaiting my reply.

I temporize. "I petition the court for an adjournment. I need time to prepare a defense."

"Mr. Devine," says the judge, looking down from his elevated throne, peering at me over the top of ill-fitting horn-rimmed glasses. He's an old man. His long white beard mingles with real white hair, thick and woolly, hanging down on each side of his head instead of a proper wig. He's a large bunch of keys in his hand instead of a gavel. No. Really it couldn't be. Could it? St Peter in person?

"You're not in The Old Bailey now," he says. His tone is stern, his eyes unsmiling. "This is the Court of Last Judgment. You've had forty-four years to prepare a defense. Let's get on with it, shall we? Do you seek representation by counsel?"

"Do you know of one better than me, M'Lud?" I query, raising one eyebrow. Dead or alive, I know the art of defense. But this time it seems I've more at stake than my reputation.

Saint Peter looks displeased. "Consider, Mr. Devine, you're charged with getting villains off. Some might consider a successful defense of yourself yet another crime."

As a ripple of laughter runs around the public gallery, St Peter taps impatiently on the desk with his keys.

There we are. I don't care who the judge is. Normal service has been resumed.

"Is Your Lordship implying I'm to be condemned whether I win or lose? Is this a court of *justice* or not?"

There's a surprised murmur. The public's taken aback by my temerity.

"The court will thank you to show proper respect, Mr. Devine." Saint Peter frowns. "Nevertheless it's a fundamental principle: innocence is presumed; guilt must be proven. The prisoner may represent himself. Prosecution may open its case."

I must think quickly. Matters of fact are hardly likely to be in dispute. I *have* got lots of guilty people acquitted. I must justify my conduct, not deny it.

"Point of order, M'Lud," I say.

"Yes, Mr. Devine," says the judge.

"The defense will concede the facts as alleged in all 8,976 instances of the first two charges." Oh yes, I can do mental arithmetic too.

"You'll what?" gasps a stunned prosecutor.

"It's true," I smile at him. "All of it."

"M'Lud, he can't do that!" the prosecutor complains.

"Beware the sin of pride, Lord Jeffreys," says the judge. "The facts of the first two counts are taken as established. Have you anything to add?"

I cast a studied glance at the prosecutor. His robes are red. His long wig is of dark, un-powdered hair, curled in the later Stuart fashion and he wears the Lord Chancellor's heavy golden chain of office draped around his shoulders. Is this really the man who presided over *The Bloody Assizes*? Am I facing a worthy opponent at last?

"Well. . . the prosecution will call witnesses on the remaining counts."

No, I rather thought not. In his day trials were not won by force of legal arguments.

"Point of law, M'Lud," I object.

Jeffreys resumes his seat with an ill grace, as though a mere defense lawyer should not be allowed to speak.

"Yes, Mr. Devine," says the judge.

"M'Lud, the third and fourth charges are faulty in law and should be struck down without evidence being heard."

"Preposterous!" Jeffreys explodes, rising from his seat. Ha! Did his pupil-master never tell him that to get angry is to lose the argument?

"Your turn will come, Lord Jeffreys," says Saint Peter. "I believe there has to be a first time for everything, though I warn you, Mr. Devine, I don't take kindly to my time being wasted. Proceed."

So far, so good. "M'Lud, to claim that compliance with God's Law is mandatory is misconceived."

A gasp of shock from Jeffreys. "You deny man must obey God's Law?" His face verges on purple. If he weren't dead already one might fear he was about to suffer apoplexy.

"I do. The claim has three flaws."

Saint Peter blinks several times rapidly. He's struggling to remain properly impartial. Good. He'll over-compensate.

"Three, Mr. Devine?"

"Three, M'Lud. First, God made man uniquely distinguished among His creatures by rationality, yet failed to provide any rational proof of His own existence. *Logically* therefore man must treat God's existence as hypothetical. To worship a hypothetical deity is superstition and thus contrary to God's Law. Revelation 21/27."

My biblical erudition produces exactly the astonishment I'd hoped for. I'm rewarded with a nod from the judge.

"Second, a charge of *failure to obey* means ignorance of the law can be no defense. In clear jurisdictions, where there's only one body of law, this axiom of course holds true. But on Earth there are many mutually-exclusive religions. A man may *believe* but cannot *know* which is correct. I submit, where to know the truth is impossible it cannot be criminal to be ignorant."

Jeffreys springs from his chair with an oath. The judge stares at him in silence until he subsides, still muttering.

"Third, and crucially." I pause and look straight at the judge. "Christianity is essentially a contract between man and God, exchanging service during life for reward thereafter. Now it's well established in law that a contract entered into under duress is invalid. Yet we're also told those who fail to enter God's service will roast in Hell. What greater duress, M'Lud, is imaginable?"

I conclude with a slight smile at Jeffreys, who's speechless and spluttering. I wonder whether I at last detect the *ghost of a smile* behind the judge's inscrutable mask.

"Let us turn to the fourth charge," Saint Peter says.

"It's self-evident this man's not humble," Jeffreys complains.

"This from a man wearing the golden chain of office of The Lord Chancellor of England?" I inquire mildly.

"Mr. Devine, Lord Jeffreys is not on trial here," Saint Peter snaps. "His case was heard long ago."

"Of course, M'Lud. My point is, Lord Jeffreys rose to his high office on merit." I never allow the facts to stand in the way of a good argument. "Were he to appear humble it would be seen as false modesty. He wears his chain of office as his due, not out of pride. To the charge of not being humble, I reply no man lights a candle and puts it under a bushel."

"Taken out of context!" Jeffreys objects.

"The third and fourth charges are dismissed," says the judge.

There are gasps and exclamations from the public gallery. Oh, but they've seen nothing yet!

"M'Lud, that concludes the case for the prosecution," Jeffreys reluctantly admits.

"Very well. The court will hear the defense on the remaining counts. Mr. Devine, your first witness," says the judge.

"The defense calls Horatio St. John Devine QC," I reply.

I look around the courtroom and smile faintly, confident but not smug. Confidence reassures; smugness patronizes. Cue the outrageous opening remark.

"M'Lud I submit the acquittal of the guilty does not pervert the course of justice. It serves it."

I do so enjoy the inability of the public gallery to restrain their astonishment.

"Justice is fundamental to society," I continue. "Without justice, there's anarchy. But justice is served through law, not vengeance. Now the typical citizen lacks legal knowledge, and since no-one wishes to see the innocent condemned, every accused is entitled to representation by learned counsel."

Jeffreys, who notoriously condemned the innocent on perjured testimony, has the good grace to squirm.

"To defend accused persons is therefore a civic duty. Not only is it not *an offense* against God, it emulates God."

"Emulates God?" Saint Peter repeats, unable to believe his ears.

Ha! If you want predictability look to Jeffreys; you're now listening to Horatio St. John Devine!

"Consider, M'Lud. God is good, yet he gave man free will. Sometimes a man freely chooses evil. But clearly God believes the total amount of good in the world is greater *with* free will than without, or he would not have given it to us. This means He accepts the lesser evil is the inevitable price of this greater good."

"I see," Saint Peter nods.

"Likewise, M'Lud, Justice is maximized by allowing the accused proper representation. It's better several guilty men go free than one innocent's convicted."

I stare at Jeffreys, defying him to show where I'm in error. Sometimes I even impress myself. Quite often in fact. This is turning into one of the times. For a dead man, I'm having one whale of a time.

"M'Lud, the failure of the second charge follows from that of the first. But I've further evidence. In Britain we have a Legal Aid system to defend stupid criminals who lack the intelligence to commit remunerative crimes and thus cannot afford good lawyers. Legal Aid's provided by lawyers who aren't good enough to find proper work, so they usually lose or plead guilty."

And only right and proper, everyone in the public gallery's thinking.

"This is clearly in the public interest. Society's better off with dim-witted thugs behind bars. As a good lawyer, it would've been wrong for me to defend violent criminals because I should've won. Therefore. . . by *not* taking on such cases I actually reduced the amount of violence in society!"

"Objection!" Jeffreys jumps up in annoyance.

Oh no, sir, you're too late; I have the public now and you're playing pantomime villain. To prove it, here comes a disapproving murmur from the gallery.

Now for the grandstand finish. It's always worked before; why fix what isn't broken?

"M'Lud, it should be clear, bad law can't be in society's interest. The better the law, the better the quality of life. *But*. . . before bad law can be improved its defects must first be exposed. M'Lud I've been more successful in exposing legal flaws than any of my contemporaries. Does not God's law enjoin a man to make the best use of his talents?"

There are cheers and shouts of 'Bravo'. Jeffreys scowls. He can do nothing now that will not make him look even more stupid.

"M'Lud, I submit the accused has no case to answer," I say.

To the accompaniment of applause, I resume my seat. I smile at the public. The public smiles back.

"Lord Jeffreys?" Saint Peter queries.

"M'Lud," grates the frustrated prosecutor, "No further arguments. *Nolle prosequi.*"

"Just as well," says Saint Peter. "But Mr. Devine, I can't allow an agnostic directly into Heaven." He actually smiles. "Fifty years' Purgatory as a servant of this court." He bangs on his desk. "Next case!"

An outburst of cheering runs around the courtroom.

oOo

In the lobby I'm approached by an obsequious, balding little man who introduces himself as my new instructing solicitor. He has inky fingers, a quill pen stuck behind his ear, and wears a Victorian frock coat.

"Amazing!" he says breathlessly. "Do you know, lots of lawyers find themselves downstairs almost before they've drawn their last breath." He gestures towards two flights of steps.

To the right, going up, the stairs are of alabaster, brightly lit from a top I can't quite discern. An angelic figure conducts upwards a white-robed vicar smiling beatifically. And inanely, if you ask me.

On the left, the rickety stairs down are dark, though fitfully illuminated from below by an intermittent ruddy glow. A smell of burning drifts up into the lobby. Being jabbed from behind by an ill-favored fiend with a pitchfork is an unhappy person bearing a suspicious resemblance to Lord Justice Featherstonehaugh.

"It's an honor to work in Last Judgment," says my solicitor. "You'll also be offered Appeals. That's the challenges brought by souls who claim they shouldn't have been damned."

"Do I get to choose my clients?" I inquire.

"Cab-rank principle, same as you're used to," he replies. "If you do well they'll all come to you; the more you win, the less time you yourself have to serve. Simple!"

"Excellent!" I say. "Bring me Jack the Ripper! Bring me Dr Crippen! I'll get them out of Hell! I can make a case for anybody." I never allow the facts to get in the way of a good argument—did I mention that already?

"Don't worry, we'll have plenty of work," my solicitor mumbles. He looks shifty.

"Are you ready for your first client?" he asks.

"What about lunch first?" I inquire hopefully. "I assume we inhabitants of Purgatory do get to eat?"

"No time, no time."

Before I can protest, he's shepherding me down a shabby corridor towards the holding cells.

My solicitor nods to the policeman on guard and enters as a cell door is held open. I blink; the last time I saw this constable he was Commissioner of the London Metropolitan Force. He was in the public gallery hoping to gloat as Frankie Arkwright was sent down. Oh my! How many of us did the widow shoot?

oOo

The solicitor begins his introduction almost before I'm through the door. "*Herr Reichsmarschall*, meet Mr. Horatio St. John Devine QC—Mr. Devine, *Reichsmarschall* Hermann Goering."

The Deputy Fuhrer's wearing an outlandish sky-blue uniform, his chest festooned with medals. He rises from his chair and extends a pudgy hand to me. "*Guten Tag, Herr Anwalt*," he says with a knowing smile.

"*Herr Reichsmarschall*," I acknowledge. Then turning to the solicitor, "What's the idea? Is the backlog of appeals this bad? Why's my client been kept waiting until now?"

"*Ja!* I like it," chortles the fat German. "My client! You hear that?" Goering speaks good English but with a guttural accent. What did you expect?

"No, there's no backlog. Your client's been waiting for an advocate willing to take his case. Many have been approached; some of the most notable ethically-challenged jurists in the world: two Lord Chancellors, three members of the US Supreme Court. All of them rejected the opportunity to defend the *Reichsmarschall.*"

"Disgraceful! It's not their business to prejudge his guilt."

"*Wunderbar!*" Goering cheers. "Such courage! This man was worth waiting for!"

"Let's be clear," the solicitor says. "In the Appeals Court, if you win they deduct five years from your probation."

"Sounds good to me," I say happily. I'll clear my sentence with my first ten cases.

"And if you lose. . ." he scratches nervously at his thinning hair.

"Yes?"

"They add five hundred years."

"What?"

"It's supposed to discourage frivolous appeals. It is the Court of *Last* Judgment after all."

I might never have anticipated the possibility of failure, but I'd never before contemplated the defense of a genocidal maniac.

The solicitor isn't finished. "There's a hierarchy of judges these days. You'll forgive me saying it, but that's why you got Saint Peter. The senior judge just takes the highest-profile cases. He's omniscient, you see. That means he doesn't make mistakes."

The little man's touching confidence makes me smile. A judge who doesn't make mistakes? Mythical beasts belong in fairy tales.

"How often do appeals against this judge's decisions succeed?"

"Do you mean how many have succeeded so far?"

"Exactly."

"Well," says the solicitor, "In total. . . approximately. . . er, none."

So. I'm being employed to attempt the impossible, am I? We'll see about that. Just because I've never defended a genocidal maniac doesn't mean I can't get one off. In any case, who suggested my client was a genocidal maniac? The clerk will strike that remark from the record and the jury will disregard it.

"Everyone has the right to counsel," the solicitor continues, "but frankly the whole thing's a bit of a formality. Rather like you were saying earlier, you know. . . about Legal Aid."

Oh! That does it! I'm almost never angry, but there are some things I cannot tolerate. One thing that matters more to me than even the fundamental principles of justice is my own reputation. Substantially more in fact. Is this miserable creature suggesting I should go through the motions? Not on your life! Not on your after-life!

"Not like *Nürnberg*!" Goering smiles. "You know for a while back there I was doing really well, even with my victorious enemies sitting in judgment. Personally I blame Speer, the coward! Mind, you have to admire his gall, claiming he'd known nothing."

"And he'd known all along?" I ask.

"Of course. He's downstairs now being roasted for his pains. But as the *Herr Rechtsanwalt* says, this judge knows everything, so he can't be fooled."

"Do I take it you've reconsidered your decision to take the case?" the solicitor asks nervously.

"*Nein!*" Goering grins, his several chins wobbling with suppressed mirth. "He has not, have you *Herr* Devine?" The fat German's eyes twinkle.

"You're correct, *Herr Reichsmarschall*. It's not my habit to walk away from a client who needs my help."

"I knew you were a man after my own heart as soon as I saw you," he chuckles. "Did you know I won the Blue Max in the First War? And I saved several Jews from the camps. Of course, they happened to be my own relatives, but we can put it forward in mitigation all the same, can't we? I also want it known I advised Hitler against invading Poland and Russia. If only the *Führer* had listened to me!"

Yes, well, there's intelligence and then there's the ability to follow the thought processes of Horatio St. John Devine.

"We won't need any pleas in mitigation," I say, turning to the solicitor. "We're filing immediately for the verdict to be quashed. A fundamental principle of justice was violated at my client's trial."

"In *that* court?" the little man gasps, stunned. "Are you sure?"

"Quite sure," I declare, flicking out my shirt cuffs and straightening my tie. "The principle was confirmed as fundamental by the judge in my own hearing. My client had the right to be presumed innocent. That's how Speer escaped death at Nuremberg; in all the chaos of post-war Germany the prosecutors couldn't find the evidence to prove his guilt."

"*Ja!*" Goering exclaims.

"For a trial to be fair, it's absolutely necessary the verdict's reached only on the basis of evidence tested in the courtroom. The defendant cannot challenge material he doesn't know is under consideration."

"*Nein! Wunderbar! Nein!*"

"Now, in my client's case the judge was omniscient. An omniscient judge, by definition, knew incriminatory facts not produced in evidence, *ergo* he was prejudiced against my client. He should've recused himself; this was a classic mistrial."

"*Ja! Ja!* Another Freisler!"

I smile at my happy client and at my astonished solicitor. Omniscient eh? No, I'm sorry, you'll have to get up earlier in the morning to catch Horatio St. John Devine.

oOo

"Well!" gasps the solicitor admiringly. "I can see they were right about you. Do you know they started to queue up as soon as they heard you were coming?"

Very gratifying. Good to know my reputation transcends dimensions. I could have five successful appeals by this evening.

"Now how about lunch?" I inquire.

"In fact, I've another client waiting next door."

This is a tiresome excess of zeal. If I were staying around I'd have to explain a thing or two to the little man about legal priorities. No matter. This shouldn't take long.

I feel my accustomed confidence flooding back. It will take more than a little problem like death to stop my run of success. There are, after all, fundamental legal principles to be upheld. And if any man can uphold fundamental legal principles, come what may, dead or alive, in The Bailey or Last Judgment, then I, Horatio St. John Devine am that man!

We leave the contented *Reichsmarschall* still chortling away, return to the corridor and proceed to the next cell.

Pride, they say, precedes a fall. I may never allow the facts to get in the way of a good argument, but incriminating evidence will be the least of my problems now. For once I'm speechless.

"Mr Horatio St. John Devine QC," the solicitor says, "meet the Archangel Lucifer."

Tit for Tat

James Dorr

Little Willie caught a cold
after the preacher's sermon Sunday,
chilled unto his very soul
he was dead by teatime Monday.

He was buried in a coffin
waiting to be sent to Hades,
there to burn eternally
with naughty boys and demon ladies.

That is what the preacher taught,
that lads like him, with reckless ways,
should expect upon demise,
the wages of their sins to pay.

But there were no flames, no perdition,
none of what the preacher roared,
just cold and damp and nibbling worms—
the truth was Will was getting bored.

So Willie swore the preacher lied
and to the church he sent his ghost,
he'd gain revenge upon that cleric,
that was Willie's spirit's boast.

He rattled papers, shrieked through
windows,
which upset the church's choir,
he kicked the votive candles over
causing danger of a fire.

He chased the preacher from his pulpit,
scared the old man near to death,
he tweaked his nose and pinched his ears,
blew in his face with graveyard breath.

And thus, this moral may be found
for those who orate of the Lord:
Should you consign lost souls to Hell,
be sure that you can keep your word.

First

Kara Race-Moore

*²⁵And after Cain SLEW Abel, Adam
begat Seth, who begat Enos, who begat
Hinnom.*

*²⁶But Hinnom did sin against the LORD,
and when he died, he did Descend to HELL.*

*²⁷And he was the first SOUL to be
received there.*

—Genesis 4:25-27, from the Gehenna

Bible

The fight between Hinnom and Kenan had already gotten out of hand by the time their father Enos arrived, yelling at them to stop acting like their reckless great-uncle Cain.

The brothers were both bruised, bloody and grass stained from fighting and tumbling their way across the field that bordered the smoking ravine near the family encampment. The sheep herd had scattered at the ruckus, but various members of the family gathered around to watch the fraternal fight.

"He lay with my wife!" yelled Kenan, trying to get a good kick in.

"Who else was I supposed to lay with?" demanded Hinnom, dancing away from the kick and then leaping back to try and land another punch. "We don't have any other sisters!"

"Oh, thanks so much," scoffed their sister Mualeleth. She angrily pointed a finger at Hinnom. "See if I lay with you again, Himmy!"

Kenan turned to yell something at her, Hinnom tried to take advantage of his distraction to hit him, but then Enos got in the way and Hinnom was thrown off balance and lurched backwards. He grabbed for whatever was nearest, which turned out to be Kenan's neck, who pushed him away, and Hinnom stumbled over the edge and plunged down the steep walls of the ravine into the smoke and garbage.

The deep, dry gully was partially filled by rubbish, it was a handy place for the family to discard waste; pottery shards, animal intestines, fish bones, menses clothes, broken tools—anything they had no use for. A few nights previously, after his sister Mualeleth had shared around a new grain drink she had invented, some of his nephews had decided it would be a great idea to toss some torches over the ravine to burn away all the rubbish. It had led to a rather large smoking mess. On the one hand, the fire hadn't spread, but on the other, it seemed to never fully go out nor fully consume all the rubbish. So, they now had a gully near their encampment filled with continually burning trash.

Hinnom felt his neck snap when he hit a large rock near the bottom as he was engulfed in flames.

And then he found himself, neither crumpled nor aflame along with the rest of the family's trash, but standing up, in the middle of an area best described as *blank.* There was a general whiteness everywhere, like walking in morning mist.

Picking a direction at random, he walked forward and found himself walking on a path of smooth, flat stones that sloped vaguely downwards. The whiteness surrounding him gradually dissipated, revealing that the path was only partially constructed. There was a vague sense of enclosure, like walking into a cave, although he couldn't see any sort of walls or roof.

There were people here and there working on laying more stones on the path. They wore dirty white robes and what looked like cloaks of dirty feathers. They ignored his queries as to where he was and who they were, concentrating very hard on their tools, some looking as though they had never picked up a hammer before.

He noticed writing on the stones, and bent down to examine them. 'For the Greater Good' was repeated on several paving stones in dark red. 'They need our help,' read another, followed by 'To keep everyone healthy.' Golden lettering read: 'Everyone will profit,' followed by the silvered lettering: 'We are here to help.'

He meandered down the half-finished road, fascinated by the thoughts laid out in stone. He was caught off guard when the road ended abruptly at a gate, large and imposing, and, like the road, still under construction.

The gate was made up of lots of twisted metal flanked with tall, chiseled stone pilings, with the occasional skull of some animal for adornment, and underneath the scaffolding there were a few projects in place that looked like they would be quite terrifying in their full artistic glory when finished.

One of the workers finally noticed him as he stood staring at the construction, and took off running. A short time later a crowd of people came rushing up to meet him. They were all wearing the same white robes that, while finer than anything his family owned, had all clearly seen better days, the shining material now streaked with dirt and starting to fray around the hems. He saw what he had taken for cloaks were actually wings, larger than any bird's, although those too looked like they were getting a bit past their prime.

Great-Grandpa Adam, whom he had always considered somewhat senile, always talked about the angel with the flaming sword God had sent to make sure no one got back into that garden he and Granny Evie had lived in. The one where there was always food, until Granny Evie had done something, they never said what, they said it was the reason she had to wear clothes. For that he was thankful. These people looked like that angel, except dirtier, and less imposing.

The group of strangers crowded around him, jabbering excitedly, most of them just repeating over and over, "He's here!"

It made Hinnom feel very odd to be surrounded by people he didn't know. Everyone in the world was a sibling, a cousin, aunt or uncle, niece or nephew, a parent, grandparent, or great-grandparent. To be faced with so many strangers made him feel as though he was falling down that gully wall again, even while standing up.

"Hi!" chirped one happily.

That one was promptly elbowed in the ribs by another. "Astaroth you fool! That's no way to great him," The second speaker turned to Hinnom. "Greetings, O Soul of the Departed!" Then turned back to the one named Astaroth and hissed, "See? See how much better that sounds?"

"Sorry, Asmodeus," said Astaroth, sounding abashed.

"Fine, fine, I am properly greeted, and greetings to you as well, O Strange Ones," said Hinnom hastily. "Now, onwards to the important question of *where am I?*"

One of the others made an exasperated noise and remarked, "Now *that* should be in the greeting, let people know right away what's happened so the whole thing can begin properly. Something like: 'Welcome, O Soul of the Departed to the Land of Hell.'"

"Oh, come now, Kochbiel," said one of the females in a bored voice, "That's a bit wordy, don't you think?"

"You think of something then, Naamah," Kochbiel snapped.

"Try shortening it. 'Welcome to Hell.' It's cleaner."

Kochbiel made a face, clearly resenting how much better her version sounded.

"So, I'm in. . . 'Hell'?" asked Hinnom.

Astaroth grinned at him with barely suppressed giddiness. "And you're the first!"

Hinnom pinched the bridge of his nose with exasperation. "I'm still a little confused."

"It's all quite simple, really," said Asmodeus, smug. "You have died and now you are to reside in Hell for the Eternity that is your Afterlife. Which one are you, by the way? Adam? I've always wanted to meet Adam."

"No, no, I'm Hinnom. Adam's my great-grandfather. So Hell is where you go when you die? But then where's my aunt Barakeil?" he demanded, glancing around the strangers. "She died last season whelping yet another brat. And little cousin Ahmik died after eating those funny looking berries. And Granny Evie is still going on about Abel. So where are they? How can I be first? They've all died too!"

"Oh yes, they died," said Naamah sardonically. "*They* got to go to Heaven." She grinned at him toothily, "This place is for the bad ones like you. The good ones go to Heaven."

"Heaven? What is 'Heaven'?"

One of the ones in the back sighed heavily, "Home."

"Shut up, Belphegor," snapped Naamah, her lazy sarcasm gone.

"No," said Asmodeus firmly, "I think we need to talk this over—and I suggest we sit down for this." He smiled at Hinnom. "And we can give you the tour of what we've accomplished so far." There was a chorus of agreement, some enthusiastic, some decidedly less so.

"You have to remember, we haven't finished everything yet," cautioned one, apologetically, as they all trooped through the half-finished gate.

Hinnom allowed himself to be swept along.

"I'll keep that in mind," replied Hinnom politely. "Now, which one are you?"

"Mammon," the male beside him replied, clearly trying to sound formal but instead sounding terribly pleased to be asked.

Hinnom suddenly wondered if meeting new people was as unusual for them as it was for him.

"And you're all from 'Heaven'?" There were several nods in his direction. He cast his mind back, trying to remember if his great-grandparents had mentioned it in their never ceasing nattering on about the old days. "And you're all angels?" he asked, vaguely recalling that might have been where the angel in front of the garden had been from.

"*Fallen* angels," corrected Asmodeus. "But we'll get to that. First, the tour!"

More joined the group as they began the tour, looking and pointing at Hinnom, some of them whispering speculatively. As they surged along someone would occasional point out a feature of Hell:

"There's the garden with the flowers that smell bad," said one of the angels proudly.

"And there's where we're setting up the cooking area that will always burn the oatmeal." Asmodeus rubbed his hands together with glee. "And there is no honey or dried fruits to go with it."

"The well here has a small bucket so it will take a long time to get the amount of water you need to bathe," indicated another.

"And this is the bathing area," said Belphegor brightly. "You notice we made it chilly and the water will be just not quite warm enough."

"And the drying towels will also be slightly damp," added Mammon. "That was my idea."

"I. . . don't. . . quite. . . understand," admitted Hinnom slowly. Why were they showing all these strange things to him?

"Hell is the land of the punishments," said Astaroth pompously.

Hinnom nodded slowly, thinking furiously, keeping his face bland.

They pointed out the beds with lumps in the pillows, and the puddles along the paths that would get people's hems wet.

They all convened in a large tent that tilted at a hazardous angle. It looked like something his younger cousins would make. Cups of tea were passed around, and gradually the voices all died down, all eyes on Hinnom.

"So," Hinnom sipped his over-steeped tea as calmly as he could, managing not to spit it out, "Heaven is where you are from." He glanced round the badly crafted tent. "What's it like?"

Many of them broke into an overlaying babble of voices.

"It's wonderful!"

"So bright—"

"Everything's made of silver and gold and clouds and—"

"And so comfortable—"

"The food—"

"And when Raphael sings—"

"And just listening to Michael talk with that golden voice of his—"

"There was just this energy of excitement everywhere at the start."

As some spoke with dreamy nostalgia, quite a few others exchanged dark looks.

Hinnom waited for the babble of voices to die down and then asked, "So why did you leave if it was so wonderful?"

The excited ones all looked at each other glumly. The others became stony-faced.

Astaroth looked down as he mumbled, "We were exiled. Living here is our punishment."

"What did you do?"

"We rebelled," said Mammon.

"Sammael convinced us," said Astaroth.

"Uh uh," corrected Naamah, wagging a finger. "Remember what he said? He wants to be called 'Satan' now. Says he's not going to go by his 'slave name' anymore."

"Whatever. All *Satan* has been doing lately is sulking. He says it's better to be free down here then a slave up there, but. . ."

"Remember?! Remember what God wanted us to do?! Satan was right, we were *right* to rebel, and better to have lost and be well out of it, rather than stuck up there doing what God wanted us to do!" said Naamah haughtily.

"How bad would it have been to acknowledge the humans?" asked Mammon.

"You are such a wimp," sneered Naamah.

Mammon crossed his arms and scowled. "I picked a side, didn't I? It wasn't like I was one of those wishy-washy ones with their noses in the air claiming to be above it all."

"What side did the angel with the flaming sword chose? The one sent to guard the Eden garden?" Hinnom asked curiously.

"That's Uriel," said one of the fallen angels matter-of-factly.

"He was loyal," added Mammon.

"So he wasn't cast out," put in Astaroth.

"Too smart to fall for Sammy's lines," muttered Kochbiel.

"I don't know," said Naamah thoughtfully. "I think Satan almost had him, given how poor Ury doesn't seem to have any end in sight to his posting. He said besides Miss Eve coming and whining at him now and then, nothing ever happens standing at that gate."

"Silly humans," muttered one, the disarray of her clothes suggesting she might have rebelled harder than most. "How could God possibly want us to bow down before such base creatures?" She glanced at Hinnom. "No offense." She paused and then smiled, cruelly. "Then again, you were sent here, so you must have done something wrong as well."

"Who sent me here?" he asked, eyebrows creased with vexation. He still wasn't sure exactly what was happening, but, given everything else that had happened to him in his life, he suspected this was not going to go well.

"God did," said Belphegor.

"God?"

"God, Yahweh, Adonai," listed Asmodeus in a bored tone. "Jehovah, HaShem, Adoshem, Elohim, the Lord, the Most High, the Supreme Being, the Exalted One—"

"Yes, yes, I know all about *Him*," interrupted Hinnom scathingly. "Granny Evie never shuts up about how if she could just talk to Him one more time she could explain about that incident in the magic garden where she and Grandpa Adam used to stroll around naked." He shuddered. "Seriously, who wants to see that? Their faces are so wrinkled, I don't even want to imagine the rest of them. No wonder God won't let them back in! Clothes on, old folks, please!"

The fallen angels all stared at him, nonplussed.

"*Anyway*," said one of the fallen, "God told us that we were to punish all the bad ones he sent down here for the sins they had committed."

"He didn't, actually," pointed out Asmodeus. "He sent his little lap dog, Metatron the Mouthpiece, to give us His judgment." He pointed at a heap of scrolls. "And some really vague directions."

"What, exactly, according to His Most Exalted One, counts as a sin?" inquired Hinnom, ideas forming rapidly.

"Oh, God gave us a list," said Mammon helpfully. He picked up the largest scroll from the pile and handed it to Hinnom, who nearly fell backward under its weight.

Hinnom had to put it back down to start unscrolling it and skimmed through the top of the list. "Well, it looks like I might be the first, but certainly will not be the last," he commented, seeing that, as he suspected, just about every action one could make was deemed a "sin" by God. Typical, considering what had happened to his great-grandparents after just one bite of fruit.

"But we've got everything well on its way to being ready," chirped Belphegor.

A lot of the angels closest to Hinnom smiled at him, proudly, hopefully.

He took another cautious sip of the tea. "Ah, yes, well, it's. . . a good start," he said diplomatically with a polite smile.

"A good start?" Mammon looked disconsolate.

"Yes, yes," he soothed, "you've done a great job constructing the basics, but now it's time to expand, don't you think?"

"Expand? But. . . but we've done so much already!" exclaimed one.

Hinnom suspected hard work was not something one had to put up with in 'Heaven'.

"Yes, you've certainly done a lot, but think of all those people about to die," he explained in a reasonable tone. "Some of the family are so old. Honestly, I'm surprised most of those old windbags are all still alive. And there's no way they qualify for this 'Heaven' of yours. So what you have to do is—"

"You don't give the orders," cut in Asmodeus.

"Why not? Who's in charge?" Hinnom demanded.

"Satan," said Naamah promptly.

"Does he want to be?"

Everyone stared at him, shocked, but there were a few whispers in the back that sounded like agreement with his scandalous suggestion.

He took an extra casual sip of the awful tea and then went on, being sure to speak loud enough for everyone to hear, "You said he's just been sulking rather than doing anything since you got here, and you said all he really wanted in the first place was not to take orders from God, not that he wanted to *give* orders."

He glanced around, taking in the feel of the crowd; they were all watching him intently, not interrupting as his family did whenever he tried to make what he felt were reasonable suggestions. Thinking of new ideas did not seem to be a strong point for angels.

"I noticed," Hinnom went on, "he wasn't exactly part of the original welcome. He doesn't seem overly invested in running things. And trust me, once the rabble starts making their way down here, things are going to need to be organized."

"Are we having a party without me?" drawled a voice from the tent entrance. Everyone looked up to see another fallen angel walk in. His robes were dirtier than most with streaks of what looked like dried blood. His hair, once combed into carefully oiled ringlets, was scraggly and unkempt. His face was craggy, like someone who had stared at the sun for too long. His wings were roughed up, but snapped with a strong crack like an ibis announcing its presence to an intruder, as he stumbled over to where Hinnom sat.

Hinnom inclined his head slightly but didn't get up. "Satan, I presume?"

"The one and only." Satan gave a mocking, stumbling bow, and then began to laugh, a hint of madness to his mirth. "Behold!" he shouted to the whole group, "O Fallen Angels, I—*I*—who, when I was Sammael, the Almighty's Favorite, refused to bow down to Adam, for he was made of mere clay after we had been made of holy fire, have now, without a thought, bowed to a son of Adam, a man of mere flesh, even *less substantial* than clay!"

He began laughing again, pausing only to take a long draught from a leather water skin he held before carrying on with his peals of mocking laughter.

There was a long, long moment of silence.

"Hey, S, so, how's it going?" one of them finally asked in a falsely cheery voice, eyes worried.

"I have drunk deep of the water made by the hands of the daughters of Eve. I have drunk. . . deeply. I. . . drunk. . ." He trailed off and took another pull from the water skin which clearly held something besides water.

"What have you got there?" asked Mammon nervously.

"Charming drink the humans invented. Points for creativity, I'll give 'em that." The angel formally known as Sammael grinned at Hinnom. "Clever girl, your sister."

"She certainly thinks she is," said Hinnom blandly. "According to this," he tapped on the scroll, "that alone might get her sent down here."

Satan grinned lopsidedly and then took another pull with a smacking noise of enjoyment. "It's going to get busy," he giggled.

"I'm glad you agree. And from what I can tell, it sounds like you all have come from a place much, much nicer than my home. Trust me when I say that we humans already have it so much worse than you that you are going to need my help if you want this to be a place of proper punishment."

Satan took another drink, burped, and said, "Do whatever you want. I don't care. I'm going for a walk."

"But the Lord said—" began Astaroth.

"So?" interrupted Satan angrily. "The worst He'll do is send me back here. Let Him. I just need a break from all His infallible plans. I'm going to walk the world for a while. Maybe start up my own group. Find some silly mortals and tell them I created heaven and earth." He grinned. "It might be fun to play God."

"Do you want some company?" asked one of the fallen angels hopefully.

"Stay, go, whatever, I don't care. But," he squared his shoulders, "it wouldn't do to end things on an informal note, so," he cleared his throat and intoned solemnly:

"I hereby do appoint this soul," he indicated Hinnom with a magnanimous wave of the hand still holding the water skin, "in charge of Hell during my absence."

Hinnom stood up, brushing his robes off. "I accept."

There was some surprised murmuring amongst the crowd. Satan turned on his heel and left the tent without any further ceremony. Caught off guard, a few hurried after him. Some looked at each other with pained expressions, clearly unsure which way to go.

In the end, some left with him, but most stayed behind.

Hinnom started going through the other scrolls to see what direction God had given. Asmodeus had been right—a lot of it was maddeningly vague. Luckily, being human, he was good at improvising.

He grabbed a piece of half-burnt wood, crushed some charcoal and spat to mix up some quick ink, then, with a brief, 'excuse me,' grabbed a feather off of Mammon's wing, and began scribbling notes on the parchment.

"I think the most efficient way to run this will be to divide the work up—put specific people in charge of different sins. Mammon, my man, you can be in charge of. . ." he pointed randomly at the list, "'Greed'."

Mammon grinned, please with the designation.

Belphegor peered over his shoulder to appraise the list of sins. "I'll take 'Sloth', that sounds easy," he said.

"Done," said Hinnom briskly. "Now, we've got a lot of work ahead of us if we want everything in place by the time people start to really die off. And trust me; killing Abel was just the beginning."

Others came closer to read the list, requesting sins to be in charge of.

Hinnom almost giggled, thinking there must be some way to pop back home for a visit at some point and let his family know they were going to a place much, much worse than a burning pile of garbage.

He glanced around at the fallen angels crowded around him, some looking excited, some looking anxious.

"And you're all going to need some new outfits—I'm thinking red and black, with lots of leather thrown in. These white robes. . . well, white just shows all the dirt. And something on your faces to make them a little more, well, startling, perhaps? Maybe get some animal parts, get you dressed up to look like some of those mixed together creatures Grandpa Seth tells about in some of his stories. Maybe we could get you some goat ears to tie around your heads? Or something. We'll work on that later."

"Looks like you've got everything well in hand, Hinnom," smirked Naamah.

He grinned back at her. "Which reminds me—I think I'll be taking a new name too."

New life, new job, new name, he thought, well pleased with how this day had turned out after all. He cast about for something appropriate and thought suddenly of the name of the star that appeared in the east right before sunrise. He'd always liked that star; seeing it meant the start of a fresh, new day.

"What name do you want?" asked one.

"Call me Lucifer."

And all the fallen angels shouted: "Hail Lucifer, Ruler of Hell!"

Dear Mary, are you there?

Megan Bee

*Hail Mary most merciful mother, hear my
cries.*
You, who bore the son of god,
welcomed his lusty cries as god
made man took his first breath.

You who watched that son,
both flesh of your flesh and yet,
also flesh of ours,
take his last breath.

*Blessed art thou who continued to live after
such a loss.*

Please, Mary, mother of all mothers,
surely you can offer some advice
on how to continue breathing while
knowing
your child is no longer on the same planet
as you.

How do you keep believing in
miracles and goodness when you've
witnessed such broken sadness?

How come the bible doesn't tell of your
suffering?
Are we to believe that you were just
magically okay
after your son was ripped away from you,

supposedly for the suffering of all
mankind
—but at what expense?

I said: *What about your suffering?*

Are we to think that you didn't weep bitter
hot tears?
That you didn't want to punch anyone
who
had the audacity to say
"he's in a better place now."
Because, if that's the case, I'd really like to
know how you did it.

How you held together when you
were faced with the idea of never seeing
your son
as you had known him, again.

And don't give me that whole "faith"
business, because,
look Mary, we are sisters here.
And it really doesn't mean anything
because

no matter how you look at it, it still is a
festering,
oozing, empty wound, piercing your side.

Maybe you didn't wake in the middle of
the night, swearing that you heard your
son cry out, cry out asking why he'd been
forsaken?
Surely you heard me, in the middle of the
night,

curled in a ball on the bathroom floor,
begging
to take my child's place, if only, she could
come back?

And if you didn't hear me then,
I know you have to hear the prayers on
every first star,
to give me a sign, a sign that she is okay,
but more!
A sign that I am okay also,

*because, lady, I gotta tell you, I'm pretty
sure I am not.*

If the scars that railroad up and down my
arms
and legs are any indication,
fine is the last thing I am, though I lie
well,
when others ask.

"How are you?",
they say, with pity dripping
down the backs of their throats,
honeyed words spilling
from their lips.

"Fine," I say. "I'm fine."

I nod numbly when they remind me
that my child, the flesh of my flesh, is in a
better place.
I clench my fists at my sides and
bite my cheeks until they bleed
when they remind me of my other
children.

"At least..."

they start to say, and I swear my soul
leaves my body.
I am an empty vessel, into which
they can pour their cherry cough syrup
words,
that are meant to coat my soul, but
instead
They just make me choke.

Mary, please, I beg of you,
give me eternal sunshine, because
I cannot take the memory of her birth.
I cannot take the memory of her death.

Mother me through this.
Stroke my hair and feed me hot tea
and promise me that I will not always
feel so broken and scared.

Promise me that I will not always
feel so helpless as I do when I wake
and remember that my child
is not in that pretty cradle in the corner.

My child is in a morgue.
Cold and alone
And I am in her nursery.
Her bed is cold and I am alone.

Mary, You have left me, all alone. I cry out
to you,
Why, Why have I been forsaken?
You reply with silence. Your statue eyes
stare back at me from my dollar store
candles.

Why?

Blessed are those who mourn, for they
shall be comforted, but
I carved your image into my thigh, called
your name with
Gravelly knees, and still you have
abandoned me here.

Yesterday, I thought I saw God.
He was standing on the corner,
with a shopping cart full of garbage,
talking to himself and I thought,
now there's a guy who has it all together.
There's a deity I can get behind.

And so, I did.

Ways of Knowing

Louise Milton

My father was a warrior and my mother a truth teller. I have no true way of knowing this except for the dreams; my memories are the barest glimpses that vanish when I clutch at them. The union between one who prizes conquest and one who seeks to know could lead only to places where love never dwells. And yet a child was permitted. The dreams and the voices visit to reveal the bones of what is no longer, but the shadows of what cannot be known haunt me.

I do not remember the exactness in time when the voices started. I only know that the voices are strong when the dreams are near. It is not safe to speak of what I hear from the voices. Once, I almost told my lover, not long after I had arrived at this place where I had not been born, but where the voices had been calling my name. I was holding Keston close, hidden by the grasses, growing wild and green. In that moment, I did want her to hold the knowing that the universe was larger than the sky above us, but I also wanted to share the burden, to be less alone. The dreams speak in flashes of color and shapes, and tell of a time before, and a time to come. But no one in my knowing has ever spoken of dreams and voices. Not even the truthtellers. So I held my tongue and longed for the company of the voices and the aching behind my eyes to depart.

I had journeyed long and far to reach this valley stretching between the blue hills that marked the east and west horizons. The proving time, the obligations, set by the Holders for me to achieve before the Gather circle drew wider to open a space was not easy. Doubt and suspicion were written on the faces of most, but was deeply engraved in the scrutiny of all twelve of the Holders. I felt their uncertainty, the unknowing if I was man or woman. Holder

Karon, was the first to see what the strength of my limbs and the nimbleness of my hands could be used for and argued that there might be a place for me in the fields where the strong bodies of the community were engaged in a continual battle with the earth to sustain the *nosta* bushes. Without the *nosta*, Holder Janes told me sternly, the *Gather* would cease to exist. Without the *nosta* there would be no reason to exist. I nodded to indicate willingness and listening.

"What is your name," Holder Karon said, more kindly.

"Dania," I answered, unsure if to add more would be unwise. There was a large and heavy silence and then Holder Janes turned and beckoned for me to follow him to the fields. In the days to come I tailed him like a silent shadow replicating all his small and large movements, watching for when the creases in his forehead signaled the need to adjust my timing to correspond to his own. The memory of those first days are blurred in a haze of salt sweat and stinging skin and a dread that the might and endurance I was demanding from the muscles in my legs and arms would be deemed insufficient despite the burning agony.

In this settlement the *nosta* bushes grow green and cling to the gentle slopes that surround the *Gather*, a settlement of huts crafted from woven roofs and walls. Existence is lived as a dance: each step a knowing each member of the *Gather* shares, what must happen now, what came before, what will happen next. A rhythm as steady as a heartbeat that plays through the cycle of the seasons again and yet again.

After the rains, the *nostas* flower, trumpets of bright scarlet, the color of red fire that the evening sun bleeds across the sky. The fragrance of the blossoms rises and sings in the air and the spirits of the *Gather* soar knowing that the blessing of the berries has visited once again.

During the fruiting and harvest times, the days are long and full, each task performed in accordance with the covenant, as told to the grandmothers and grandfathers, as was told to them. Each member of the *Gather*, the old and the young, know their part and do their duty without question. They rise at dawn to recite the prayers, the sacred words used sparingly to guard their strength. Earthen vessels are carried to the river in the morning hush, slip below the surface for filling and are carried up the hill in slow steady steps to quench the thirsting roots. Gently the nests of earth shielding each bush are combed and tilled to ensure invading pests cannot threaten or foreign growths will not compete for nourishment in the sparseness of the soil.

Only the Holders who walk the fields from end to end know how to select the strongest and truest of new green shoots that are carried off for transplanting, nurturing a new generation. As the *nostas* grow, plump and plentiful, an urgency swells in the *Gather*, waiting for the day the Holders pronounce the beginning of harvest which unleashes a frenzy of activity. Each berry must be gathered in the rightness of time so that each precious fruit is used to the fullest. While a portion of *nostas* are enjoyed fresh during harvest season, most are saved for drying, roasting, pounding. The resulting grounds, dark and sweet, are stored and enjoyed as brews and cakes, and sustain the *Gather* throughout the year.

A full circle of the season had unwound before the Holders agreed that I would be welcomed to the *Gather*. I had not believed Keston when she leaned in close with a glimmer in her eyes to whisper this secret. I had not told her of my encounter with Holder Janes a few days prior after walking back from the fields south of the river where the wild grasses grew. I went there often, not only because it served well as a place for Keston and I to meet up to sip the pleasure of each other's bodies, but also because the voices of the dreams had been calling.

That day I had trailed through the tall golden stalks, stopping to cradle the golden crowns between my fingers, curious about their meaning. When I rounded the corner and caught the full bore of his fierce and angry eyes, at first I thought he had guessed that Keston had been lying with me. But then I noticed his stare was intent on the stalks of golden grasses in my hand.

"Dania. What are you doing?!" It was more of an accusation than a question.

"Exploring the field grasses," I said. And then thinking

to distract him further I added, "Have we ever thought of harvesting the grasses? There are so many and perhaps we should..." I had no opportunity to finish as the Holder's wrath exploded.

"May the sky break open and the bright light strike you if I hear you use those words again!"

"But..."

"We shall have none other," he shouted. And then more quietly, but the tone of his words continued to hammer. "We shall have none other. None other."

The chorus in my head was crying. I dropped the grasses on the ground and covered my ears, not knowing, never knowing, how to invoke silence.

He said nothing further. He bent and picked up the grasses and marched away. I watched him cross the *Gather* grounds over to the pit where the evening fires were lit. He dropped the grasses into the pit and turned away, not watching as they caught fire and blazed away in a handful of stars in the dusk.

So no, I had not believed it possible that I would ever be welcomed to the *Gather* after that. But indeed, Keston's knowing had been true for on that very evening at the *Gather* circle, the Holders stood as one to make an announcement. They called me forward to stand before them.

"The *Gather* circle draws wider to welcome another to the people of the *nosta*." It was Holder Janes himself who held out his hand to me for the clasping, a fresh *nosta* berry sacrificing its bloody juices between our palms. "We are a gathering of the *nosta* people. The wise ones blessed us with the gift of *nosta*, the gift of life."

"Thanks be to the wise ones," I responded.

"The *nosta* is the source of all life, said the wise ones. Eat and drink of the *nosta* and see that it is good. Happy are they who put their trust in the ways of the wise ones."

"Thanks be to the wise ones," I responded again.

"We the many, become one when we share the gift of the *nosta*," we sang together. "Thanks be to the *nosta*. Thanks be for the gift of life."

A ceremonial *nosta* cup was passed around the evening circle and for the first time I lifted the sacred cup and sipped. For the first time in my living awareness, a place in a circle, belonged only to me. I thought about how each morning, I drank deeply of the morning *nosta*, the dark smoothness slipping down my throat and the sweet bite that lingered afterwards in the mouth. I thought about how it was true that one cup of *nosta* sustained my body for an entire day in the fields. And I decided not to think about the grasses anymore.

Now that I was welcomed, I was helped to build my own hut. The very first night I left the *Gather* circle to sleep under my own roof, Keston also stood and followed me. I stopped at my threshold and turned to see the women tittering. Keston crossed the doorway and pulled me in. She placed a gentle hand between my breasts and my heart filled and filled with a warmth that burst out in spokes of light and heat that could no longer be contained.

"Dania," she said. "My heart is yours. I want to share a roof with you until the end of time." Fear fought with want and I shook my head. Her hand reached out and stroked my face. "Dania," she said again, "the *Gather* and the Holders will not care as long as I bring forth babies." She laughed at the perplexity showing in my face. "Dania, do not fret, I know how to bring forth the babies. But they will be our babies and they will grow under this roof." She paused. Solemnness flowed in and filled the space between us. Her eyes searched my face. "That is, if this is what you want."

I extended my hand to her heart and echoed the words of her people. "Keston, my heart is yours. I want to share a roof with you until the end of time."

The first season after the welcoming was much like the one before. Except that this time I had my own roof, and Keston beside me, and a place in the *Gather* circle that I trusted would be held for only me. Keston's belly began to swell and soon our daughter Neesha was brought forth.

The voices were troubling though and allowed me no comfort. After the harvest of the second season, I learned how to quiet their plaintive cries. I walked through the fields and used my knife to scythe and sweep up armfuls of grasses. I plucked their golden heads and rubbed the heavy heads between my fingers. Blowing gently I watched their golden berries spin and fall into my basket. Keston and Neesha would join me sometimes; our daughter would laugh, delighted when she saw the golden grass berries pirouetting in the sunlight. I told them it was a way to pass the time. I did not tell Keston of what the voices spoke. That the golden berries were a food. The ultimate sacrilege: that *nosta* was not the only source of life.

Three more seasons passed, the forms and rhythms as I learned them. I knew my place, I sipped the *nosta*. I sang the chants beside my sisters, my brothers, the grandmothers, and the grandfathers. I let myself be soothed by the knowing order of *Gather* life. See, I told my voices. The order of the *nosta* people has its own truth.

It was the fourth season when the troubles began. Missteps in the tidy symmetry were small at first, not worthy of significant unease. That batch of *nosta* seemed slightly off. A number of the young developed a slight cough. One of the Holders came late to the *Gather* circle and then misspoke the ritual words. Someone observed that the weight of the *nosta* sacks this harvest were just a little less heavy than the season before.

And then without warning, when Holder Karon's spirit left her body to join with the wise ones, the *Gather* was overcome with a tearing kind of grief. Keston said it had been known to happen before, but not within her lifetime. The Holders consulted the covenant texts, then followed them devoutly to anoint her replacement. And all agreed the circle had not healed the breaking of her space and would not for some time to come. But when the *Gather* finally knew the meagerness of the season's harvest, there was no more doubt that disorder had entered uninvited.

Although the Holders offered answers, fashioned from their secret hoard of knowing, few were satisfied, craving easement for their fears. It was known throughout the *Gather* that the *nosta* reserves were depleting at rates faster than had been replenished. How could one be content with a half mug of *nosta*, I heard someone mutter.

I worried about our waning strength in the fields as I, like the others, worked more slowly, stopped more frequently. And it was Keston who said when we were whispering in the dark of night that the numbers of babies brought forth that season numbered less than ten. I knew from my dreams and my voices that a time was coming for the *Gather* to bring forth change. But my knowing did not speak of what or how and I was afraid.

The blossoming of a new season arrived. One morning, after a night of foreboding dreams with dark and twisted paths where I could not find my way, I rose late. I was weary and aching, my belly pinching with hunger. I entered the *Gather* circle, murmuring greetings and regrets. Keston joined me, handing me a cup of steaming *nosta*, touching me on the shoulder as if to balance herself. But I caught the warning. An argument had ensued between the Holders, an occurrence not commonly witnessed. The *Gather* watched in a brooding silence. An entire section of field had been discovered stricken with a wasting disease, the *nosta* blossoms black and wilted, dropping to the ground. Some of the Holders wanted to tear out the offending bushes at once and plant again. They did not appear to hear the others who countered that the numbers of available transplants were lacking. Two of the Holders said there was a need to consult the covenant texts for solutions. Another Holder stood up and spoke at great length, oblivious to the silent groaning of the circle, blaming the disaster on the far away season when it had been agreed that the nesting circles could be dug two fingers smaller.

Holder Janes watched the anger and fear silently crackling and leaping round and through the *Gather* circle and held up a hand.

"We are a gathering of the *nosta* people," he said, as he had said a thousand times before. "The wise ones blessed us with the gift of *nosta*, the gift of life."

"Thanks be to the wise ones," everyone responded as was expected, but I did not join in.

"Happy are they who put their trust in the ways of the wise ones," Holder Janes recited. This time only the Holders responded. "Thanks be to the wise ones."

I stood in the stillness that felt like stones and the eyes of the *Gather* turned to me.

"The people are hungry. The children are hungry. We are becoming weak and ill. It is time for change." I looked at Holder Janes' lined face and empty eyes, reaching for a knowing we could not share, that I could not name.

"We the many, become one when we share the gift of the *nosta*," he continued on. "Thanks be to the *nosta*. Thanks be for the gift of life." I turned to leave, the circle parted to open a space for me.

Life continued on, but without the forms that guided order. The disease plagued bushes were ripped from their nests, the fields replanted. The Holders persisted in their futile rituals, poring over the impotent truths of their texts. A miserable and paltry yield of *nostas* ripened and were harvested and celebrated according to the covenants as it was written. But a silent seed of knowing was taking root; the commandments of this *nosta* no longer served, a time for a new covenant was becoming.

And then one night, we woke to Neesha's crying. After we rocked and calmed her, I led Keston to the hiding cache I had dug and covered with a mat. Deep within the earth I had lined up rows of baskets filled with golden grass berries. She drew back swiftly and her eyes were wide.

"You said it was just for fun."

"Keston," I said. "We must try to find a way to use the grass berries for food. You know how to grind the *nostas* into meal. Could you find a way to try that with these berries?"

"But this is not our way," Keston cried. "It has been promised. *Nostas* are the source of life." I knew her fright was born of having the last remaining stones cast away from what had sheltered her from the falling skies all her life. I tried again.

"Keston, I know your people have lived forever on the *nosta*. And you taught me to love the knowing ways of the *nosta*." I paused. "But this too I know. *Nosta* is not the only source of life." And the moment the words left my mouth something deep inside locked and tight broke open and flooded through me like a river of light.

"It is my knowing," I finished, and my voices rejoiced and stilled.

Neesha rolled and tossed in her sleep again and woke

coughing. Keston went to her, but this time she could not be calmed. Keston turned to me and I saw in her eyes that the choice had been made.

"This is *my* knowing Dania," she said with fierceness. "I will not let the children die."

Keston gathered the women she knew and trusted; they worked in stealth over a period of days. She brought me a handful of golden meal and poured it into the cup of my hands.

"When we stir it with water in a pot over the fire it makes a kind of mush." She wrinkled her nose. "The taste is not good but the babies are eating." She hesitated. "It might be helping."

I sifted the golden sand through my fingers, thoughtful, reaching into my mind for deeper knowing.

"What is it?" Keston asked.

"Bring me some more of this meal," I said.

The next morning I filled a large earthen bowl with two handfuls of the meal. I dipped a cup in a pail of water from the stream and stirred it in. I covered it with a *nosta* sack and left for the fields.

"See. Just mush," Kestin said that evening, poking a finger in it and screwing up her face.

For the next several days I added two handfuls of meal and a cup of the water to the mush in the bowl. I would sit and watch the foaming that sat on the surface before I left for the fields. Then came the morning Keston and I lifted the sack and realized this living sponge was growing and climbing, reaching for escape.

"It's a creature," she breathed in awe. "Dania, what have we done?"

"This is truth," I agreed. I picked up the ball of meal, squeezed and pinched the softness, rolled it between my palms. "If the *nosta* is the source of life, what heresy can this be? For this grass berry meal will truly be a food born from life." I smiled.

"What does your knowing tell you now Dania?"

I closed my eyes. "That we must take this ball of mush and cook it over the hot stones. Like we do with the *nosta* cakes."

"This we will not be able to hide," she pointed out.

I went to Holder Janes with a proposal. I brought him the thought that the Holders and field workers should hike to the far north field. The field had not been used for several seasons and was a source of contention for the Holders. An argument was waging about the suitability of the location and possibilities for improving the potency of the soil. I suggested mildly that many voices together might assist the Holders in seeking a truth. The distance was far though and would take half the day. Holder Janes, no longer able to cover his black despair, seized the idea at once, making it his own.

The march was long and strenuous, the discord incessant, and the piety of the Holders unrelenting in the face of their weakening explanations. It was a defeated group that returned to the *Gather* circle when the sun was low in the sky. Feet were bruised and bellies were empty; exhaustion with no hope of remedy.

Keston and the women were waiting near the heart of the *Gather* circle. This band of women, who had worked for days with their hands in the shaping of a new truth, were prepared for battle. Keston stood in the center, flushed and triumphant, a stack of pale oval cakes laid out before her. A new scent, warm and strong, wafted from the firestones and my mouth began to water.

"Welcome grandfather," she said to Holder Janes. "We have prepared for you a new nourishment. I hope you will find it pleasing."

"What is this," he demanded.

"A new type of cake. It comes from the grass berries." The women began to pass out the cakes to the returning field workers who fell upon them with eagerness and exclamations.

I went to stand beside Keston and Holder Janes who was turning the cakes over and over in his hands in disbelief.

"Stop at once!" he cried out. "It is forbidden!" He turned to me. "Is this your doing?"

"It is," I replied.

"We are the *nosta* people. We welcomed you to us and you have caused us to betray the wise ones."

I knelt before him. "Holder Janes, I was humbled and

proud to be welcomed to the *nosta* people. I wanted nothing more than to live the way of your people. My people." I was quiet for several moments. I closed my eyes and reached out to listen to my voices, to feel the thrumming silence in the *Gather*, to hear the knowing and the not-knowing pulsing in the air.

"But the people are hungry. The *nosta* has not sustained them and it is time for a new truth to be known."

I picked up the cake made with the golden meal of the grass berry and took a bite. The taste of the cake flooded my mouth with a delicious sweetness and flowed through me with a kind of rapture. I smiled as I lifted the cake high for all to see.

"We are still one people, the people of the *nosta*. The people will no longer live by the *nosta* alone. These cakes are a new gift for the people. Taste and see that life is good."

"Taste and see that life is good," the *Gather* echoed.

And I picked up a cake and gently placed it the Holder's hand.

Louise Milton

Izzy Tells No Lies

P. James Norris

I step out of the air-conditioned quiet of the Basilica and into the cacophony of Colfax's incessant traffic and its attendant smell of auto exhaust. I do what I can to shut out this assault and cross myself. "Lord, grant me the strength to bring Your comfort to those who most need it."

Only then do I allow myself to look south across Colfax. To do otherwise is to invite a nearly paralyzing despair over the quiet desperation of the far, far too many lost souls who wander up and down the street looking for sex, drugs and, often times, oblivion.

But *she* is there, as though she has been waiting for me, knowing exactly when I would emerge from the nave and out into the hot, muggy August twilight. As she seems to every night, she comes to tell me of her latest vision.

For a moment, her eyes focus on mine, and I see *her*. Not what her brain's natural chemical imbalances have made of her. Not what the drugs, prescribed and not, have made of her. Not what her guilt has made of her. Not what her parents have made of her by throwing her out of their home, like Jezebel, on her eighteenth birthday.

I see her—I see *Isabelle*.

Such sadness. Such compassion. Such thwarted strength.

As always, it is her cornflower blue eyes that first draw my gaze. But then I notice her dish-water blonde hair is even dirtier than normal—when was the last time she showered? Would it be a brighter, more lustrous blonde if she had the opportunity to wash it regularly? The slight Adam's apple. And good Lord, is that stubble or is it just dirt from living on the street, or wherever it is she sleeps at night?

But then the confusion takes grip, and *Izzy* starts lashing the air before her face, as though swatting at a cloud of gnats. She turns east and starts walking, almost stumbling, toward Pennsylvania Street.

When she reaches it, she will turn around and pace down to Logan Street and back to Pennsylvania.

Over and over.

Until I approach her and she tells me of whatever vision it is that has brought her all but to the steps of the Cathedral Basilica of the Immaculate Conception. Steps I know she will never climb because she is convinced God can no longer love her—would no longer welcome her in His house. But God is infinitely forgiving, and He *would* welcome her in His house as readily as He once welcomed. . . Isaac.

I grit my teeth to push thoughts of that poor, tormented boy from my mind—they still have the power to push me to a despair worse than the contemplation of all those who choose, for whatever reason, to desecrate their bodies and souls on Colfax.

That her parents—"good Catholics"—could not accept their son's inability to see himself as a boy.

That they would throw her out of their home for. . .

With the determination of a man who knows he's lost his way in the desert and yet must soldier on, I walk down the steps to let Isabelle tell me of her latest vision. But, of course, I'm forced to stop before I reach the sidewalk.

"Heypaaadre."

Benny manages to slur even just those two words. He's an elderly. . . gentleman. Every night he scoots up and down five blocks of Colfax on a wheeled walker with fluorescent orange tennis balls on the rear legs. He's not fat, but is portly. His legs are bowed, and the same quarter inch of grey stubble covers his liver-spotted head as his throat and jowly cheeks.

He wears a Marine baseball cap—claims to have served in Saigon during the war, claims to have saved more than twenty people during the evacuation. A cigarette dangles from his lips even as a portable oxygen tank pumps what he claims is "pure oxie" directly into his nose. If it were, indeed, pure oxygen, I suspect he would have blown his head off long ago while trying to light one of his ever-present cigarettes. I've seen him thumb his zippo a dozen times before managing to light a cigarette to his satisfaction.

Even from five feet away, I can't tell which odor is stronger, the stink of his nicotine saturated clothes, or the whiskey on his breath.

Ignoring the man would be rude.

He comes to a stop just a foot from me.

I breathe through my mouth to avoid *some* of the stench. "Good evening, Benny. How are you tonight?"

"Same'ld, same'ld. Ya know-oww it is, paadre."

The words are a little less slurred—practice makes perfect, I guess. "Well. . ."

"Say, padre"—he's making a real effort to speak distinctly—"Ya wouldn't happen to have some spare change, wouldja?"

I fight down a sigh. "Benny, I do have some change, but. . ."

"Honest, padre. I'm headed down to MikkiD's for some coffee and a burger."

Isabelle's on her third round. Though I know she'll keep going for as long it takes for me to get to her, I hate to make her wait.

Experience has taught me that if I give Benny money, it will go for either more smokes or more whiskey. Luckily, I have an out, and I must play it quickly. "Benny, I remember giving you two dollars last Thursday night when you told me the same thing. And you told me you'd bring me the receipt to prove you bought food and not cigarettes or whiskey. But you didn't. So, tonight, you're on your own."

"Tat's fair, paaadre."

His head sags, as does my heart. The slur is back in full force even as he pulls a piece of cardboard off the side of his walker. He hangs the sign from wire clothes hangers on the walker's front cross-bar. It reads, *Viet Nam War Vet—Every quarter helps—GOD BLESS*.

That done, he starts wheeling down toward the McDonalds. "Ya hafa gude evenin', paaadre."

"You as well, Benny."

Who knows? Perhaps he *was* telling the truth. And perhaps I have committed the sin of unjustified condemnation.

But now I'm free to go to Isabelle.

As I step into the inner eastbound lane, she stops her pacing and swatting at the air. She doesn't look at me, keeping her attention on the ground a foot or two in front of her. By coincidence or not, she has stopped just where the traffic leads me to walk up onto the south sidewalk.

It would be arrogant to think that the Lord had arranged the traffic so I could cross all four lanes of Colfax at little more than a brisk walk. Nonetheless, I give Him my thanks.

I know that using her full name will cause the swatting to start anew, and several minutes will pass before it stops again. So, "Good evening, Izzy."

Only then does Izzy look up to meet my gaze. "Father Grigori." It is not Isabelle who says this, it is Izzy's scattered, diffident gaze.

Everyone else to whom I minister addresses me, as is Catholic tradition, by my ordained name, "William." But not Isabelle. In fact, I don't know how she could know my given name. Just another one of the mysteries that is Isabelle.

From the basilica's portico, I had not noticed the light, open-hand shaped bruise on her left cheek nor the bruise around her right wrist. "Izzy, what happened to your face and wrist?"

"Michael is coming."

Still Izzy—is this her prophecy? But I don't care—what I *do* care about are the bruises.

"*Izzy*, what *happened* to your face and wrist?"

"Isabelle needed money, so she tried to turn a trick. But the Jane was a lesbian who didn't appreciate Isabelle's little Isaac."

This isn't the first time Isabelle has tried to prostitute herself to a woman who subsequently abused her when the Jane discovered biologically, Isabelle is a man.

"I see." I want to take her right hand in mine to examine the bruise, to wipe the dirt from her face so I can better see the bruise there. But in the six months I've known her, we've touched only once. In the church's hospice. And she had fled immediately afterward. But come to think of it, it was after this that she started calling me by my given name.

Though it costs me terribly, I respect her self-denial of human compassion. "Who is Michael?"

"Michael is coming for Benny."

For no longer than it takes her to answer, *Isabelle*, not Izzy, looks up at me. Direct and self-assured, not afraid and confused.

By both her tone and the way her eyes hold—almost grip—mine, *Isabelle* implies that I know this Michael.

It is always Isabelle who tells me what will come to pass.

And as always, the intensity of her gaze starts to fade.

She is Izzy once again.

And even though I know to expect it, I flinch at her first swat at the things she sees before her eyes but aren't really there. And as she turns and stumbles away, I pray in whispered words, so that she cannot hear, "May the Lord watch over you, Isabelle."

oOo

For the next hour, I stand in front of the Cathedral, inviting all who pass to the midnight Mass.

But my heart's not in it—another sin for which I will have to atone.

Michael. Archangel *Michael?* The Lord's warrior, His bringer of death? If it is the Archangel coming for Benny. . .

There are so many ways to die on Colfax, and so many do.

Worried for his physical safety, I keep an eye out for Benny. But I do not see him before it is time to go in to celebrate the Mass.

oOo

Attendance is sparse, and giving the sacrament to the handful in attendance does not take long. Another sin to account for: my prayers are only half-heartedly for those to whom I offer the sacrament—mostly I pray that the Lord will show Benny mercy this night.

oOo

As I remove my vestments in the sacristy, I can't help but think about when I first met Isabelle.

It was just days after I had arrived at the basilica; I had not even led my first Mass, when the Monsignor approached me about a girl in the hospice. She had been badly beaten.

As he led me to her bedside, he told me Izzy and Isabelle's story.

Told me how Julia, one of the cleaning staff, had found Isabelle lying, nearly unconscious and bleeding, by the rectory door. He hoped that I would be able convince her to go to the police to report the beating—she had told him only that Jane had done it.

When I first saw her I could not believe that anyone would do anything so brutal to such an obviously tortured soul. But my own experience with the *Bratva* back home in Moscow forced me to acknowledge that such things happen. Far more often than a loving God would allow. So often to the least able to. . .

The Monsignor introduced us: "Father William, this is Izzy. Izzy, this is Father William. I've asked him to look after you."

Isabelle did not reply.

At first, I tried to console her, but she did not need consolation.

In a very matter of fact manner, Izzy—it would take me some time to recognize the difference between Izzy and Isabelle—told me that what had happened *happens*.

This was the beginning of my trek into the moral and spiritual desert that is East Colfax.

I spent hours by her bedside.

It was a long time before she would tell me the story.

It was the same story as Izzy had told me earlier today, only with more dire outcomes.

Then I tried to show her sympathy, but she did not want it.

Sympathy implies a connection, but the desert is a desolate place.

Eventually, she announced her need to relieve herself.

I offered to bring her a bed-pan and give her privacy, but in an act of will the likes I had not seen before and have not seen since, she forced herself up out the cot in which Julia had laid her.

With her first step, she stumbled and when I took her by the arm to steady her, she froze like a statue.

I said her name, apologized, worried that I had wrenched her arm.

But she did not respond. Did not move.

Eventually, not knowing what else to do, I let go.

Only then did Izzy look at me and say, "Isabelle needs to do this for herself, Father Grigori."

I was startled by her use of my given name, convinced that the Monsignor had given my name as "Father William."

Odd, how only tonight, it should come back to me that this was the first time Izzy had called me Grigori.

But her poise forbade questions.

I escorted her to the restroom and then found the Sister Nurse to ask if Izzy had suffered physical harm not visible to the eye.

When I returned scant minutes later to the restroom, Izzy was gone.

The desert is also a lonely place, as I truly began to learn that night.

oOo

I am on my knees, praying for guidance regarding both Isabelle and Benny when there is a shockingly loud knock at my door.

"Father William! Are you awake? There's been a. . ."

Julia's voice trails off as I open the door. Her eyes are wide with fear, her mouth gaping with dismay, her aged, dark Colombian skin pale. Her right hand is still raised in a fist, as though she doesn't know what to do with it now. The other trembles at her breast.

"Julia, what is it? What's wrong?"

She starts to answer in Spanish, too rapid for me to follow, but stops herself after just a few words. She swallows hard, and her eyes plead for comfort.

When I reach out to touch her still raised fist, she starts and snatches it to her breast as well. I gently take both her hands and hold them between mine. "*Julia, está bien.*" My Spanish is not yet as good as I want it to be, so I continue in English. "Whatever it is, it is the Lord's will." Doggerel theology, but Julia's faith is a simple one.

This seems to steady her, but I can see the effort it costs her to suppress her normally charming accent. "Father, there is man in the courtyard." She swallows again, before adding, "I think he is dead."

It takes me a moment to process this, but then, letting go of Julia's hands, I spin and stride to the small window that looks out over Logan and the rectory courtyard. I thrust aside the heavy drapes and. . .

Red-and-blue lights flash balefully.

Uniformed officers stand around a body.

Paramedics rock back on their heels, remove an oxygen mask from. . .

The body lies in a smudge of something black against the courtyard's limestone and marble tiles.

Blood.

In this light I can't make out his face, but there, a few feet from the body, is Benny's unmistakable walker with its bright orange tennis balls.

I bow my head, close my eyes, and quietly utter "I commend you, my dear brother, to almighty God and entrust you to your Creator." I suspect Benny is already dead, so the Prayer of Commendation may not be appropriate, but when I look back, the Monsignor stands in the background, and I trust that he has given Benny his Last Rites.

Then my eye is drawn across Logan to a person standing in a shadow. She seems to be standing witness, her head bowed.

And as I realize who it is, Isabelle looks up at me.

oOo

I run down two flights of stairs like Satan himself is at my heels. Bursting through the rectory's front doors, I startle the two police officers still standing near Benny's body.

But even before I get to the sidewalk, Isabelle is gone.

oOo

As the Monsignor and I walk together back into the rectory, he volunteers that Benny died of a single small-caliber gunshot.

Suspects? None.

Motive? No money on the body. But for a homeless person like Benny, that means nothing.

His walker was his most valuable possession.

On the other hand, maybe he had just bought a pack of cigarettes or a bottle of whiskey.

oOo

Though I lay on my bed until the sun rises, I never really make it to sleep. For no reason I can express, even to myself, I know Isabelle was there when Benny was killed.

On Colfax, people have been killed for less than nothing.

Lord, it is I who need comfort.

oOo

I don't know what to do. If Isabelle witnessed Benny's murder, then she could be a target now.

But it's entirely possible that the person who killed Benny was so drunk or high or both that they don't even really know what they did or that they were seen doing it.

oOo

During the day, when my duties allow, I go out onto Colfax and ask after Izzy. Many of the people I speak to know of her, but no one knows, or is willing to reveal, where she spends her days.

oOo

The Monsignor, a very intuitive man, doesn't ask why I'd like him to take the evening Mass. Today is August 15th, the Night of The Assumption, so the evening Mass is starting later than normal—at sundown, at 7:56 p.m.

By the time the Monsignor has begun his entrance procession, I am on Colfax asking its nighttime denizens if they've seen Izzy or know where she might be found. I walk a few blocks to the east and then back a few blocks to west of the Cathedral several times.

I expand my search, on my next eastbound trek, I walk an additional block before turning back to the west, and then walk an extra block in that direction.

It's a Friday night, and so the traffic is insane. More than once I nearly become a statistic myself when crossing Colfax to speak with someone I've seen in Izzy's company.

Perhaps the Lord is looking out for me, but I take no comfort in this thought.

I am convinced it is Isabelle who needs His protection.

oOo

By nine o'clock, my search pattern has extended to the east end of the 16th Street Mall. I've never seen Isabelle on the mall, and it's earlier than I've seen her anywhere, but many of the Colfax homeless panhandle on the mall until around eleven. I hope someone there might know how I can find her.

oOo

An hour and a half later, I'm back in my rectory cell. My feet and legs ache. I haven't walked so much in such a short period of time in. . . most likely, ever. And the hot, humid August weather has left me a sweaty and smelly mess. My collar is tight around my neck.

Not wanting to waste time, I spend more time on a hand-towel bath than a shower would have taken.

As I put on my shirt, I immodestly look out my window.

As I do, Isabelle looks up at me from the very spot where she'd stood last night.

Buttoning my shirt fully isn't possible as I run down the stairs, but modesty be damned.

This time, she's still there as I blow through the front doors.

In seconds, I'm standing before her—it's Isabelle, not Izzy. Without thinking, I blurt out, "Isabelle, I've been looking for you all night."

Her eyes widen at the sound of her full name, and her hands start to twitch.

I fear even Izzy will retreat into swatting the air, and I squash an urge to take her hands in mine in an attempt to keep her mind from fluttering away. Instead I quickly correct myself, hoping to minimize the damage. "Izzy, I was worried about you."

Her jaw clenches ever so slightly, and her hands become still. It may not be Isabelle looking at me now, but at least Izzy is.

I want desperately to ask if she witnessed Benny's murder, but I fear this may not be a good tack to take. Perhaps the tried and true. "How are you tonight?"

I'm probably kidding myself, but it looked like, for just a moment, Izzy, or possibly Isabelle, was thanking me with her eyes.

"Michael is coming."

My stomach plummets to my feet. I know she's just answered the question I wanted to ask. "Izzy. . ."

"Michael is coming for Isabelle."

The Earth seems to spin a day's turning around me in but a moment.

The next few seconds pass in a fraction of one but take an eternity to play out.

A glint of light behind Isabelle catches my eye.

A shape emerges from behind a trash dumpster in the Archdiocese parking lot.

A flash of light.

A sound of a .38 snub-nose.

Isabelle gasping.

Stumbling a step toward me.

Her hands coming to rest, unbelievably lightly, on my chest.

The sound of the gun hitting the ground.

A guttural, angry voice saying, "You won't rat me out to the pigs, you bitch."

The sound of feet running away into the night.

Without being aware I'd taken a hold of her, I gently lower Isabelle to the ground.

"He's here," she says in an absurdly matter of fact way.

And suddenly, night becomes day.

Or rather morning, as the light illuminating Isabelle's face feels like the sun rising in the east behind me.

She is only nineteen years old, but her face has always looked many years older. Those extra, unwarranted years fade away in the golden light illuminating her face.

Isabelle is the beautiful young woman she was meant to be. Her dingy, stringy hair takes on a brilliant flaxen sheen. The dirt on her face evaporates. The only thing about her that doesn't change is the cornflower blue of her eyes.

And then she smiles—Isabelle smiles. "Grigori, I brought Michael for you."

I am stunned—Isabelle has never in my experience referred to herself in the first person.

Perhaps what she's said should scare me, but the look in her eyes tells me there was nothing to fear.

Following her gaze, I look over my shoulder.

"Child, forgive yourself and know the forgiveness the Lord God granted you the day you were born. Come with Me, and never know pain again."

In my ears, the Archangel's words are English. In my mind, I hear him in my native Russian. In my heart, the Latin of the Holy Church. And in my soul, every language ever spoken by any of God's creations.

He is beautiful. Divinely beautiful.

But not so beautiful as Isabelle, when I turn back to her.

Her eyes close, and as they do, she says, "I brought him to lead you out of the desert."

And as they do, the light of the Archangel fades away.

oOo

I am still standing there looking down at Isabelle when the police arrive. They try to question me, but the look of peace on her face arrests their natural suspicion. Their natural cynicism.

It is a look I am certain that Isabelle never knew.

But that is of no concern now.

All that matters is that Isabelle tells no lies.

And in this, and the light of the Archangel, I find a comfort that will last me all of my days.

Christopher Nadeau

Ultimate Messiah Smackdown

Christopher Nadeau

Don't ask me how it started.

I came in after the two of them ran into each other. I was on vacation in Branson, Missouri, talking to some Mormons who assured me they were "this close" to locating the ever-elusive Garden of Eden when people started yelling and running. Hearing no gunshots, I excused myself and joined the crowd, hoping to see something more exciting than the ads for washed up country singers that assaulted the senses.

"Do you think it's really him?" a woman asked me, panting between each word. "Is he back?"

I just shrugged. This was one of those towns where not knowing worked just fine.

"I'm coming, Jesus!" a man yelled up ahead. "It's me, George! Remember?"

Now I was really confused. What kind of expression was that?

The rabid press of humanity pushed me forward, there was no option for questions and ponderings. This was an event, a happening, and I would apparently experience it no matter what.

The shouting ahead grew more intense and, as one, the crowd surged forward and we stopped and gasped at the sight greeting us.

It was Him. I mean the Him we all heard about. He looked just like the painting, too. He had long, sandy blond hair, a neatly trimmed beard and mustache, pale white skin. The only difference was that now he was wearing a blue suit with a red tie and carrying a leather briefcase.

"Step forward for the growth opportunity of a lifetime!" he intoned. "This is a limited time offer! Sign up now for the true salvation that only I, the returning Jesus, can provide."

Dozens fell to their knees while reaching for their wallets and purses.

"Don't listen to him," someone out of my range of vision said. "He's a fake!"

"Who's that guy?" someone yelled.

"Some hippy," a woman replied with a wave of her pudgy hand.

I wove through the crowd until I could see who "him" was. The first thing that struck me was, he was short. Like five-foot-five if he was an inch. He also had wooly, curly black hair that ran haphazardly along his head and a filthy white robe. His sandals had seen better days, and his dark brown skin matched them almost perfectly. Who was this unkempt weirdo?

"Pay no heed to this impostor!" he yelled. "I have returned to collect my loyal followers."

The other, the one that *looked* like Jesus, chuckled. "Yeah, you're really gonna have a successful conversion rate looking like *that*."

People laughed and started talking to him, begging him for his grace, offering to follow him anywhere. The more he talked about salvation not being free, and the need for meeting the bottom line, the more their eyes glazed over and the more they ignored the dirty little dude standing to my left.

"Ask him why he's here," the man said.

Something in the little guy's tone combined with the passion in his eyes persuaded me to do as he asked.

"Why are you here," I shouted. The crowd grew disturbingly silent as all eyes turned to me. As if Moses had joined the party, they parted until nothing but a litter of empty wallets separated us.

"Excuse me?" Portrait Jesus said.

"Answer him," the little guy said, his confidence growing.

Portrait Jesus smirked and raised a perfectly groomed eyebrow. "Just who do you think I am, Samuel Franke?"

Okay, he knew my name. I was sold. He was the real deal. That other guy was some sort of nut. I felt ashamed of myself. "Never mind," I said and began to turn.

"Don't back down now!" the little guy hissed at me. "Make him admit who he is!"

"I'm the Lord and Savior of mankind," the walking, talking painting said, his grin wide as he turned in a circle, his hands out, palms up. Making good eye contact. "This was all vetted two thousand years ago."

More people in the ever-growing crowd fell to their knees, many of them placing their faces flat on the ground. Some people sobbed and threw their hands in the air, their heads back as if the Father would appear to them next. For some reason, I didn't join in. Only a few of us didn't.

"You're leading them into pointlessness," the little man yelled, wagging his index finger. "You have perverted the message."

Portrait Jesus made a *pshhh* sound and looked around. "These people seem to get it. It's all about brand recognition, hoss." His grin again, "And I am the brand, the truth, and the light."

My head ached. My stomach had a pit in it. My hands wouldn't stop shaking.

"That ain't none of *my* Jesus!" a woman yelled from somewhere deeper in the crowd. "Everybody knows Jesus was black!"

This started a whole new chaos within the crowd as someone yelled, "You people think everybody is black!"

The response, "Everybody *is* black!" didn't go over well either. Yelling and shoving ensued.

"Stop fighting!" the little guy yelled.

"And just who the hell are?" some new arrival asked.

The little guy looked at him and smiled. "I am Jesus."

That resulted in raucous laughter.

"Is that the best the devil could do?" someone said.

The little guy stomped up and down, looking for all the world like a disheveled cartoon character having a meltdown. This drew more laughter, but not from me.

"People don't want a Jesus who looks like a homeless beggar," Portrait Jesus said. He waved his hands down his suit. "Who wants to feel guilty about being successful?"

This was met with cries of "Yeah" and "Good point." The crowd slowly moved closer to the handsome, picture perfect Christ they'd all grown up seeing on peoples' walls. A few people shouted, "Amen."

"Whatever happened to the dignity of living simply?" the little guy said. "This phony wants to call himself your savior while advocating greed as a way of life. Is that what makes a Christian?"

"Sounds like class envy to me," Portrait Jesus said. "Good people, how many of you think God wants you to be poor?"

Very few people raised their hands and the ones that did lowered them immediately upon noticing the disgusted looks of those around them.

"Of course God doesn't want you to be poor!" the little guy yelled. "But He also doesn't want you to horde everything for yourselves while your fellow men suffer."

Portrait Jesus snorted. "Now we're supposed to take care of the people who don't want to work?"

"'Blessed are the meek, for they shall inherit the Earth.'"

"The meek, not the lazy!"

I felt bad for the little guy. He was clearly outmatched on the charisma scale. In fact, it was safe to say he didn't know any of the current buzzwords and catch-phrases. I looked away as he hung his head.

"Anyway," Portrait Jesus said, "we're still in the process of evaluating our options, so we're not ready to make a final decision yet. If you'll step forward, I'll hand out our assessment forms to get a little positive momentum going on this thing."

I frowned; since when did Jesus talk like a real estate tycoon?

"Obviously, I'll be the point of contact on this," he continued. "And there's a pretty intense evaluation phase. We used to do it all in-house but it was more cost effective to farm out some of the work to the lesser realms."

The more Portrait Jesus talked, the more blissful the majority of the crowd became. Even I felt a bit swayed by his spiel. With each person he signed up, the dirty little guy in the old sandals seemed to diminish.

I decided I had to know what this was all about and grabbed an application form from one of Portrait Jesus' voluntary helpers. It took only a moment for me to raise my hand when he asked if anyone had any questions. I was the fifth person he called and the only one who questioned the wording of the application.

"I'm just a little confused over why you need to know if I am now or if I have ever been a member of the Communist Party?"

Portrait Jesus air shot me with his thumb and forefinger. "Excellent, question. It's just for our records."

"Uh-huh," I said. "And this part about 'Islamofascism?'"

His grin faltered. "We're looking for a very specific type of person for this project."

"But that isn't even a word," I said. "In fact, it's impossible to be an Islamic fascist."

"Everybody has their own viewpoint."

"Listen to him!" The little guy said from next to me.

I didn't even know he was there, but he seemed empowered by this moment.

"Samuel Franke speaks with the voice of one who sees truth."

That gave me goose bumps; nobody had ever said that about me before.

Portrait Jesus placed his chin inside his thumb and forefinger and nodded absently. "I'm thinking you're probably not a good fit for this organization. But I'd like to thank you for coming out and I really enjoyed meeting you."

"Oh, stuff it!" the little guy said.

Many in the crowd gasped.

"Save your hollow corporate speak for your next power meeting." The little guy turned to the crowd and raised his hands. "*I am* the Light and the Way. Only through me are you saved. This guy is just a wanna-be poser dork!"

Portrait Jesus shook his head. "Another disgruntled former employee."

"Screw you guys," the little guy yelled. "I'm going somewhere else!"

Before our eyes, He floated right up into the sky and vanished in a flash of white.

The resulting awe only lasted a moment, however, as Portrait Jesus started making a speech about profit and how those who didn't believe in his business model should probably be erased from the face of the Earth.

I yelled as loud as I could, over and over, until people started to notice me. It was as if I'd been chosen to do this, my voice withstanding the constant strain as I spoke to the crowd.

"Don't you see?" I said. "This isn't Jesus. The man who left, that was Jesus. This guy is the Jesus of selfish men. The Jesus of bigotry and greed. He only has power as long as you buy into his agenda!"

A bottle came sailing from somewhere deep in the crowd and landed at my feet, spilling brown liquid all over my tan khakis.

"Why do you hate freedom?" someone yelled.

Despite my protests to the opposite, I was shouted down.

"If you didn't hate freedom, you wouldn't have a problem with us doing whatever Jesus says!" someone else yelled.

I looked down at the bottle and sighed; if I tried again, the next hurled object would most likely find its target. The idiots in the crowd continued to swarm around the Jesus who looked like the man in Da Vinci's paintings, signing their lives away for a slice of the pie.

The news featured a report of a small brown skinned man in a filthy white robe somewhere in Mississippi who had been targeted by unknown assailants. For reasons that had yet to be discovered, they'd beaten him to a pulp and then tacked him to a tree with carpenter's nails. Three days later, his body disappeared from the morgue.

Meanwhile, Portrait Jesus and his followers are sweeping the land, eradicating poverty. Not by feeding them or anything crazy like that. I won't go into the details, but I think their catch-phrase, *"Cutting away the fat so the meat can thrive"* should give you a pretty good idea how they're accomplishing this monumental task.

And me?

I took a one-way trip to Northern India, where I hear there are two Buddhas, one who preaches about Enlightenment, and the other who hangs out with celebrities and preaches nationalism.

Maybe I'll meet them some day.

Christopher Nadeau

The Audit

Colin Patrick Ennen

Two figures materialized mid-stride in the shadow of a looming red pickup truck. A smattering of orange Dorito dust stained each man's white, billowing linen robes.

The larger of the pair, tall and broad-shouldered, a bushy white beard cascading from his square jaw and a full head of white hair blowing in the gentle breeze, gave off a blinding glow, putting to shame the intense Albuquerque sunshine. A life-sized Charlton Heston-shaped light bulb.

"Uh, sir," said the other, squinting and hustling to keep up. "Could you turn that down a bit?"

"Huh? Oh, yes. My apologies, Peter." At once the radiance diminished to a barely noticeable level. Mr. Look-At-Me peered over his shoulder at his companion. "What about you?" he asked, pointing to the golden circle floating above the shorter man's bald pate.

"Shit, did I forget?" Peter tapped his halo with a finger and it disappeared. In his other hand he carried an iPad.

The pair lumbered through the packed parking lot that surrounded the eyesore of a church. It looked like a disused Walmart excreting a shiny office building.

Okay, the Big Guy lumbered; the shorter fellow more waddled the best he could in the Almighty's footsteps. With fingers more suited to untangling fishing nets, he managed to open the spreadsheet, tongue sticking out against his own ivory beard.

"Make a note, will you, Pete?" his boss said as they reached the perimeter curb. "Next year we pay less attention to football season and more to the heaven audit. We really shouldn't give a crap about football anyway."

"Well, sir," Peter replied, slipping a hand over the Cowboys logo on the back of his iPad. "I'm sure you can give a crap about whatever you want. But I agree, it's best we not get behind like this again."

Of course, they weren't *really* behind. What kind of Paradise would it be where anyone, let alone the guy who held the keys and kept the book, could get behind? This was more a case of the boss looking to meddle again. And it wasn't like Peter needed the help—this was what occupied much of his infinite time, after all. But he'd learned long ago not to stand in the Almighty's way when he got bored or was feeling officious. Nevertheless, he thought the plan was stupid. Car decals as a measure of piety?

His boss wore a satisfied smile as they turned to survey the scene. Satisfied, or smug. For all the Almighty's. . . almightiness, the dude had an egotistical streak—hence the meddling.

The whole ego thing should have been obvious to Peter 2,000 years ago, the signs were all there—the whole build me a temple, no other gods, floods, his sayonara Sodom/goodbye Gomorrah act, that pestilence fetish. He *had* done the reading. But back then, Peter would have done almost anything to get out of the fishing racket.

The view before them was imposing—a couple thousand automobiles used to bring close to 3,000 people to worship His Beardedness. Who wouldn't be a bit smug in those sandals?

Where the boss had gotten the idea remained unclear, unless it had been that swag bag he'd snagged from the Southern Baptist Convention—the thing was loaded with kitsch, a dozen bumper stickers included. Looking out over the parking lot, it seemed to Peter that almost every car displayed at least one relevant decorative adhesive. Which meant a shit-ton of people would be slipping past the Big Guy's revised standards.

"Would that be so bad, Pete?" his boss asked with a wink, aware of Peter's opinion on mind-reading. The Almighty shook his head, smirking at his gatekeeper. "Disruption, dude. Isn't that the buzzword? That's what we're doing. Thinking outside the box." He flashed a toothy grin. "Anyway, I don't remember you having any better ideas."

Peter sighed. "No, sir," he said. He'd only been doing this for, oh, 2,000 Earth years. "You're right, sir. Shall we begin then?" He gestured for his boss to lead the way.

With a middle finger extended over his shoulder at Peter, Yahweh made for the car at the end of the first row, a red Corvette, late model and shiny. On its back window was a single sticker, three white, stylized letters, intertwined: AGC.

"Which one is this?" he asked.

Peter consulted his tablet. "Uh. . ."

"No, wait. Let me guess. It's. . . Apostolic Grace Church."

"Nope. Sorry, sir," replied Peter. "Try Abundant Grace Cathedral. The other AGC is next, though. But what are your thoughts on this one?" He pointed to the Corvette and smiled. Best to get down to business.

"Hmm. Well, she's only got the one sticker, Pete. And it's kind of a fancy car. Depending on whom you ask, I'm either totally cool with such ostentation or totally against it." That smirk again.

"I'm asking you, boss." Peter held his stylus above the tablet's screen, waiting. He had background ready on everyone, just in case the Good Lord needed more data.

Glaring at his factotum, Jehovah twirled his beard in thought, twitching his lips left and right as he tapped one of his enormous feet. Finally, the Big Fellow balled his fists and bopped them on his thighs as he began to sputter. Far above, a faint rumble of thunder. "I don't know," he whined, slouching like a pouting toddler. "Gimme a hint."

Peter sighed again. "Well, sir. Tanya here got the money for her fancy car from her grandmother. Actually, Grannie insisted she use the money to buy herself a—and I'm quoting here—'zoomer'. And Tanya teaches fourth-grade at a school down in the ghetto. So. . ."

"She's in," his boss said. "Next."

Peter breathed a sigh of relief, this might not be so bad.

They stepped up to an older vehicle, a Ford Explorer that had seen better days. Mud and filth covered the bottom half of the sides and much of the back window.

"Could use a wash," Yahweh said, snapping his fingers. With a whoosh, the SUV was clean, revealing a collection of decals that required the inspectors to step back for a better view. Three of the intertwined AGC, another proclaiming the driver to be fiercely pro-life, two advertising a Christian radio station, and one American flag. "Okay, this one's a piece of cake. Am I right?" He turned to Peter, beaming with smugitude.

The auditor hissed through his teeth, shaking his head. "It's not so simple, sir," he said. "Jacob Summers does indeed come to church nearly every Sunday, and he screams about abortion online all the time. All caps, boss. Come on." Peter snorted. *Luddite.* "However, according to my records here," Peter pointed to his tablet's screen, "he's been divorced three times, has four children by four women, and owns a small arsenal which he does not keep well-secured." He peered at his boss from under bushy eyebrows.

The Almighty scowled back, biting at his beard. He looked from Peter to the car and back. Licking his lips, he repeated the motion again and again, his auditor waiting patiently.

"The stickers, man," said his boss finally, counting them on glowing fingers. "He's in." Jehovah moved to the next vehicle.

Next car, more modest than the Corvette, had only one sticker, though it was twice the size of the others they'd seen. A cross hung from the rear-view mirror.

"He sells cell phones and is only here today because some girl saw his sticker at the gym and that provided an in for her." The auditor shrugged.

Yahweh pointed to the sticker. "But it's a big one," he said. "He's in."

Peter shook his head and marked Carlos Roybal as saved. Apparently they were cool with a sex-for-church trade.

Most cars had but a single sticker, normal size.

Susie donated to a vehemently anti-choice politician and got the thumbs up, while George, with a WOLVES BELONG sticker, gave as much of his money to environmental causes as the church and earned himself a raspberry.

Annie drove a green Chrysler, and it turned out she'd been haranguing the school board for years to get creationism taught on the curriculum—"Winner, winner, chicken dinner," the Chief sang as he danced a little jig. He was rather proud of what he'd wrought.

Franklin, Benny, and Pierce, and their families, were the Scouting types, of the no-gay-Scout-leaders persuasion, earning them all checks in the saved column.

Thus far, nothing Peter couldn't have decided on his own, though some might have gone another way. In fact, on his spreadsheet the auditor had three columns to mark the decision: Saved, Damned, and Maybe. He didn't think the boss knew about the last one.

A small number of cars boasted no stickers at all, at least none signaling the driver's virtue. This was where Pete's trusty database should have come in, the process he'd used for centuries. But on each the boss beat him to it, and with an impish grin bestowed upon Angelo—immigrant rights attorney and vegan—a thumbs down, and Chelsea—bikini model, social media influencer, climate change denier—an entry pass.

Daniel Robertson's colossal SUV triggered a little tiff. He had three AGC logos on the rear window alone, one on each back-side pane of dark-tinted glass, earning a fist pump from Jehovah. But then Peter pointed to the bumper. In a line running its width were four stickers, all pro-gun to some degree. One made use of an impolite term for the act of procreation regarding what some folks could do with their opinions on the matter.

"Dude," said the Almighty. "Five church stickers. That's awesome. So he's got guns." He gave a dismissive wave that rustled the leaves of a tree across the street.

Peter let slip a "tsk, tsk." He covered his mouth, but too late.

"What?" His boss turned to him, arms crossed, and grew. Physically grew. Got to about 18 feet before the auditor shook his head.

"That won't change my recommendation, sir," he said. "I've seen you much more frightening than this. Anyway, you're the one who said 'Thou shalt not kill'." Peter put the phrase in air quotes, nearly dropping his iPad.

Jehovah shrunk back to above-average size. He stared at his auditor, who, staring back, refused to quail.

"Five church stickers, Pedro," he said, spinning on his heel to continue on.

Peter checked his Maybe column.

A three-sticker car here—saved, despite a history of spousal abuse. A zero-sticker truck—damned though she volunteered at the animal shelter and had adopted a kid from Cambodia. Lawrence—one-sticker, but a prolific Fox News re-Tweeter—saved. Shelly—two church stickers, but another promoting a progressive candidate—damned. At least that's what the boss directed. In a few of these cases— alright, a lot of them—Peter simply checked his secret column. *Omnipotent my ass.*

After what seemed like hours—though of course God had stopped time to accommodate their labor—the pair finally neared the building itself, a stucco and glass monstrosity, the reverend's name plastered on each side in three-foot-high letters. In the shade of an awning near the back entrance stood a new Mercedes SUV, gleaming, with tinted windows so dark they might as well be black. A posted sign marked this as the pastor's parking spot.

Walking around it with his boss, Peter noted four normal-size stickers, distributed tastefully among the many windows. In addition, a fake-chrome cross adorned the back hatch next to the license plate, which was framed by some words from a psalm. From the rear-view mirror hung another cross.

The Almighty beamed as he continued lapping the SUV a second, then a third time, admiring the adhesive adulation. When he finally stopped, he clapped Peter on the back, and chuckled.

"Now this is what I like to see," he said. "Eh?"

Peter stared at the ground and began to fidget.

"Just give it to me," Jehovah said with a sigh.

"He's a cheater, sir," Peter said. "And he ran over a homeless person as a teenager but never reported it."

The Almighty frowned. "Doesn't look like he's a teenager anymore." He swung his arms towards the church.

"Two kids out of wedlock, whom he doesn't support. One time, on a 'business trip'," more air quotes, "he paid a kid to—"

"But the stickers, dude!" The metal awning above them shook at the power of God's voice. "He's in, Pete."

The auditor consulted his tablet one last time.

"Um, sir?"

Yahweh looked down at his auditor. "Yes?"

Pete fumbled for the right phrasing. "Now, he claimed it was only because the other guy was Mormon—" The Almighty rolled his eyes. "But Pastor Joe voted for a liberal, sir."

A crack of lightning startled Peter, and he jumped back, his hair and beard splayed by a sudden gale. He squinted and covered his ears as the boss began one of his tantrums.

Each sticker-bearing window on the Mercedes shattered as the tires deflated, hissing. The hood popped open, spewing steam while the leather seats inside the vehicle tore as though rent by a vicious beast. Heck, even the sign marking the parking space crumpled like a piece of paper. Jehovah let out a growl, again bopping his fists on his divine thighs.

Peter struggled to hide his smile. "Damned, then?"

Colin Patrick Ennen

A Liberal Prayer

Gwyndyn T. Alexander

May the gods of Justice and Liberty hear our
prayer:
Give us this day our daily bread,
that we may feed our brothers and sisters
who have none.

Forgive us our trespasses,
if they have hurt none,
and bring justice to those who have
done harm to others.

Give us reason, and facts, and logic.
Give us science, and progress, and the means
to save our planet, our children, our future.

We know, too well, that prayer alone will not
suffice.

So give us the strength to act on our prayers,
that we may march, and protest, and vote.
That we may create actual change in the
world,
that the world shall be better for having us in
it.

Give us the will to make our voices heard,
to amplify the voices of those who have been
silenced.

Give us the courage of those who have faced
gun massacres and said 'No more.'

Give us the persistence to continue the fight
for equality and justice,
against all odds and opposition.

Give us the power to change:
to change minds
to change policy
to change
our world.

Give us the tools we need
to feed the hungry,
provide healthcare for all,
to reverse climate change,
to enact sensible gun reform.

Give us legislators who will work
for us, and not the lobbyists and corporations.

We do not ask for miracles,
or for the work to be done for us.

We ask only for the tenacity
and determination
to fight for everyone,
even those who trespass against us.

For ours is the duty to create
a democracy
that serves us all.

Ours is the kingdom, the power, the glory. . .
and the hard work and heartache to achieve
it.

In all our names, we pray.

A Conservative Prayer

Gwyndyn T. Alexander

Republican Jesus
save us from liberals
bless our sacred guns
protect us from regulations
we pray.

Republican Mary
Lady of Gerrymandering
hear our prayers.

Give us this day
our daily kickback
from the NRA.

Give us high capacity magazines and
bump stocks
Give us Stand Your Ground laws
so we may slaughter
unarmed children
because black people are scary.

Give us universal concealed carry
so we can shoot
those we imagine have trespassed against
us.

Give us our Congressmen
bought and paid for
to do our bidding.

Give us the Second Amendment
that we may be shielded
from all common sense
from those who would deny us
these guns we worship.

Give us the power
to kill all we want
to hoard weapons of war
so that we may feel powerful,
so we may forget our empty lives.

Give us more, O Lord,
more ammo
more guns
more school shootings
to drive up gun sales.
Give us our guns
our fear
our lies
for without them
we are nothing.

Give us 'both sides are bad'
'my vote doesn't matter'
'I voted third party'
'I didn't vote at all'.

Give us our due
for we are the scared
white male minority
and all others are
disposable.

Bless our guns.
Bless our guns.
Bless our guns.

In thy name, we shoot.

Forgiveness

Irene Radford

"Oh, woe is me. God hates us. He's going to kill us any minute now!" Adam lay back against the cave wall and pressed a dirty palm against his face.

Eve glared at him, from deeper in the small cave. "He won't have to if you don't get off your ass and help me gather some food. Otherwise, I'm going to kill you first. Or let you die of starvation." The words remained unsaid but strained against her throat for exit. Instead she kicked the empty baskets; all of them empty because *he* had eaten the contents. "I'm going out to look for food," she said.

Adam picked up one of the baskets that had bounced against his outstretched legs. He looked randomly into it, picked out a sliver of grain caught in the weave, and then flipped the basket away. "What is the point? We are doomed." He sighed heavily. He lay against the cave opening, his legs stretched across the entrance, scratching absently at the rash he seemed to have developed where Eve had bound fig leaves with a stringy vine.

"If God had wanted us dead, Archangel Michael would have skewered us back in the garden," she said. "I don't think God particularly cares what happens to us now." She gathered the six baskets and stepped over him into the rising sun. In the mornings it shone under the rocky outcropping that shielded the cave entrance. She paused to add wood to a fire ring where she'd left clay pots baking. They held water better than a mud lined basket.

Adam wasn't done yet. "It's all a joke to him. *Dominion over all that lives on the earth under water and flies in the sky*," he mimicked in a deep and sonorous voice. "Remember when we tried to eat those eggs. That bird nearly pecked my eyes out. God is going to kill us in the most painful way." Adam leaned his head against the cave wall. "Well I am finished, let him do his worst."

Eve looked up at the sky. Clouds were beginning to gather. Already portions of the sky looked heavy and gray. She still had several hours of gathering time before the skywater made the grains too mushy to gather, or sent the rabbits into their burrows rather into her line of snares. She had gotten the idea for snares from watching the spiders. There had been many failures, but now she knew the taste of meat and she liked it.

The baskets under one arm, she picked up a long shaft of wood. She had ground one end to a point and hardened it in the fire. Lazy or not, Adam was right about the animals. They were no longer docile, having learned wariness from her hunting. She absently looked at the small scar on her hand where she had tried to pet a ring tail. It had bitten her. She made the pointy stick the next day. The day after that she cooked that ringtail over the fire.

If she could only get Adam to hunt, with his broader shoulders and larger muscles, he could bring home better meat.

She used her stick to shift the wood on the fire. She needed to keep the coal bed hot. "You aren't too fearful of the wrath of God to eat what *I* put in front of you," she muttered as she blinked away the tears brought on by the irritating smoke.

"Could you look for some of those sweet red berries?" Adam said plaintively from the cave entrance.

Eve turned, her pointed stick in her hand. "You know," she said, "you could take the advice he gave us." She flipped a small basket towards him. "Get a little sweat on that brow. There're some berries ripening down by the stream. Maybe even get a fish?" She gestured toward the stream with the pointy stick.

Adam settled against the wall. His eyes still closed. The asshole was taking another nap!

He didn't open his eyes, but a smile crossed his lips.

"He also commanded us to be fruitful and multiply?" His fig leaf began to quiver.

Eve turned away in disgust and picked up her remaining baskets.

"A man needs more than food."

She ignored him and stalked away. Soon she was away from the rocky outcropping and walking through stalks of tall grasses with heavy seeds growing on long stalks. She carefully shook them off, slowly covering the bottom of the basket. It took a lot to keep Adam fed. She might have given up on God, but she wasn't done worrying about Adam. He didn't want to do anything, not even tend the blessed fire that kept them warm and cooked their food.

Past the grasses, low bushes marked the entry into the trees. A berry bush beckoned her. She sampled one fat red berry. "Sweet!" A double handful went into the basket. She gathered them despite Adam, not for him. The wild almond tree tasted just as bitter as it had yesterday. But, next to it, another tree with nuts very like the almond tasted sweet. They looked the same, but one would feed her, the other would make her sick.

Quickly she plaited together long strands of grass that had already given her their heads of grain. When she had a strand long enough, she tied it loosely around the trunk of the good tree to mark it.

Onward she trekked, throwing grains and nuts and berries into separate baskets. Then she stopped by a dry creek and used a stick to pry up some meaty roots. They went into yet another basket.

The sun rose high above the horizon, warming the land and her back through the thickening clouds. She sniffed the air. Instead of the usual dry scent of baking plants and drying manure—good for fuel when dead branches grew scarce—from the grazing beasts in the distance, she smelled the coming of sky water.

Their first encounter with bad weather had frightened both of them to their core. They had walked for many days away from the garden before the skies had exploded with sheets of light and the crashing of clouds that brought a deluge of water from the sky. They had sought refuge in the small cave.

The first time they'd needed shelter. Now it was home.

Eve had decided then and there that she was done wandering. God had shown them the cave. She accepted the gift and would not insult God by abandoning it. Now she wasn't so sure it was a gift from God. She didn't think He was in much of a giving mood these days.

Adam hadn't cared. Or even noticed for that matter. From the day Michael had banished them, all Adam did was moan and groan in despair. And eat. He was as good at eating as he was complaining.

She had consoled herself with the thought that God created her to take care of him when he couldn't—or wouldn't—take care of himself. But she did wish he'd stop moaning and do something, anything.

She moved on, watching the clouds thicken and feeling the air grow heavy. Sweat dripped from her brow and down her back. Now and again she paused to stretch and scan the landscape. From the carcasses she had found she knew there were animals that would kill in these lands. But not today. She had the plains of tall grasses all to herself.

On the horizon, the sky flashed, and a dull rumble rolled across the land, she knew she'd stayed too long. A sudden gust of wind tore at her hair. The baskets, heavy with the fruit of her labor, strained against her arms and shoulders. With regret, she left the heaviest of the baskets, the big one with the mud lining. She couldn't deal with the storm and hope to get to the cave with all of her foraging. She tucked the baskets more firmly beneath her arms and began to run. Lightning cracked above her. A wisp of smoke taunted her nose. The bolt of light had sparked a fire.

She hoped the sky water would douse it before it spread.

She needed shelter fast.

The cave was too far, an hour's slow walk or half that if she ran. She couldn't run fast burdened with her baskets, but she needed the food, Adam needed the food.

At the next slash of lightning, the water began to fall. First it came in heavy pellets that quickly turned into sheets of falling water. She crawled under a bush. She knew the sizzling light would seek the taller trees over the lower bushes. She hoped the broad leaves would shelter her until the storm passed.

In time, the sky grew lighter and the falling water slackened to a drizzle. The rumbling skies and flashes of light moved on. On the horizon, the clouds thinned. Scattered bursts of sunlight streamed through the openings. She shivered in her wet rabbit skin clothing. Water still dripped from her hair, but she gathered her soggy baskets and trudged through wetness, back to the cave.

"You're late," Adam said almost before Eve dragged herself across the threshold of the cave. At least he'd stirred himself enough to stoke the fire.

Eve set her baskets down and crouched in front of the hot flames. He said nothing as she wrung extra water from her hair, then used a twig to straighten the tangles. She noted that the sun had begun to bleach and straighten the strands while Adam's hair and beard remained dark and curly.

"I said, 'you're late'," Adam repeated.

"I got caught in the storm."

"That was careless," he said and rolled onto one hip to reach for one of the baskets. He pulled the basket of the sweet berries into his lap and began to eat them by the handful.

She stood up, fists clenched. Red swam before her eyes. She wanted to kick him, knock some sense into him.

But God had said she needed to take care of him.

But then again, she'd broken more than one of God's silly rules.

Ruthlessly she turned her back on him and began sorting the food, spreading it on a rock slab to dry.

"Aren't you going to cook those?"

"Why should I?"

"Because I like it when you toast those nuts."

"Then toast them." She thrust a basket of acorns at him, and kept her eyes focused on the cave floor. If she faced him for even a moment she'd kick him.

"Ah, Eve don't be like that," Adam cajoled.

Her shoulders relaxed for a brief moment as memories of the garden came back. When he used that charming and winsome tone of voice, soothing like warm honey, she remembered all the good times they'd had together. Before. Before God had cast them out to fend for themselves.

She stiffened again.

"Eve, sweetheart, I was worried about you." He gestured toward the puddles of water outside the cave entrance. "That's why I snapped at you." He crouched down and rested his berry stained hands on her shoulders. "Forgive me, sweetheart. It was only the worry that made me angry." He began to massage the tension from her muscles, warming her through and through.

"Show me how to roast the nuts?" He whispered into her ear.

She ended up doing all the cooking herself as he proved too clumsy to do anything but make a mess. They laughed at his crude attempts to mash the acorns with the remaining berries into a paste for frying. As the sun set, they fed each other tender morsels. But in the end they went to their separate pallets. Adam had grumbled but Eve still carried her pointy stick.

The next morning repeated the pattern as the previous day. Eve took her now dry baskets to the east where she knew some bees kept a hive. Adam had reminded her they'd had no honey since leaving the garden. She smeared her arms and legs and face with mud—plenty of that from the rains—and a noxious smelling weed to protect herself from the angry bees.

She hastened back to the cave with her prize.

Adam looked at her with disdain, as he took the basket containing the dripping honeycombs.

"I hope you're going to wash that mud off," he said. He wrinkled his nose. "And you smell bad." That was when she took her pointy stick and left.

Eve sat beside the river and watched the water split endlessly around a rock that jutted above the rushing water.

"Why do you make me put up with him!" she demanded of the sky. "Why did you make him so helpless?"

No answer. God never answered her anymore. Even in the garden, he seldom actually spoke with her, it was always Adam this and Adam that. Did she get to name the animals? Nooo. She just got to sit and smile at the stupid names. Kangaroo? What in the world had inspired that?

"Well see if I care about you and your commandments. See if I take care of your precious Adam anymore. See if I gather the food and cook it for him when he does nothing but moan about how you deserted us. And as for that 'be fruitful and multiply' thing, you can both forget about that.

That night she assumed Adam went hungry. She built her own small fire an hour's walk from the cave where she cooked and ate her own diner. Two small fish wrapped in leaves with some brown grains cooked soft. She ate it all.

"But. . . but. . ." Adam spluttered in bewilderment when she returned to the cave that night, empty handed. "But I'm hungry!"

"Then go look for food." She stomped over to her pallet of fresh grasses and lay down with her back to him.

"But. . . but. . . it's dark out. How am I supposed to find food without the blessing of the sun that God makes rise every day?"

Eve wasn't so sure that God made the sun rise and set, or that he sent the storm as one of his temper tantrums. She closed her eyes but only feigned sleep. *Let him suffer a bit*, she thought. She ignored the grumblings as Adam scrounged for stale mouthfuls in the baskets she had left behind.

Her rebellious thoughts kept her awake long after the moon had set and the wheel of stars in the sky faded toward dawn.

When a bird chirped the first greeting of the new day, Eve crept out of the cave with her gathering baskets.

Adam stirred at her leaving. He muttered something in his sleep and rolled over to put his back to the cooling embers.

Eve spent the day wondering how to evict him. He wouldn't leave willingly. But the pattern of life he had settled into couldn't continue.

"God," she said, if only to the plants and the birds, "it's not fair that I do all the work and all he does is moan and complain. If you mean to kill us, then just do it. I'm tired. You created me. If you wanted me docile and compliant you should have done a better job on Adam."

But I created both of you in my own image.

It was a small voice in her mind. Where did that come from? Was it God? When had he stopped booming out his words from the sky?

She wandered on, thinking about God and his relationship to his creations. Created in his own image and therefore curious, and resilient, and smart enough to figure out ways to survive and thrive on their own.

A smile crept across her face. Maybe. . . just maybe Adam would come to a similar conclusion after a night and a day of hunger gnawing at his belly. No, Adam might need more time. He was stubborn.

As stubborn as God?

She paused in her thoughts and looked around. "I was standing right about here when the storm hit," she said aloud, just to hear the sound of her voice in the quiet. She began to look around.

Baskets required a great deal of work to make them large and tight. She didn't want to lose the one she'd left behind, filled with grains. And, there it was. The basket sat upright on the ground, only a little worse for wear after the beating the rain had given it.

"What's this?" She stared at the golden sludge of sprouted grain inside the basket. Water sat atop the soggy mess that had matted together to seal the bottom and sides of the basket against leakage.

She'd never seen anything like it before. "I'm supposed to keep the grain dry so it doesn't invite the demon of mold and mildew. But this. . . this looks like new grain growing from the old. And the water. . .?" It looked cloudy, but still that marvelous golden color, like ripening grain. Tiny bubbles rose to the top from the mass of sprouted grains and burst when they reached the surface.

They sent out an enticing fragrance.

As with everything she gathered or discarded, Eve stuck her finger into the water and tasted. "Not bad." The flavor burned a bit then blossomed into a backwash of raw grain flavored with. . . something exotic she couldn't place.

Her throat was dry and she was thirsty. She took a sip. And then a longer one.

Her body demanded more.

She drank nearly half the basket full. It was a big basket and there was plenty more. Her tummy bloated and felt a bit uncomfortable. But then she burped and tasted the marvelous blend of flavors all over again. And she felt. . . good!

She raised the basket to her mouth again. Then paused before tipping the liquid into her mouth. "I need to share this. God gave me this wonderful stuff, I must share it with Adam." She repressed the voice in her mind.

Then an idea struck her. She took one of the baskets of grain she'd gathered today and set it where the previous one had rested. It took two trips to gather enough water to fill it. She would be back in a few days to check.

"Adam!" she called the moment she could see the cave entrance. "Adam, where are you?"

"Here," he said tromping through the undergrowth from the direction of the spring. Mud spattered his beard and hair. Scratches and more mud covered his hands and arms. Idly he scratched at the mat of hair on his chest where red welts marked insect bites.

"What have you been doing?" she backed away from the scent of rotting vegetation and male sweat. The clay pots beside the outside fire ring gave her an excuse to avoid him. Deftly she poured the precious liquid off from the sludge of sprouted grains, noting that the number of bubbles rising to the surface had increased. Mind abuzz with ideas she wondered if the sprouts would prove useful. A quick taste told her they were the source of the nutty under-taste in the liquid.

One bite and her tongue begged for another. Were the sprouts best raw or cooked? Perhaps roasted dry then ground up with nuts and berries before a second cooking?

"I've been digging roots in the swamp beside the spring," Adam announced proudly.

Eve swallowed her surprise. "Find any?"

"Quite a few actually, but they don't taste right raw." He proudly thrust a handful of bulbs the size of her thumb toward her. Half of them were brown with over-ripeness and would have to be tossed. "Can you roast them?" Adam asked eagerly.

She fought the urge to tell him how useless his gathering had been, but she knew if she did, he would simply resume his seat at the cave entrance. "Very nice," she said as he held up a basket for her inspection.

She held out one of the small crocks of the cloudy liquid. Part of her wanted to keep the miracle to herself. Part of her needed to share her own triumphant discovery.

"Taste this while I cook." She placed the crock in his hand, then, with a small sigh, picked up the small basket of roots. They would need to be scrubbed.

"What is it?" Adam asked skeptically.

"Just taste it. If you don't like it, I'll finish it." Her mouth longed for more.

Adam's face worked as he puzzled out the advantage of depriving her of what she clearly wanted and the disadvantage of trying something new.

Eve turned her back while she sorted through the roots and discovered only a little bruising from his rough handling and not much spoilage at all.

"Bah!" Adam spat out his first mouthful. "Tastes like spoiled piss."

"Fine. I'll drink it. I like it fine."

"On second thought, it does leave a nice aftertaste." Adam swallowed a large gulp. His eyes grew wide in wonder. "What is this?" He held the pot close to his chest possessively.

Eve shrugged. "I have no name for it."

Adam belched, "Bee...rr."

She caught more than a hint of the fragrance of the brew.

"Beer?" She grabbed the pot and downed half of the remnants.

"As good a name as any." Adam took back the pot and finished off the fine beer. "Needs something though. Where did it come from?"

Eve related losing the basket and coming back to find it filled with liquid treasure.

"Can we do it again?" Adam asked hopefully.

"I have another basket set out," said Eve.

"Can we do it here?" Eve shrugged even as she transferred three handfuls of grain to her largest clay pot and took it to the spring to fill it with water. "Now we wait."

"How long?"

"That first batch took three days."

Adam's face fell in disappointment, then brightened. "Then I suppose we'll have to start a new batch every day. I can make more pots. Do you suppose God tricked the rain into turning grain into beer?"

"Probably." Eve began preparing a meal, already longing for more beer.

"Maybe," said Adam, "this is proof that He has forgiven us!"

"Yes." She remembered the small voice in her head. "Yes indeed!"

"He has forgiven us!" Adam raised his arms into the air and pranced in a circle, celebrating the glorious event. "God has forgiven us!"

An Atheist at the Movies

Adam-Troy Castro

I recently got the following comment on Facebook:

"The thing is, Adam, you're an atheist yourself! Of COURSE you'll sneer at religious films!"

NO! You won't lay that on me.

Look, I love any number of movies where the characters are moved or defined by their religious faith. You can strongly move me with such scenes, even if you don't draw me into the prayer circle.

For instance, there's *Lars and the Real Girl* written by the talented Nancy Gillespie, in which a community's conspiracy of kindness protects a painfully withdrawn man who has come to see an anatomically-correct sex doll as his real, living girlfriend. The doctor says that he needs to be humored as Lars works this out, even to the point of taking that girlfriend to church. The church elders are conflicted: would this not be unseemly? Then the reverend says, "I keep coming up against the same question: what would Jesus do?"

Boom. Destroys me. I may not buy into the gospels, but I buy into that moment.

Another great moment in a bad film, *Delta Force,* the fact-based scene where the Catholic Priest, Father O'Malley, played by George Kennedy, refuses to let the airplane hijackers separate him from the Jewish passengers. He declares, "I'm a Jew. Just like Jesus Christ." That happened, actually. In real life. I will sit through that largely terrible movie for that moment.

I'm an absolute sucker for benevolent clergymen, in movies.

I will never stop sobbing at the incident of the Bishop's candlesticks, in any version of *Les Misérables,* or in the musical, Jean Valjean's appeal to God, in "Who Am I?" which leads him to make a life-ruining but morally correct decision.

I adore it when Gandhi tells the Hindu rioter, "I know a way out of hell. Find a small boy who has been orphaned by the rioting. Raise him as your own. Only make sure he is a Muslim boy, and raise him as a Muslim."

It may be, indeed certainly is, that what I'm reacting to so powerfully, in these scenes, and any number of others, are those manifestations of religious faith as engines of human goodness.

I absolutely adore the intense religious parable that is The Poseidon Adventure, right down to the closing crucifixion of Reverend Scott to save them all—all while the valve forms a halo over his head.

I love that stuff.

I can watch several dramatizations of the life of Christ without squirming. I think Zeffirelli's is a beautiful piece of filmmaking and can watch it right alongside the most religious Christians. Of course, I also feel the same way about *Life of Brian* and *Last Temptation of Christ,* whereas many of them do not. I am reacting to the storytelling, not the fundamentalism. But the storytelling can get me.

What I loathe in the evangelical films of Kevin Sorbo and Kirk Cameron is that they don't hinge on goodness, but on scorn and just desserts for anyone outside the club. THAT is, I think, an evil force, an encouragement to stupidity, a way of handholding audiences through things they already believe.

Not the same thing at all.

Everlasting Due

M. J. Holt

The building stretched as far as he could see. The morning sun glinted off the marble and granite.

"Do you like it, sir?" said a voice behind him.

"It's beautiful. Even more magnificent than Mar a Lago."

"Would you like to look around, Mr. President?"

The President felt frumpy beside this man. He had never seen a man as beautiful or as well dressed as his Host. The man's dark bronze skin and highly styled silver-white hair, ramrod straight back, long slender hands, and sculpted face awed him.

At the entrance, the man held the door, as one should for the President. A Scottish Terrier skittered across the marble floors. "Fala, Fala, come boy, my cousin Teddy is here and he wants to give you treats."

"This is the FDR wing. Teddy Roosevelt has his own wing with miles of wilderness and horses. I think that FDR and Teddy plan to go riding today."

Happy sounds and the commotion of many women drinking tea and coffee while sorting papers came from down the hall.

"Here is Eleanor Roosevelt's wing. They felt it best to be separate. They meet for a martini every so often, and all is good." The beautiful sound of an operatic call, "Hello everyone," announced the arrival of a casually dressed woman.

"There are black people here?" asked the President. "She doesn't look good enough to be a servant."

"She's no servant. That's Marian Anderson. Her wing is huge. Two opera companies and several symphony orchestras have their own wings off of her wing. Marian, Beverly Sills, and Maria Callas hang out there. I cry from the beauty every time I visit them. Their singing—magnificent."

The President followed the Host who pointed out wings as they walked down a long hallway into a construction area. Pallets of marble and granite tiles, and the beautiful appointments that would be added upon completion, stretched as far as he could see.

"Who is this for?"

"President Obama. We work on it sporadically, since he won't be here for quite a while. Presenting this will be a challenge since he is such a modest man."

An older man hailed the Host. "Hi, Pete, you're going overboard here. All my grandson needs is a hut next to an ocean."

"I know, Mr. Dunham, I know, but this is such a labor of love. How do you like your beach?"

"Heavenly, sir. We give thanks every day."

They continued to walk further along the hallway, past countless wings. The Host noticed that the President did not recognize the names of many who got their wings before the President was born. As they passed, the Host just said the names. "Jonas Salk. Zhang Heng. Queen Njinga. The great Hindu philosophers have wings of wings." The Host started to say more but the President interrupted him.

"Where are the Christian people who were the great businessmen, the generals, the great preachers?"

"There are hundreds of Jim Jones wings, but not one for the Kool-Aid preacher. Destroyers aren't here."

"How can that be? They were great Americans."

"Remember the part about not harming things? Love does no harm to a neighbor. Remember the last commandment to be kind? It's all in the Testaments, Old and New, and every other religious book. How about 'Those who do not abandon mercy will not be abandoned by me'? That's Kami, another speaker for the Father. You missed that, too."

"What nonsense are you talking? You do what you gotta do."

The Host nodded. "I am enjoying our little walk and talk. Do you want to see the wine cellar?"

"Of course," said the President.

They walked through miles of bottles and amphoras of wine, all dusted and clean. At an old wooden door, the Host led the President down a set of stairs. These were old and worn as though from millions of feet over the ages. At the base of the stairs, an ill-lit hallway lead to another set of stairs that were yet more worn. Damp and stale air assaulted the President's nose. The Host never turned a hair or breathed hard. The President huffed and sweat trickled down his face.

"What's down here?" the President asked.

"Many friends and people you admire."

The President followed the Host down hundreds of steps. He felt so tired that he didn't look around as he concentrated on keeping up.

The Host opened an antique door, its wood aged until the grain stood out begging for oil. The President shuddered with revulsion as the gentle hand of the Host guided him into the shabby room. A wobbly bed, table, and chair sat on a cracked cement floor. None of the furniture had two legs the same length. Cold seeped in through the rough gray rock walls. Three candles lit the small room. A moth-eaten blanket and an oily sheet covered the broken straw mattress. A dingy cracked cup and plate rested on the table. A chair with a cracked toilet seat over a large old ceramic pot occupied the far corner and smelled as though it had been used. The President saw no sink or bathtub.

"Disgusting. Poor people live like this."

"I must get back to the new construction," said the Host. "Ask for what you would like. What you're due, you will get. That's why there are no servants."

The door closed and the Host disappeared.

The President looked around. "I need a new chair," he said. Nothing changed.

"How about a glass of water."

The dingy cup filled with water.

"I want a glass of wine."

The water turned to wine. The President tasted it and spit out the sharp sour drink that burnt his nose.

"Serve lunch."

A stale sandwich with unidentifiable meat appeared on the plate.

The President pulled on the door, but it was too heavy for him to open. He gave his orders to the invisible servants, and each time nothing changed.

oOo

"Put eight-forty a.m. on the form," said the doctor who Walter Reed Hospital had sent. He read the paper, signed it, and left. The President's head lay on top of the eagle on the Presidential rug.

Across the Oval Office, a Secret Service agent spoke into his cellphone. "Yes, Sir. It's time to tell Mrs. Pelosi to go to the Supreme Court."

A weeping Ivanka rushed to the agent, "You reported this, already? Why would you do that? We have a plan. No. No."

"Calm down, ma'am. I just did my job. I follow the protocols and report to my superiors."

Jared went to Ivanka and put his arm around her. He spit a little as he said, "Why would you say anything about Pelosi or the Supreme Court?"

"The Justices are gathered to swear her in. That's protocol."

"Swear her in?" Ivanka yelled. "You can't do that. His term isn't up. We've got things to do."

"Ma'am, his term ended a couple of hours ago when he died."

"She's a Democrat. This can't happen. This is his administration and his worst enemy is going to take his place? No. That's not right." Ivanka clutched her blouse.

"Ma'am. He's been dead on the office floor since Fox and Friends showed the former Vice President's perp walk.

In the meantime, the succession protocol went into motion. After the midterms, she *is* the Speaker. Most of the Justices are waiting to swear Mrs. Pelosi into office. I heard they are going to do this together. Never been done that way before. They all seem quite delighted. Of course, they will send their condolences, but they are making history. President Pelosi will be here in a few hours."

M. J. Holt

Extinction Level Non-Conjunction Event

Anton Cancre

All I wanted was a baby. A young life to guide and nurture as it grew into adulthood. Someone to share love and hope with. An opportunity to add something beautiful to the world.

It didn't seem like too much to ask. How many times a year do you still hear about some tiny blue-faced angel found in a dumpster? Or turn on the TV to see someone working on their fifteenth—just to hold onto their 8pm primetime slot? Or have *another* rosy cheeked, beaming coworker or friend hand you a pink or blue invitation to *another* baby shower? It's never a big deal.

Unless it is.

Sometimes, I wonder if nature and my own body were conspiring against me at every turn. Maybe something was, and still is, wrong with me, down to the genetic level, that made this minor dream impossible.

Or, maybe, Mr. Lawson was right. It was all part of God's plan. An invisible, soft hand guiding everything to the place it needed to be. *Nothing more than a cog in the great clockwork machine that keeps the skies and the sun and the winds and the waters in perfect motion around us all.* He always tended toward the dramatic.

I never said anything to him about the fears and doubts that gnawed at me. My conversations with God. *Why make me so ugly? So clumsy? So foolish?* Even Mary was granted a husband and a choice. Not me.

No, I was always too skinny. Lanky, every joint jutting out at some extreme, angry angle. My lip pulled into a constant snarl—from a bad fall at eight years old. Once you add in the brittle, translucent hair and sagging, flat breasts, you aren't left with the type of image that sets fire to the imagination.

Not that it mattered once Mr. Lawson presented me with his offer.

According to him, our meeting was pure providence. *Ephesians 6*, the companion care agency I worked for at the time, placed me with him. Nothing particularly grandiose about it. He had the money and I had rent to pay.

Maybe my shyness was my saving grace with him. I didn't feel comfortable talking to most people and he, like most of our customers, just wanted someone to listen to him. Most seniors, even the rich ones, spend all day being told what to do, what to think, by family, friends, doctors and often strangers. Too withdrawn to speak, I simply listened.

He filled my ears with tales of his misspent youth and rants about the vicious nature of business. He laid out his dreams and regrets, his hopes and fears. Mostly, he talked about his fears.

"I don't worry so much about myself," he'd say almost daily. "I'm old enough that I'll be resting in the arms of my savior well before the worst comes. But I worry about you and my children. I see the world. I see what we are doing to each other and I weep for the future."

Mr. Lawson didn't speak with the fervor and excitable panic you always see on TV. There were no burning eyes or manic movements. No desperate pleas or hollered demands. No gnashing of teeth or rending of garments. Just calm, resigned terror.

The reasons were no different than anyone else's. Overpopulation. Moral decay. Violence in the streets. Children either fornicating with, or murdering, each other.

"God is turning his back on us, child." I was thirty-eight, but Mr. Lawson called everyone younger than him 'child'. "We've broken three covenants and I think he's going by baseball rules. I think it might be somebody else's turn at bat."

It wasn't anything new. Nothing that wasn't being shouted by a hundred fools on street corners every day. But he had a plan. He saw a small window of opportunity in the field of genetic engineering, of all places.

"That's the genius of God, child. The tools of the Enemy, created in an attempt to subvert His divine will, turned to salvation instead of damnation."

I believe I mentioned before that he tended toward the dramatic.

Eventually, he began to let slip that his plan might include me. Might depend on me. Especially since modern ethics—more like a lack thereof, he would smile and nod while elbowing me and saying this—made it harder to find women in my *unique position*, as he put it.

I probably should have felt offended by his assumptions. Should I have stormed out at that moment? We'd never discussed anything remotely resembling the subject. He had no reason to know—and less of a right to guess. But that calm, sad manner of his made it almost impossible to get angry over anything he said. Also, it was true.

Scattered across a hundred conversations, it became clear, I was to be his Mary, and he would be my Joseph. We could bring forth the Messiah. The future could be saved. For some, at least.

There would never be a legal union, he'd been clear about that from the start. But that was just a rebellion against the laws of man. One of his enduring rants.

But he could make it happen, with my help. Mr. Lawson had built the right contacts over the years. He knew people in genetics firms and still had the best fertility clinic in the country operating under his company. There was no need to involve the prying eyes of the government.

He explained to me that pieces of the Shroud of Turin had been snipped off years ago for DNA testing. The basic genetic material was there. So was the technology. All that was needed was the will and the desire.

I would be taken care of. He spoke endlessly about the marvelous care the baby and I would receive. The best the world had to offer. No expense would be spared. I would be pampered. I would be revered. Most of all, I wouldn't be alone. I would finally have what so many others achieved so easily and He would love me unconditionally.

Don't start thinking that I jumped right in. It didn't feel right, and I argued it with him. As hard as it was to speak up, as much as I enjoyed his company and my job, I couldn't sit back and abuse the foolishness of a dying old man. I wasn't Mary. Wasn't even a believer—anymore.

"I know that I sound like a fool," he told me. "I might actually be one. All the same, if I am wrong, what have I lost? There are worse things to do with your time and money than give a good woman a child of her own. To bring a life into the world. A life that will be cared for and loved by a mother who truly appreciates the miracle of his existence.

"But if I'm right..."—he paused, adding dramatic effect—"...if we bring our savior forth into this world, then your faith can have no choice but to be renewed. For who can deny the light and grace of the Son when He is suckling at their own breast? I will have played a minor part in your salvation and in the salvation of the world. You can take it as a calling from heaven or you can take it as a gift from an old man. Just take it. Please."

I agreed.

The conception itself was more clinical than immaculate. Lots of sterile, white rooms with too-bright fluorescent lighting. The smell of bleach. Cold stainless steel and latex gloves. Passive faces hidden behind surgical masks issuing muffled instructions and muted encouragement.

The pregnancy? That was as horrifying and ecstatic and excruciating and beautiful as I have been told every pregnancy under the sun is, was and shall be. I got scared. I got sick. My back hurt. My ankles swelled to the size of twin baked hams. I aggressively glowed at every person I met. It felt as holy as the sunrise to me, even if it was just as mundane.

The first sign of something outside of the scripture of plan came with an early ultrasound. The Ob-Gyn wouldn't talk to me. He was clearly concerned but refused to speak to anyone other than Mr. Lawson. However, the doors were thin, and I overheard something about nuchal translucency and a request for a blood test. I didn't like the idea of anyone poking a needle into my son and neither did Mr. Lawson.

"We've done what we need to," was his response. "The rest lies in the hands of God."

Within a week, I was seeing a different Ob-Gyn and I spent the remaining months enraptured with the life inside me.

My memory of the birth is a blur. I'm sure there was pain. I'm sure I yelled. I'm sure there were tears and fear and hope and regret and a whole mess of emotions and sensations that shorted out something because I don't remember much in the way of specifics. I've been told that your brain does that, blots out the pain, so that you are willing to go through it again for the sake of the species. I don't know. The only part that mattered were those final, glorious words from the nurse.

"Ms. Reynolds, it's a boy."

The real terror came after. The Doctor immediately shushed her and became oddly silent himself. I didn't know if this was normal or not. The silence drew on too long. All I wanted was to hold my little baby. To make sure this being, so new to the world, understood that it was loved. It wouldn't get that from the cold stare of a stranger.

I tried to be patient. Something felt wrong, though. He was crying, so I knew he hadn't come out blue and motionless. My boy was alive, but they weren't handing him to me.

I tried to remember the contract. Of course, there had been a contract. Accounts full of someone else's money were established for his health, education, clothing and lodging. But I was certain it specified that the child would not belong to Mr. Lawson. I was promised that, regardless of how it worked out, the baby was mine to care for and to raise. What if I missed a subheading or some piece of fine print that allowed Mr. Lawson or someone else to take my baby away? What if they never let me see him?

I panicked. I yelled out to see him. To hold him. My stammering revealed my fear, I am sure.

"Yes, of course," the doctor responded calmly, "but I want to warn you that there are some abnormalities. I need you to remain calm. The important thing is that he is healthy."

I think anyone would be forgiven for losing their mind at that point. I was exhausted, in pain and just told that my baby was abnormal. I didn't. I kept my calm.

"Please," I asked, "just let me hold him."

They handed him to me, bundled loosely in soft white cloth. He squirmed a little, then nestled against my chest

He relaxed. He stopped squalling. Maybe it was the familiar rhythm of the heartbeat that had been his companion for nine months, something safe and familiar after so much noise and stress. Maybe he knew me already. He might have been too tired to care.

I didn't see what the concern was. Sure, his forehead was a tad big. Babies always seemed to have giant heads compared to their bodies. And his ears were small. Of course, I had never bothered to pay attention to relative ear size in babies I had seen. His eyes were a bit wide, alien looking, but everyone talked about how weird babies looked right after they were born. If my little boy just didn't look enough like the paintings of Jesus for the good Doctor's taste, so be it.

I laid my head back onto the pillow. My child rested his head on my breast. Our hearts pattered slightly against each other through walls of skin and bone. As I dozed, I noticed Mr. Lawson enter the room. He and the doctor were talking softly, and the color seemed to drain from his face.

I didn't let it concern me. I had my baby and we would be fine. Together.

The doctor was there within an hour after I woke. His smile was a bit too broad, his manner too casual for someone who had been pure business until now.

He laid his hand on mine and explained. All preliminary, of course. No one could be certain until official blood and DNA tests were run. He spoke softly. Words were given little or no emphasis. He said something about the spacing of the eyes. The extra distance between the big and little toes. Microgenia. Brushfield spots. Trisomy 21. None of it meant anything to me.

"Ms. Reynolds," he continued, "Mark. . . that is what you've decided to name him, correct? It's a wonderful name. My grandfather was a Mark. A good name for a good man."

He patted me on the shoulder, as if to reassure me that everything would be fine. As if I could possibly believe that when he was talking to me this way.

"There's no easy way to say this," He paused. Time dilated as his mouth finally began to open again. "Mark likely has Down Syndrome."

The strong thing, the brave thing, to say would be that I didn't care. He was my baby. I'd love him.

Of course, that was true. It was just as true that I wasn't prepared. As if anyone can be prepared to hear something like that. Images of college, of grandchildren, of someone to care for me in my old age withered and fled out the window. Chased away by a blurred, uncertain and terrifying future.

But Kathrine. Dear Katherine—I didn't yet know her, she was just a strange lady in floral print—stepped in and put a warm, strong arm around me. Who whispered every secret fear that flashed through my head into my ear. Whose murky green eyes looked into mine without the slightest bit of judgment and let me feel the fear. Then took it all away in a wash of hope.

She told me there were programs. Plans. Schools for me and for my child to allow as good of a life as he could possess. Didn't lie about the increased potential for heart problems. Didn't hide mental retardation behind neoteny. Just told me that he would live whatever life he found. Would love as deeply, hate as profoundly, be as joyous, as petty, as caring and as cruel as anyone else.

Then she lifted Mark from his crib. As she held him, her eyes welling up, she called him beautiful. In that moment, I knew that he was. Years later, he called for Katherine almost as often as his mommy and I never took offense— the love was earned.

Mr. Lawson didn't fare as well. From the way the tabloids put it, my baby killed him damn near on the spot. After good old Doc whatever-his-name laid it all bare, he left the room and calmly, quietly slumped in his chair. You can call it a heart attack or simply giving up, but he was done with the world; with me and my child.

I keep thinking things would have been different if he had held it together for longer. Maybe things wouldn't have gotten so crazy. Maybe the two of us would have faded into humanity without a whimper. Maybe it was all going to go this way no matter what.

His lawyers found the papers. The plan, the surgeries, the payoffs. A great story for the ages: "eccentric billionaire spends half of his fortune funding the second coming".

The hunt was in full force. TMZ, the National Enquirer, and every other tabloid from the *Sun* on down were offering unheard of sums to find the nutbag Lawson impregnated. Televangelists begged and pled with their audiences to share anything they found in hopes of getting in with Jesus on the ground floor.

I didn't notice any of this while it was happening. I was too busy caring for my child. When I wasn't feeding or wiping or bathing him, I was sleeping or had my face in a book. My head was too focused on the path immediately before me to see the clouds building. Didn't even notice the stray raindrops until it all came pouring down.

It started with a knock on the door. Maybe I was imagining that it was so loud. Maybe I've blown it up in my memory. Maybe I was just angry at the disturbance and it sounded excessive to me at the time. I know it was loud enough to wake Mark.

At first, I thought he was shocked by the way I looked. Answering the door in a rumpled robe, with my hair ratty and disheveled and the requisite purple bags under my eyes had to be a bit surprising. There was even a moment where I worried that the robe had slipped someplace. Until I realized that he was stammering and staring at Mark.

He was little more than a boy. Definitely not an adult yet. But dressed well. A crisp black suit and clean, pressed white shirt. Short hair, simple. The small silver cross dangling from his neck reflected the midday sun into my eyes, blinding me for a moment.

"I just. . ." he stammered, eyes never leaving my son. "I wanted to. . . say. . ." Then he abruptly ran off down the street.

I found out later that he wasn't out for the money. He was just curious and desperate to justify his faith. Apparently, the information was out there in the world. It just needed to be dug through and followed and it eventually led to me. That poor, polite boy apologized to me in his suicide note.

He must've said something to someone who said something to someone else who said enough to bring the vultures down in droves. There were days where I couldn't see the street through them all. Demanding, never asking, for interviews and pictures. Calling out for personal appearances and explanations, apologies and affirmations.

My name started popping up on AM talk radio. Then NPR. Then local, and eventually national, TV talk shows. I was alternately a fool and a savior and the foulest kind of con. That one huge televangelist praised my name as the *Glorious Birth of a New Age* while another fat faced pundit said I should be *strung up for taking advantage of an obviously senile old man*. People camped out on my lawn, singing beautiful and beatific hymns even as the police escorted them off my property. Others yelled hideous, unintelligible curses at me from their cars as they drove by.

Apparently, Mr. Lawson had anticipated all of it. His contract earmarked funds for a security firm and someone to deal with the reporters. There was even an isolated house on a private island waiting for me and my boy, even though I told Lawson I wanted to stay in my own house.

I changed my mind once the real news got out. The news about Mark's *condition*, as the doctor was determined to put it. Not much in all this had yet truly angered me, but that did. He wasn't sick. It wasn't a disease. He didn't suffer from anything. Sure, he was different. Always would be. Might need special care and wasn't likely to live the same as the rest of you. But when the hell was being born different considered a *condition*?

Apparently, that is a minority viewpoint, if you go by the reactions. The news vans and camera crews didn't go away. The hymns did. No one called me a savior anymore, only a fool or a con who had gotten exactly what I deserved.

I gave up on watching news, but accidentally stumbled on that same televangelist on a late-night rerun. There I was, sitting in my rocking chair, feeding my boy and hearing that man. . . hearing him refer to my little boy. . . my beautiful, sweet angel as an abomination. A "just punishment against the hubris and insolence of that silver-tongued Jezebel and her modern-day Judas." Saying that we should live out our lives in shame and poverty until the good Lord chose to send us into our "rightful place in hell."

He railed on for the better part of an hour. Getting more and more worked up, red faced and screaming. Started talking about sins made flesh. About how God worked every day in the concrete world and how the *condition* of my boy was proof. By the end, the very boy he had once called everything but the Christ was now labeled a "demon spawn of the Satan walking among God's loyal servants".

I finally found the will to change the channel to a late night political comedian with the same look in his eyes. He may have been laughing, but the smile ended at his bared teeth. He was saying how it all made sense, really. That he had always known *they* weren't right in the head. No one who believes nonsense like that could be. Only someone exceptionally stupid or a bit *special* would believe. He said it exactly like that, sneering and drawing out "special" with long, dramatic hand movements.

That night, I couldn't even cry as he said it. Just stared dumbfounded. Blank faced and boiling over with rage and terror as his jackal-smiled tirade built to its punchline. I'm sure he thought it was brilliant. Shocking and punchy in a simplistic way built for tweets and hashtags. The captive audience seemed to think it was hilarious. Then, the fu. . . the *comedian* looked straight into the camera and, through teeth as big and sharp as a shark's, said "Of course, their god is a retard."

I wasn't prepared for such anger, such bald hatred for my boy. I could see hating me. I made my choices. I didn't believe the things Mr. Lawson did. I didn't want to be the mother of a God, even if I could. I just wanted to be a mother. Wanted it so bad that I pretended to not know how illegal it all was. Pretended to buy into his claims that we had to be secretive because of the "agents of the Enemy" instead of the agents of law enforcement.

I was the criminal. I was the liar. I was opportunistic and greedy and maybe even sacrilegious. I could and would face anything anyone had to say about my actions. But Mark wasn't any of those things.

He was innocent.

Maybe one day, when he's old enough, I'll be able to explain what happened. The cushion of time may just soften the wounds. Maybe he'll be able to forgive. I have neither the strength nor faith for that.

The next morning, I woke to find "Retard Jesus" spray painted across the garage. In between the words was a crudely done image of a tiny crucified stick figure. Wearing what appeared to be a helmet. The dark red paint was laid on heavily and oozed down the slats in thick rivulets.

I had plans made by the afternoon and we were on our way to the airport that night.

I don't know or care what's happening in the world outside of our little shell. I don't watch TV. Don't use the internet. My own world collapsed to just me and my little boy.

He's getting anxious, though. I know he needs children his own age to play with. Someone who isn't an adult to talk to. Someone who can keep up as he runs through the grass and hides among the trees.

I got him a puppy, hoping to alleviate the need. To buy myself a little time. Mark named him Luke because he loves eggs. I don't need to understand the boy to adore him.

The two of them are beautiful to watch together. Luke is calm and gentle, even when Mark plays a bit too rough. But Mark's smile nearly swallows his face when they're together.

There was a scare last week, though. I was taking a shower when I heard Luke yelp. A loud, high pitched and painful thing that echoed through the yard. Then Mark began wailing. His screams surrounded the house like thunder and I knew something horrible happened.

I didn't bother getting dressed, just threw my robe around me and ran outside. Mark had stopped crying, which worried me more. Our deck stood five feet off the ground and I could see a ragged hole in the safety fence. Slats of wood were splintered, the raw white of the breaks stained with drops of red. I was so frantic as I ran down the steps that I almost didn't see him by the edge, cradling Luke's head in his lap.

Tears streaked down Mark's face and I knew immediately what must've happened. They were playing on the deck, and the poor thing took off after a squirrel or something. Luke still had too much puppy in him, was too impetuous to look where he was going, but had gotten big enough that the thin boards of the fence didn't stand a chance. The hit and the fall combined were enough to break his neck.

I was trying to figure out how I was going to comfort Mark. How I would explain to a five-year-old that his best and only friend was dead. How I would explain what dead meant. My eyes were already welling up over the poor beast who didn't know any better.

Through the blood rushing in my ears, I barely heard Mark laugh. I had to wipe the wetness from my eyes to see Luke's tail wagging. He was breathing heavy but licking the water from Mark's face with what I am sure was a smile on his face. Bastard must've broken lucky in the fall. I couldn't even see any cuts on him. I tried not to think as I rinsed the blood off the broken fence slats.

Anton Cancre

Ruby Ann's Advice Column

C. A. Chesse

Q:. . . *I first suspected something when I saw the way Maria was touching her stomach, and how nervous and jumpy she looked. . . Now I know that Maria, engaged to wonderful, virginal Joe, is pregnant by another man. What should I do?*

A: The first and most important thing to bear in mind is that Maria is cursed by God. When God cursed Ham in Gen. 9:25-27, the curse was manifested in dark skin, which her people partially bear. Indiscretions of darker races must be viewed more tolerantly than indiscretions of white people, because "to whom much has been given. . ." What is really disturbing to me is that Joe, from your description, is white. I should not need to tell you that a white man has no business being engaged to a woman from a cursed race! This is the danger of excessive interracial fraternization: it leads to unnatural outbreeding.

Another thing that I found uniquely disturbing was the self-delusions that both Maria and Joe suffer from. You say that Maria claims to have become pregnant because of a divine miracle, but we all know that God is spirit and does not sully himself with the flesh! Further, if God *were* to cause a miraculous pregnancy, it would be within the safe confines of marriage—not as an assault on family values! The traditional home is God's domain, and it is insulting to His name to be associated with anything as vulgar as an unwed pregnancy!

As for Joe's dreams, which encourage him to accept Maria anyway, I would remind you that sinful passions naturally lead to mental instability and demon possession (see Pastor H. Howard's sermon on "Prozac: The Devil's Mind Control.") He has clearly stepped outside of God's will by planning to marry a non-white woman, and so is more susceptible to the devil's lies.

Once this is established, we can move on to what needs to be done. As I see it, the church can either tell Maria to keep the baby, tell her to abort the baby, or stone her.

If she keeps the baby, Joe will, doubtless, leave her, because what legitimate man would marry a woman pregnant by someone else? Then Maria would be left alone to raise the child. I am sure others are beginning to realize that Maria is pregnant, and churchgoers often experience discomfort as an unwed woman's belly gets larger. This is the Holy Spirit reaffirming what is natural and good in His true people. Our churches should continue to offer neither physical nor emotional support to unwed mothers and the divorced. In so doing we discourage what God hates most (promiscuity). If a picture is worth a thousand words, a public example is worth a million.

I should not need to mention the second option, but because of liberal infiltration I will simply say: it is entirely out of the question to suggest an abortion. The church has clearly stated its position on this issue, and its opinion of women who use abortion as the coward's way out, not wanting to face the consequences of their actions or the church's retribution. (However, if Maria repents after having had an abortion, the church can forgive her, labeling her as a "woman with a stained past"—a perfectly acceptable church role.) It is only those who keep their babies, and have the gall to appear happy, that provoke the wrath of the sexually pure.

This leads me to the third option. Traditionally, churches have stoned such women publicly. I would encourage, in this instance, a public stoning. This is particularly appropriate because the stonee is a minority, as most who get the death penalty are. I would also encourage you to talk this over with others—this is not gossip, only verifying how widespread your belief is. Once most of the church knows about Maria, it will be time to approach Joe. Clearly Joe, being a righteous man, would never try to put her away quietly.

Thus we can see God's blessing even in this, since He Himself probably sent this child to reveal to Joe, and the church, the folly of waywardness.

C. A. Chesse

Nature Does Not Always Know

Jane Yolen

"Behold: 4 New Species Of Tiny Frogs
Smaller Than A Fingernail"—
The Two Way. Breaking News from NPR

If there is a God, and note,
I am not taking a public stance,
He/She/They sure have too much time
On his/her/their hands.

First the new planets, lined up
Like pool balls, ready to be racked,
And now this, a jewelry-sized frog
You can wear on your thumb.

Come on, God, we've got dead children
floating onto our beaches, fished out like
cod.
A vice president who believes
In angels dancing on the head of a pin.

We've got drones almost as small
As the fingertip frog, but more deadly.
And seven kinds of poison (possibly ten)
Entirely undetectable by our science.

Don't get me started on the escalation
Of cancers and that old stand-by AIDS,
Your little party trick
To keep us upstarts in line.

So folks, it's up to us, not God
And His/Her/Their newest toys.
While you're cooing over these frogs,
The world goes to ruin,

One major highway at a time.
I can't blame the amphibians.
They don't even have webbed toes.
Means we can't strap miniature bombs

On their backs and point them towards
China
Or Korea, or anyone else we will soon be
At war with. Next 100 days
And we should know all about that.

The Lost Gospel Writers

Charles Walbridge

"He drank out of this very cup. But I'm not worried. Getting crucified isn't contagious."

"This bloody wine has no body."

"Very true; 31 AD was not a vintage year."

"Things were going so well. . . ."

"He did make waves."

"Hell, he walked on 'em."

"We need to get a positive spin on his being dead."

"They can't kill him anymore."

"He can't correct us if we misquote him."

"Your words live beyond you, until they reach the editors."

"We need to make it look like this was the plan all along."

"Somebody who dies for your sins?"

"That would be popular but way too convenient."

"Right. Why would anybody change their ways if they think their sins have already been taken care of?"

"He wasn't really against the Romans or the Temple, he just wanted us to be better Jews."

"Good point. We need to recast this, not as a political movement but as a spiritual movement."

"What does that mean?"

"Survival. We won't oppose bad leaders, just bad ideas."

"What about bad leaders with bad ideas?"

"We try to correct them. Gently."

"How gently?"

"Just firmly enough so that we don't actually get crucified."

"Just tortured."

"Thanks a lot."

"Stick a crucifix up front to remind people how far is too far. Let them work it out themselves."

"Like watering the wine. Just enough, but not too much"

"Speaking of that, my cup runneth empty."

"This plan may look different after we sober up."

"Let's not sober up."

Don't Get the Bible Wet

Debora Godfrey

Mary Sue was going to get a whipping for sure. No way was Papa going to believe that Brother Luke's perfect son John tripped her on purpose, only that's what he did. It hadn't mattered so much the other time, she was able to mend the tear in her stocking without Papa noticing, and by now her knee was almost healed up.

This time John knocked her in the mud, and she was afraid her book bag was full of muddy water.

Even that wouldn't have been so bad, but she had been carrying the Goodly Bible in the bag.

Every girl got a Goodly Bible when she turned eight, just like Mary Sue did two years ago when she accepted Jesus Christ as her Personal Savior, but her Bible was extra special, with its white cover and gold-edged pages. Brother Luke gave it to her right up in front of the congregation, telling her that the Bible was a Sacred Charge.

What made it a Goodly Bible was that much of the Book had its Pages glued together in the Forbidden Sections which were not for women who had tempted Adam out of the Garden. She didn't care about that since her Goodly Bible naturally opened up to her favorite verse "Suffer little children, and forbid them not, to come unto me: for of such is the Kingdom of Heaven." Papa said that's what Jesus told her little sister right after He killed her (only Papa said He called Lily Beth Home, which was the same thing as far as Mary Sue was concerned).

Mary Sue had visions of Lily Beth sitting up in Heaven on a Cloud with a little gold crown, looking all happy and healthy, not scrawny and sick and coughing all the time, the way she'd been just before she died.

Mama said it was the bad air from the coal plant that killed Lily Beth. She said it was gonna kill all the children, and that they used to have clean air before That Man changed all the rules and let the plant start spewing out black smoke from its chimneys. Papa told her to hush up, saying it was in the Bible that you couldn't talk like that against the President who made the Government stop sticking its nose into everybody's business. He said it was in the Forbidden Sections where the pages were glued together so that not just anybody could read them, meaning the women, because only the women had the Bibles with the glued pages.

Mama said she didn't see how the Bible could know about the coal plant spewing black smoke, but Papa quoted Scripture about how the coal plant was given to the town by Jesus and the President, and Mama needed to have more respect and be thankful that Papa had a job.

Mama said she didn't think That Man was fit to be Dog Catcher, much less President, and that the black smoke was why all the babies were dying. Papa got real mad after that, saying it was in the Bible that a wife had to obey her husband, and he hit Mama across the mouth because she blasphemed against the President that Jesus picked personally to save the country. Mama didn't say anything else, just sat and cried for Lily Beth, and maybe for her other dead children, all except Mary Sue, now in Heaven with Lily Beth on her Cloud. Or maybe they each had their own Cloud, Mary Sue didn't know.

In any case, Mary Sue had learned not to get too attached to her brothers and sisters because they didn't last. She doubted Mama was ever going to learn that.

Mary Sue snuck in the back way and up to her room which she had by herself since Lily Beth was on her Cloud, and found everything in her bag was soaked. Her Sacred Charge was a soggy mess. She put the Bible inside a wadded up towel and stepped on the towel to squeeze out some of the water, but it was still pretty wet. She considered for a moment putting the Book on the radiator next to her wet mittens, but she was afraid the drying paper wouldn't smell like the usual scorched wool and Papa would find out.

Maybe Mama could fix it. Mary Sue could hear her moving around in the kitchen, so she took the Goodly Bible wrapped in the towel downstairs. She and Mama agreed it would be a bad idea if Papa knew about the Book getting wet, and that she'd try to see if she could get it dry without him knowing.

oOo

Mary Sue forgot about the problem until Sunday morning, when Mama told her to get her Goodly Bible in a hurry because if they didn't get out the door THAT VERY MINUTE, they were going to be late. Being late was not tolerated, and Mary Sue always had to bring her Bible to Services because it was her Sacred Charge.

She ran up to her room to get the Goodly Bible from the shelf where Mama had put it, hoping that it hadn't been ruined by the water. Luckily for her, the Bible seemed to be dry, although it didn't close on account of all the wrinkled pages. She was afraid some of the pages might be loose, not to mention the beautiful white cover that wasn't as white as it used to be, and the corners looked to be peeling. She hoped no one would notice.

Mary Sue felt safe as she and her mother walked past John and he couldn't do anything to her even though he and Sister Jane were sitting right behind the pew where Papa and Mama and Mary Sue always sat. She felt safe sitting next to Mama and holding her Goodly Bible while Brother Luke gave a sermon mostly about how the Forbidden Sections told that anybody who wasn't a member of their own church was going to Hell and how Jesus said that everyone needed to have a gun for when the Time of Judgement came, which would be any day now.

It was when Brother Luke said that the coal plant was doing Jesus's work that Mama had clearly had enough. She snatched the Goodly Bible out of Mary Sue's hands and sprang to her feet right there in front of everybody. Mary Sue no longer felt safe.

"It doesn't say what you said." Mama riffled the pages of the Bible, now without any sections stuck together. The water must have washed away the glue. "I read what it says, all the Forbidden Sections, and it doesn't say that. It says. . ."

Just at that moment, Papa grabbed Mama and put his hand over her mouth. She dropped the Bible, and Mary Sue tried to catch it but missed. Hitting the floor, the Bible disintegrated, and the pages were knocked every which way as Mama struggled.

With the vague idea that she could put the Bible together again, Mary Sue scrambled for the pages all over the floor, Mama kicking them by accident trying to get away from Papa. Brother Luke was shouting for him to get his woman under control and that the Goodly Bible was now ruined, and it needed to be destroyed lest it lead the Righteous astray, just like it had led Mama down the Path to Eternal Damnation.

Everyone was picking up pieces of the Bible and Mary Sue was dodging to avoid getting kicked by accident, so all she managed to pick up was a single page. Hoping no one would notice, she shoved the gilt-edged paper into her pocket.

Just as though Papa wasn't still holding Mama, Brother Luke talked some more about how the Forbidden Sections said that if a wife didn't obey her husband, Jesus required a Penalty. The way Brother Luke said it, it was clear that the Penalty was an important thing, just like a Sacred Charge. Mary Sue didn't know what the Penalty was, exactly, but from the noises coming from behind Papa's hand, Mama knew and really didn't want to have it.

After a while, Brother Luke and most of the congregation went out into the back courtyard, Papa hauling Mama who fought him every inch of the way. He was much stronger than she was, so her struggling didn't do her any good. Sister Jane kept watch over the children, preventing any from leaving the room, even when the screaming started outside.

When the rest came back in, Mama wasn't with them. After the service, Mary Sue noticed there was a new pile of stones in the courtyard, joining the two that had been there before.

Papa told Mary Sue she could never talk about Mama again, and nobody else did, either.

Afterwards, Mary Sue occasionally pulled out the page she'd managed to save from the Goodly Bible, the one with her favorite verse. "Suffer little children, and forbid them not, to come unto me: for of such is the Kingdom of Heaven." She hoped that Jesus welcomed Mama too, up on the Cloud with Lily Beth and her dead brothers and sisters.

And Mary Sue hoped that Lily Beth was saving a piece of Cloud for her. She was starting to cough.

Prayer

Rebecca McFarland Kyle

I grew up in the 60s, in Oklahoma, in a Southern Baptist household. At school, I was ducking and covering for bomb drills while asking the teacher what good being under my desk would do if everything was supposed to evaporate. Every Saturday at noon, the tornado sirens shrilled reminding us to be vigilant particularly in Spring. I spent more time in the cellar with my Western Oklahoma grandparents than I care to recount. At least, there we had cookies and stories told by lantern light. And every Sunday, our pastor yelled hellfire and damnation from the pulpit.

With that triple threat hanging over us, I pretty quickly came to realize that I could not live my life in fear or I wouldn't get anything done. "If this world is ending, we're just one day closer," has been my motto since. I do my best to love my neighbor and treat others as I would like to be treated.

The *Bible* really hasn't been updated for the Internet, but I suspect my forebears would claim that a bona fide sign of the End Days would be when Christian groups ignore the Gospels.

The first time I encountered this was when a politician decided to have a massive prayer tent vigil for his presidential run, which he claimed God had told him to do. I posted Matthew 6:5-6, which was one of the first Christian practices I learned along with memorizing The Lord's Prayer.

> *5 And when you* pray, *do not be like the hypocrites, for they love to* pray *standing in the synagogues and on the street corners to be seen . . .*

6 But when you pray, *go into your room,*
close the door and pray *to your Father, who*
is unseen. Then your Father, who sees what
is done in secret, *will reward you."*

The post literally disappeared before my eyes. I refreshed the screen and it was not there.

I reposted.

The third time I was blocked and advised not to post again by the site administrators. Note: That particular candidate didn't even win his party's primary and has not held an elected office since.

As my Mom wisely said, "Sometimes God says no."

I forgot about the incident until my cousin, who has a terrible habit of spamming people with every urban legend around, sent me something supporting public prayer and prayer in school.

I recall the latter with shudders. "Coach" led the school prayers every morning. The man had a distinctive Okie twang worsened by chain smoking and alcohol. Coach also used to bellow into a megaphone which meant the subtle nuances of microphone speech volume completely escaped him. I don't remember Coach asking God for much for the general student body, but a frequent imprecation featured "stomping, annihilating, bashing," whatever team our school was playing against next week.

I sent my cousin the *Bible* verse regarding prayer. While we have spoken since, she hasn't sent me a single SPAM email.

So You Want to Make Gods. Now Why Should That Bother Anyone?

David Brin

o *How can optimistic futurists effectively communicate with those who are 'creeped out' by talk of transcendence and life extension?*

o *(Presented to the Singularity Summit, New York, October 2011)*

It's thrilling to join you brainy alphas, sharing insights and eagerness for a boldly transformed human destiny. As most of you know, I feel that I'm one of you, having explored non-human, trans-human, extraterrestrial, and all sorts of other exotic prospects for intelligence in books and media.

But you folks don't need another cheerleader for the Singularity today. As an ornery contrarian, my job is to *poke* at the viewpoints of whatever group I'm with, shining light on potential problems. And my, you folk have plenty of them!

So I plan to poke. And some of you will *not* be happy, especially you New Atheists out there—militant in your perceived struggle against the "pernicious mental disease of religion". Indeed, I propose to teach some of you, today, how to *talk to* your neighbors, especially those you heretofore viewed as implacable opponents. Indeed, some of these tricks—and altered attitudes—may offer the best way for a scientific enlightenment to win overall, let alone survive.

This is important—as we are currently in the midst of a so-called "culture war" that's getting ever-deeper, plunging especially America, but more broadly civilization, into what's more and more resembling Phase Eight of the American Civil War. Any general will tell you that, under such conditions, the best thing to do is to *break up* your adversaries' coalitions! You do that by making friends with moderates—turning them into *your* allies, instead of driving them into the enemy's arms.

Let there be no doubt, we who believe in progress—in science, in the potential for incremental and wisely-chosen self-improvement for both individuals and humanity—we do face enemies! Inherent in human nature is a deep divide between those who believe improvement is possible and those who reflexively reject the possibility as inherently loathsome. . . an attitude that comes not only from the hyper-religious but also a dour wing of the intelligencia, typified by Stanford Professor Francis Fukayama, in his grouchy tome: *Our Posthuman Future.*

It is important to study and understand the roots of this rejection. . . of renunciation, nostalgia and gloom. For indeed, *your ambitious optimism* is the unusual—some might say crazy—attitude toward the time-flow of wisdom. In fact, most civilizations across history shared the opposite core mythology! Nearly all looked backward to a Golden Age, when people were supposedly better, wiser, more knowing or closer to God. We are the exception: we who take a forward-looking attitude toward better days, possibly even a near-utopia, that we might build in the future. . . or else we might build the builders of the builders of that bright age—our smarter children and wiser grandchildren.

(You might say that some religions *do* propose better days to come, but only in a very specialized sense—after some catastrophic event or upheaval or externally-mandated transfiguration. If it's a sudden end-of-the-world leading to transcendent bliss, well, I don't consider that to be a look-forward view to a better-managed human civilization. If it relegates us and our civilization to be helpless bystanders and recipients of a prophesied set-piece drama, then we can rightfully consider that to be another version of the look-backward mentality.)

This distills the essence of our dilemma and struggle, and *not* the distracting side issue of belief in God. If you manage to turn a person's gaze from the past to a better, human-crafted future, then he or she becomes an ally, regardless of what differences remain. It is the critical issue. In an era when science and the very notion of progress are under attack, we do need to keep fighting for an ambitious problem-solving civilization. That's a daunting task. If it were easy, the galaxy would be filled with prior success stories.

Why no sign of successful predecessors?

For thirty years, I have collected theories to explain, as I coined it back in the 1980s, the *Great Silence* in the cosmos—the lack (at least till now) of any clear sign of extraterrestrial sapient life. It's also called the Fermi Paradox. Having gathered nearly 100 possible or plausible explanations for that Silence, I must conclude that *something* is keeping the numbers down. Some think that the explanation is a filter that suppresses the factors on the left side of the famous Drake Equation—those factors *leading to* a civilization's emergence, making that event rare, but leaving a galaxy that's open for us to explore and to make our own mistakes. These uniqueness proponents are opposed by those who focus on factors on the *right side* of the Drake Equation. . . who think the filter is waiting for us in our present or future, in factors that winnow down civilizations *after* achieving sapience, or that limit their visibility across the sky.

One thought is both creepy and alluring. What if we're the first to make it? Further, suppose we go forth and *rescue* a myriad other races who would otherwise tumble into failure modes that *we* somehow barely evaded, by foregoing nuclear war, or discovering environmental stewardship (barely) in time? Under this scenario, our can-do problem-solving zeal might not only save humanity, but also light up the galaxy! Talk about a good reason to engage in self-improvement projects.

If so, it won't be easy. Nor will such a destiny fall into our laps. We'll need to use humanity's most-recently evolved organs, the ones that fold into shape during the very last moments of the pre-natal period. These organs still continue to take form, as-yet incompletely functional, during human adolescence. (This explains teenagers!) They include the paracingulate sulcus, which lets us evaluate memory accurately, and the prefrontal lobes, those future-probing lamps on our brows. We know this because people who have had prefrontal lobotomies remain intelligent and conscious, but they lose interest in projecting what Einstein called the *gedankenexperiment*, or thought experiment. This involves our ability to imagine: what outcomes might occur if I propose this project and try this joke, or what would happen if I try to run this yellow light? It is also where empathy lets us contemplate: "what might be going on in *that* strange person's head?"

The prefrontal lobes may be the seat of humanity's greatest gifts and powers. . . and yet, even those who have access to both memory and foresight still divide between those who are optimists and grouches. Among the former, picture Ray Kurzweil and Vernor Vinge, who believe we may become indistinguishable from gods, while on the other side, are not only religious fundamentalists, but politically-driven authors with scientific backgrounds, such as the late Michael Crichton. . . whom I turned into a character in my novel, *Existence*.

Which brings us back to those 100 explanations for the Great Silence—reasons why extravagantly successful alien intelligences seem so rare. The "Fermi" hypotheses that I find most interesting are those things that most often thwarted human advancement across nearly all cultures and history. These were societal: oligarchy, secrecy, suppression of open and fair competition, and rejection of the very idea of progress.

One obstacle was the pyramidal social order, which reigned in nearly all human societies over the last 6000 years. Most of these generally-feudal cultures practiced *renunciation*—relinquishing rapid progress that might destabilize lord-centered hierarchy. This same impulse underlies today's "war on science".

It's an old, old fight

Is this a new problem? The 1930s book and film *Things to Come,* by H.G. Wells, shows how deeply many of our grandparents fretted about the tradeoffs between ambition and renunciation, in some respects pondering such issues more deeply than you would-be "godmakers" do.

Yes, "godmakers". Isn't that what your agenda boils down to? I mentioned Ray Kurzweil, whose book *The Singularity is Near* forecasts an approaching technological transcendence, overcoming most of the ills to which our mortal flesh is wont. We in this generation already *fly through the skies* and make light happen with a flick of our fingertips. Now, you aim to overcome the next obstacles of mortality, our limited mental capacities, and to surf atop the tsunami of Moore's Law, arriving (alongside our cybernetic-AI progeny) at a towering state of being that's akin to what our ancestors were promised by religion.

Woof. An astonishing ambition, yet it describes *you lot,* here at a conference on singularities and trans-or post-human destinies. Accept it. You are would-be god-makers.

So. . . what should be your top priority as godmakers? What pre-requisite should top your to-do list? How to design artificial Intelligence? How to make sure AIs stay loyal. . . or at least tolerate us, in the manner of our previous experiments in creating greater minds (our children)? All those imperatives are important, and they pale next to what *should be* your number one priority! I refer to a very basic thing, so fundamental that you may never have thought of it till now. So consider this an IQ test, indicating your mental *worthiness* to design new gods.

Give up?

Your top priority

At the very top of your list should be to *avoid the fate* of one early singularitarian, Giordano Bruno, who was burned at the stake for heresy in 1600, just thirty years before the infamous trial of Galileo. None of your goals will come to pass if the streets outside your hubristic, godmaking labs are filled with torch-carrying mobs! Yet I've not seen even one "transhumanist" address this matter of *survival*, which comes before issues of technical success or failure.

This will require adjustment! Abandoning snooty-smug detachment, for one thing. The blithe assumption that the hoi polloi don't matter. If your godmaking efforts alienate them without your having ever tried to soothe their very human fears, then the fault—when flames lick your feet— will be your own.

You are supposedly the sapient, logical ones. Find ways to connect with those who might burn you at the stake! As the guys like you burned in *every* other culture.

Reaching Out: 101

Step one: don't deride your neighbors—understand them! Can smart-aleck geniuses manage that? Hey, some aspects *are* interesting!

And so, for example, let's turn to. . . *the Bible.*

What? You haven't read it? You, who can parse computer code and arrogantly claim to grok quantum mechanics—are you *so* emotionally insecure that you must snort disdain, instead of using a few spare neurons to explore one of your own culture's mythic linchpins? Even in a spirit of curiosity? Millions view this book as their core postulate. Derision only solidifies Culture War, making you a *them-enemy* who thereupon can never, ever influence those neighbors about anything at all, even whether or not they ever actually burn folks. *Why would you deliberately disarm yourself, that way?*

Heck, it's always a good thing to be able to speak another language.

Experimenting with this approach, I've found it powerful at combating preconceptions and building mental bridges, even with deeply religious people. Yes, even those who come knocking at my door, fervent to convert me. Using *their* terminology, their myths, their holy book, it is possible to draw them toward a greater appreciation of largeness, of potentiality, of wider ideas and a much bigger cosmology. And a greater willingness to posit wisdom in science.

Metaphors of great power

Opening our Bibles, we'll *start at the beginning* of the relationship between the first man and his creator, with an episode that is potent and telling. In Genesis, the Lord. . .

". . . *brought (all the animals) unto the man to see what he would call them. And the man gave names to all the beasts and to the fowl of the air, and to every creature of the field.*"

Amazing, no? Especially since it is portrayed as the *first* interaction between God and man, and the only time we were ever asked a favor, independent of any consideration or repercussion of sin. Theologians generally dismiss this passage as cute. . . and largely irrelevant.

Irrelevant? *(Hey, that's one of the names Adam gave one of the largest creatures!)*

No, seriously, this is the only interaction in the entire Bible that preceded all the complications and subsequent tsuris of sex and transgressions and all that. In that case: what better hint at what we were made *for?* Note that we weren't asked to pray or to flatter or to beg, but to perform an early act of naming things.

Let there be no mistake: naming stuff is god-like power. Doesn't God use names to create everything? Ask any physics student who contemplates Maxwell's equations, which underlie the statement: "There is light." Ask yourself—and your religious neighbor—what is the act of naming things other than an apprenticeship in co-creation?

And what activity embodies that apprenticeship other than *Science?* The naming of distant moons, of hidden molecular codes, identifying never before seen species, or grubbing under alkaline mud to come up with new *beasts* to name. You can assert, convincingly, that the sheer purity

David Brin

of this moment. . . the *only* pure moment in the Bible. . . constitutes evidence that—

—we were made to be scientists. Continuing to name new 'beasts'–planets and microbes and all the stars in the sky—is sacred activity!

Time and again, I have found that this bold assertion—talking scripture to those who consider it paramount—almost always gets through. It penetrates. It persuades. . . and even makes folks smile.

What is "destined" for us?

So much for the very beginning. All right, then things got complicated. Sin happened, according to the mythos believed by millions of our fellow citizens. But even then, are they interpreting biblical events correctly?

This is where you get aggressive, as a smart-guy or gal who—though rooted in science, ambition and the future—was also able (with ease) to dive into the literature that your neighbors deem fundamental.

Yes, *aggressively* (though always with a friendly smile) you are free to get in their faces and cite scripture to them, defending science in terms that leave them no escape, because the passages you'll cite have authority. Remember, you're all descended from priests and rabbis who handled this stuff with ease! It should be trivial for you alphas to have a look at these cultural keystones, and show your neighbors some light.

All right, so let's get back to Genesis, a page or so later, after that darned snake talked us into seeking the fruit of knowledge. Take this passage:

"The man has now become like one of us, knowing good and evil."

Excuse me? Become like us? Hold that thought, because the next line is even better:

"He must not also be allowed also to reach out and take from the tree of life and eat it and live forever."

Oh, you dullard singularitarians and transhumanists, not to have taken part of that as your motto!

". . . take from the tree of life and live forever."

Okay, that required some editing—removing the *"he must not"* part! But set that aside for now. What all this passage says, above all, is that man is *inherently capable* of using knowledge to be like god and to live forever. Half of the argument over your godmaking ambition is settled! The Bible clearly agrees that we *can* do it. Now we're only haggling over when it's *allowed*.

Hey. Maybe it just wasn't *time* yet for Adam and Eve! What if there was stuff to accomplish first, the way children have to experience the world (and burn their fingers) before graduating? Perhaps that stuff has now been done! Maybe the time has arrived.

Only now, let's flip forward a few more pages to another crucial event that theologians mostly ignore. *The Tower of Babel* is shrugged aside, as a morality tale about the cost of human sin and the price humans must pay for hubris and arrogant pride. Take a look at what it says:

"And the Lord said: See, they are all one people and have all one language; and this is only the start of what they may do: and now it will not be possible to keep them from any purpose."

There it is again, the combination of two themes. Number one: humanity is inherently godlike, with limitless potential to achieve anything with cooperative effort and the power of words. It's right there, utterly inarguable.

But so is point two—that this is something God prevented, as when Adam and Eve were expelled from Eden because they just might grab some fruit from the Tree of Life. And hence, amid the ambitious endeavor of the Tower, mankind was cast into confusion, speaking a thousand tongues, leaving the great edifice in ruins.

Only, once again, the modern mind is drawn to ask: *Was it to be prevented forever?*

If so, why make us this way? Capable of greatness but perpetually denied any chance to fulfill it—except through endless flattery (e.g. prayer)?

Again, might the expulsion from Eden and the confusion at Babel have been *limited* measures applied just to those situations? Ways to stymie and prevent us from achieving things too easily or too soon? After all, we achieved other, later ambitious enterprises, without obvious interference.

In any event, we're about to test those limitations again! As many of us have depicted in fiction, modern technology is ensuring that language will be no barrier to cooperative effort, anymore. One worldwide culture, will, we hope, both unify us and enhance our individual eccentric creativity. The new Tower of Babel we're building is no simplistic ziggurat, but a flat, broad foundation for ambition, allowing us to assert every godlike power that our inherent natures equip us to pursue, along with, we pray and hope, the wisdom to do things honorably and right.

Just look at the hubris of the preceding paragraph—the singularity-seeking aspiration. Make no mistake: this is one of the core things frightening our neighbors! It underlies the war on science, that is being cynically manipulated by evil men, who wish to continue their oligarchic putsch aimed at ending the Enlightenment. Fear of punishment for arrogant pride helps propel a rising trend toward Renunciation. . . and it is one possible explanation for the Great Silence, if this happens widely in the cosmos.

Indeed, given their axioms and postulates, can you honestly blame your neighbors for reacting this way? The proper response is not ridicule, but to show them that some of their postulates are simply wrong, *even in terms of their own sacred texts.*

Because God never actually punished humanity for hubris. Ever.

He was. . . not. . . angry!

Let's compare two kinds of events in the Bible. In the first category are plenty of incidents, when the Old Testament God got extremely pissed-off. This happened at Sodom and Gomorrah, or before Noah's flood, when men buggered children and sold their daughters to rape-crazed mobs. Sure, on those occasions God responded with hot-tempered rage: fire from the sky, or drowning everyone in sight, pillars of salt. Hey, I am not here to defend or even discuss those legendary snits, only to draw a sharp contrast against a completely different class of events.

How were Adam and Eve punished for eating the apple? God said, *"OK you kids think you're so smart? Go get jobs!"*

Likewise in the Tower of Babel story, there's no tantrum. A page earlier, he drowns the world! A few paragraphs later, he is torching cities. But in the Babel story? In fact, there is no sign of actual anger or wrath! God says, in effect: *"Huh, nice try kids. . . but not now. Not yet. Disperse. Experiment in ten thousand lands. Become many and diverse. Make mistakes. Learn."*

Reiterating: nowhere in the canonical Hebrew book of Genesis, is there an expression of wrathful anger toward the hubristic ambition of Adam and Eve or the tower-builders—nothing even like the mass slaughters of flame and water and plagues we see elsewhere. [1]

In fairness—later writers, in the Talmud, the Koran, and the Book of Mormon, interpret God's reaction to the Babel Tower as genuinely angry. But there is not one whiff of rage in the original Hebrew Bible text, just calm deliberation and decision. Paraphrasing, those two passages boil down to: "Humans are capable of doing godlike things. Let's stop them, for now." There is no mention of "forever". In effect, God thwarted humans, but with minimal force, and with the distraction of new tasks.

Hence, you are at liberty to assert this clear interpretation: *Ambition isn't punished as sin. It is rewarded with challenge.* [2]

---

[1] I dismiss the doctrine of inherited Original Sin, a much later invention that is spectacularly stupid, insane, and an insult to God.

[2] There are other issues I could go into. For example, the recurring fixation on the Book of Revelation—currently the fetish

Will you automatically win this argument? Of course not! It is a theological assertion. Many of those who hear it are going to argue with you. But here's the deal. They will argue with friendliness and *respect* for someone who's taken the time and effort to come to their bailiwick and argue in language and terms they can understand. And it's an assertion that is worthy in scriptural terms.

A worthwhile endeavor

These talking points, all supported by scripture, are just a beginning. At minimum, they might help in those tedious tussles with your uncles, cousins and neighbors. If you're friendly about it, they will often say, "Hmm. . . I'll have to think about that." And they're no longer your enemy. You've become someone to argue with. Even if you don't manage to sway even one of them, you'll be doing what alphas ought to do: using a tiny sliver of your giant brains to reach out, to demonstrate that you can cross the divide, and speak their language. And hence, maybe now they are behooved to visit your realm a little bit.

I have found it effective to talk about how Moses had "lamps on his brow" and how this seems to speak of the

---

that transfixes millions of fundamentalist Americans into relishing hate-drenched fantasies about horrid agony for their neighbors—is one of the most loathsome things that has happened to America, of late. Do you know that Martin Luther didn't even want it included in the bible? Computerized rhythm patterns that studied the wordage of the Book of Revelation found that it was closely similar to the ravings of schizophrenics. Perhaps you can help them turn to other, more wholesome parts of the bible, like the actual words of Jesus. But the simplest answer to the Book of Revelation is to be found in the story of Jonah. It says right there: God can change his mind. Think about what that says to any smug, 2000 years-delayed rant of vindictive prophecy.

prefrontal lobes, just above our eyes, that are the seats of foresight.

Or how about *this* little thought experiment, that I've found especially effective—a comparison of prayers. Say you are a creator who came up with Maxwell's equations, the Bernoulli Principle and Quantum Mechanics. What would you consider to be better praise?

Prayer #1: *"Oh you're so great. Oh, you're so magnificent. . . please don't squish me."* repeated over and over, ad nauseam. Or—

Prayer #2:—some students in a high school chemistry class, carefully doing a titration they had calculated the night before. And it all pops out! The sedimentation and separation. . . all as clear as a bell. . . as day and night! And the students say, in awe: *"Oh, that's neat!"*

Which would *you* consider to be better praise? A nicer compliment? One can imagine a respect-worthy, craftsman-deity replying to the students: *"Why yes, thank you. I was kind of proud of coming up with that. How good of you to notice."*

Here's another thing that's effective. Find a railroad cut not far from your town and invite some of those neighbors—those you are reaching toward, in order to draw into the light—in order to actually show them exposed sedimentary layers. Most have never actually touched or examined the physical reality, especially layers with fossils. Staring at the variety of bands, they will be hard put to claim "it all happened in Noah's 40 day flood!"

Then find out when your local planetarium is holding a Star Party and talk to your uncles about how long the light took to get here from Mars, from Jupiter, from Vega. . . from Andromeda.

Why should you engage your neighbors? Again, one reason is to shift frightened minds, to ease the kind of populist fever that evil men may someday use to burn *you* at the stake.

Another is curiosity and the intellectual challenge of taking on yet another puzzle interest for your voracious mind, that should be able to tackle theology, no? Or else to give proselytes a delicious taste of their own medicine! *How does it feel, to be talked into questioning your own dogmas, for a change?*

Anyway, why not? It's interesting. . . and good practice, especially for would-be makers of gods. Shouldn't you be thinking about all this? Not only to reach out to your neighbors, but because you'll be going through these issues yourselves! With the Artificial Intelligences you create.

The theology of hubris

In summary, *naming* is called sacred, innumerable times, in scripture. . . and naming *is* science and we're good at it. Further, our potential is unlimited. Even conquering death—it's right there in the holy books. Regular, mundane obstacles of ignorance are toppling. . . as if in a training program. Hence, it is not unreasonable to demand a second look at the purported ties on Eden and Babel.

In those examples, god didn't punish ambition, but merely thwarted it, delaying things. And clearly, we are at the cusp of a time when all the issues of those fruity trees of Eden and towers to the heavens are being raised again. Now, it's possible that God will intervene again, thwarting all you would-be makers of immortal-brainy successors. Perhaps he's going to delay us again.

So? Should we let that stop us from trying? We're only doing what we're built to do! Moreover, humanity will *keep* taking on these challenges, no matter what the setbacks, because perseverance is also an integral part of our nature.

It's time for another Tower of Babel, we're building it now. And let the chips fall where they lie.

What we've covered are only a few of countless ways to assertively confront your neighbors on their own ground, to make your fellow citizens stare and blink and think new thoughts. And getting them to re-evaluate *you* as more than a caricature mad-evil scientist. Perhaps as someone to defend from being burnt at the stake. Even if you disturb them with these things, *they will be more friendly,* because you actually took the time and effort to speak to them in their language.

Oh, you singularitarians and transhumanists—whether you are atheists or techno-deists, you are already theologians! Because you plan to create (with Artificial Intelligence) what any other generation would call gods. Some of you hope to *become* gods. Fair enough. Then justify it. Sell it. Protect yourselves. Prevent torch-and-pitchfork mobs by relating to your neighbors. Prevent the Renunciation that could prevent your dreams from coming true.

Even if you despise religion, stop over-reacting. These cultural keystones matter. They are powerful metaphors; they are useful. Use them.

David Brin

The Faithless Angel

E.E. King

I've seen it all. . . and long ago. There is nothing new under the sun, not even the sun. There is nothing new above the sun either.

I should know, I'm an angel. Oh, not a big guy like Peter or Gabriel; I'm just a guardian. I get assigned here and there, watching my charges until they die. Then I get a new one.

I lived my life as a believer. First, as a fisherman, then as a fisher of men. Many spend their time angling, never realizing it is not fish they are after. I was more fortunate.

Now, I regret slaughtering those innocents of the deep. Now, I can relate. An angel caught between faith and reality, is like a fish between a net and a hook.

Still, even BD (before death) I knew there was more to the world than my paltry senses could perceive. Then I died and got my wings. I took to the job like an osprey to water, diving for spirits in the sea of life. But now? Now my heart's no longer in it. . . that's just a figure of speech of course. I don't actually have a heart—no heart, no lungs, no spleen, no pancreas. I do have a soul, though. In fact, I'm almost all soul. A soul and an appendix. Don't ask.

I keep it secret, my lack of faith. If the big guy ever finds out, God knows what he'd do. He's a vengeful sucker, that's for sure.

I can pinpoint the ending of my faith. It was early in my career as a guardian angel. I'd just been allotted Aliza. It seemed an easy assignment. She was a sweet, pretty, Almighty-afearing girl—much good it did her. She came from a big, close-knit family who were pretty well set.

At first I thought she'd be just another charge, a well to do, well behaved child of a Deity-dreading family, but she was more, so much more. Even as a child she watched each fledgling as it fell and tried to save it. She sensed the threads of infinity in every bird and beast.

I watched her, marveling that such a flower of compassion could sprout from the arid desert.

She was no work at all. Indeed, she could have taught the big guy a thing or two.

So I, not having much to do, was hanging out in heaven, watching God deal cards. God has often been accused of playing dice with the universe, but God favors poker—and he has a hell of a time finding anyone willing to play. That is why on this day that I'm telling you about, sometime before 2500 BC—I always lose track before the AD switchover—I suck at counting backwards—God and Lucifer were playing a few hands.

Lucifer? I can almost hear you thinking. Surely God would never hang out with THE DEVIL.

Most people forget that Lucifer was God's favorite, the smartest, most charming and loveliest angel—hell, his very name means "bringer of light."

That is why God occasionally invites him up for their particular brand of poker, otherwise known as "let's fuck with the humans."

Well, that day God was in a chatty mood, going on and on about his favorite new pet—Job. It was Job this and Job that. "Job is handsome, rich, strong and so righteous that after every feast he gets up at the crack of dawn and sacrifices one of his seven thousand sheep, five hundred she asses, three thousand camels, or five hundred oxen—just in case one of his sons or daughters accidentally curses Me in their hearts," God said.

As far as I know none of Job's sons or daughters ever cursed God. Usually that was done by the sheep or ox, and who can blame them?

So, as I was saying, God and Lucifer were playing and Lucifer said, "Job only adores you so much because he's got it all. I bet that Job wouldn't be so sycophantic if things got a bit tougher."

"Naw," God said. "Job would praise me no matter what."

"I bet I could make Job turn against you in just one day."

"You're on," said God. "Just don't injure him, that's all I ask. He's got lovely skin and it's rare in the Sinai."

It took no time for Lucifer to round up some bored Sabeans who were always looking for someplace to pillage and directed them to Job's 500 yoke of oxen and 500 donkeys. Next, he found a few Chaldeans and gave them keys to Job's camel coop.

Then he goaded God into firebombing Job's 7,000 sheep. Let me tell you, the sheep's guardian angel was pissed! The Shepherds didn't fare so well either, half were toast, literally, and the rest were just out of work.

I had gotten tired of the game and was watching over my charge, the sweet, pious Aliza. She was at her brother's with the rest of the family, teaching her nieces and nephews about birds, bees, and desert flowers. She had just freed her nephew, Elon's pet lark, and he was crying.

"Do not weep," she said. "God made birds. Man made cages. They are like angels these bright feathered beings. It is wrong to imprison them. I know you think your room will be made silent and bare by the empty cage, but look, up into the sky as it circles and sings and rejoice!"

Elon looked up, his tear stained face shone like a diamond made of flesh, clear and brilliant under the ancient sun. And my heart soared with his lark singing hymns to heaven.

"How come birds can fly and we can't?" asked Elon.

"Because they have a perfect faith," she said, gently kissing his cheek. "Divine boy, always remember that God is here, there and everywhere. The birds and sky are his eyes and ears. He sips from the oasis of your soul and feels the wetness of your tears. As long as you love the Lord and cherish his beings he will protect you."

Then—WHOOSH—God ups the ante. With a mighty wind he destroys Job's house and all ten children. They were torn limb from limb, their body parts scattered like dice over the desert.

I flew up to heaven fast as my wings could take me. . . "Yahweh," I said, "Lord of Lord, Host of Hosts, Master of the Universe, the Cosmos and Creator of Everything," (God likes titles almost as much as praise.) "Aliza, my ward, a good and Creator-cringing girl as you could hope to find, has been ripped into little pieces by a cruel wind that has blown nobody any good. . . surely you can't allow this to happen."

"The sins of the fathers. . ." God begins. He is a God of few words which he repeats a lot; maybe that's why He is so fond of prayer.

I interrupted, "Yes, that's fine, Lord." I said. "But, her father is JOB. He has no sin. So perhaps you could just do a little miracle, reassemble my ward and we can forget this ever happened?"

The Guardian angel of the sheep was in a corner pulling his wool out. But he knew better than to complain. God hates sheep. He's not too fond of oxen either.

Nor apparently of me. I became unable to speak. Nothing more, no lightning, no threats, just a simple silencing and he turned back to his game.

I should have known better. It was like telling fish stories to a trout's relative.

Lucifer crossed his lovely legs, grinned and dealt a straight.

An angel caught between God and Lucifer is like a fish caught between two cats.

So far Job had held true. Sensing a winning hand, God raised the stakes, disregarding his former objections to preserving Job's skin and health, and gives Job a horrible case of acne and herpes.

Job wept and prayed and looked around for something to sacrifice, but all was already destroyed.

Job's wife, who had taken the slaughter of their children a bit harder than Job, cut right to the chase. "It's time for you to stop offering stuff up to Yahweh, Job. He destroyed all the sheep, oxen, she-asses, camels and our ten children. Now all you have to offer him is okra and Brussel sprouts, and you know God hates veggies. Just look what happened to Cain when he offered the Lord greens. The only decent thing for you to do is to curse Yahweh as a child killer and die with honor."

"Silence, Woman," said Job. "Don't you know suicide is a sin?"

Just then there was a knock on Job's door, which oddly enough had survived the destruction of his house. It stood like a small hinged monolith rising out of the ruins. Behind the door were three of Job's friends—Eliphaz, Bildad, and Zophar. Instead of being welcomed by servants and ushered into Job's lovely home as usual, now they were greeted by the charred remains of sheep, oxen, and a few fingers and toes—the remnants of Job's children that had blown into the yard.

"What evil have you wrought," they cried. "You must have sorely offended The Lord our God to make him punish you thus."

"I have done nothing wrong, praise the Lord," Job cried. "For no known reason I am become desolate, lacking cattle and kin. I curse the day I was born. My birth should have been shrouded in darkness. Light and life only intensify my misery and make my skin itch."

"Well, Job," said Eliphaz, "you always made out like you were so holy, telling everyone who had ill luck to 'bear up' and praise Yahweh. But now it's clear to me that you've never really understood their pain. A few pustules and you fall to pieces."

"Is that contagious?" asked Zophar, rubbing his cheek.

"No," said Job, "I love the Lord with all my heart and all my. . ."

"Herpes," said Bildad and the three fled as if bad luck were catching.

"How, God," asked Job, "can you judge people by actions since you, oh Lord of Lord, Host of Hosts and all that, can easily alter their behavior? How can we appease you oh Omniscient One, you who are beyond all comprehension? Why do you let the wicked people flourish while I suffer?"

Job looked around hoping for an answer, but no one was there. He was talking to himself, a sure sign of madness.

"Talk to me, Yahweh of Yahwehs. Don't just inflict all this shit on me and remain silent."

But the day was still as death. In fact, the sun blazed more brilliantly than ever, making Job's abscesses ooze.

Out of the desert a wind arose, circling and swirling like a gigantic dust bunny.

"Hey," said the voice of Yahweh, calling from inside the whirlwind, "do you realize who you are talking to? How dare you question me? Not only did I create the world in seven days, I also made the Behemoth. He eats grass like cattle, the Big Behemoth. His strength is in his loins but his power is in the navel of his belly. It's all in the core; it's where I got the idea for Pilates. You couldn't make anything like that, could you?

"You never even invented the wheel, let alone a Behemoth, or an entire discipline that exercises every single part of the body.

"I also created the leviathan. You couldn't catch the leviathan with a fishhook if your life depended on it. Could you make a pet of him or put him on a leash for your girls. . .or rather, could you if you *had* any living girls. . .which I believe you don't, now, do you?"

As if to emphasize his point, Aliza's little fingertip somersaulted onto the barren ground at his feet, as naked as a newly hatched chick.

"No," bellowed Yahweh. "You know nothing! I am God, motherfucker—QED, bitch."

(QED 'Quod Erat Demonstrandum', is Latin for 'I haven't actually proven anything, but believe me anyway.)

Job wasn't satisfied, but no one wants to argue with a whirlwind.

"Sorry, Yahweh," he muttered. "You are of course right. I could never even draw up plans for a behemoth or a leviathan, let alone make one."

Thus, God won his bet with Lucifer. It put Yahweh in a generous mood. With a wave of his hand, he cured Job's herpes and gave him a tube of Clearasil, clearly a miracle since neither acne cream nor tubes would be invented for centuries yet to come. He deeded Job twice as much property as he had had before, some new children, and one hundred and forty years in which to enjoy them. In fact, Job's new daughters were so beautiful that he even put them in his will, which was most unusual.

But Aliza, my sweet, loving, innocent girl was still dead, her dust blown to the corners of the earth along with her siblings. For her there was no return from the beyond and no forgiveness.

E.E. King

St. Patrick 1, Snakes Nil

Jane Yolen

He rolls up the sleeves of his robe,
flexes saintly muscles,
hand-wrestles the first bunch of adders
into a leather carry-bag,
then heads across the pond.
England is the kind of place
that can support snakes,
not the green island he's made his home.

A harvest of first sinners,
narrow, vile ribbons hung
on the lapels of liars and thieves,
sooner out of sight, out of mind.
He's doing God's work,
he reminds himself each time
one of them wraps its sensual slink
artfully around his wrist.

Jane Yolen

Temple Tantrum

J.W. Cook

"911 what's your emergency?"
heavy breathing and loud excited voices
female voice
"Hello?"
"This is 911 what's your emergency?"
"Oh, sorry it's hard to hear with so many people around. We're at the Lord's Covenant Church on Meadow and Pine. There's a fundraiser here today and some indigent just came in and started tearing down booth's and attacking our vendors."
sounds of falling and crashing objects
"Is he armed?"
"He beat the man who was collecting tithes with his own charging cable and threw his iPad through a window. Hold on honey, no you can't go see the lamb. There are no lambs here."
child's voice
"But Mommy it's the Lamb of God, we should go help him."
"We are going nowhere near that crazy homeless drug addict. C'mon honey, let's get you back to the car."
"Ma'am do you require assistance?"
"What the hell do you think?"
child's voice
"Mommy, that's a bad word."
"Yes, get someone down here to haul off this crazy man. Right now! He's scaring my child and destroying the church. He's spouting that he's the Messiah."
"Are you sure he isn't armed ma'am?"
"Just with the iPad cable."

sounds of a whip cracking

"Describe the man please."

"He's Arab looking so he could be a terrorist, and he is definitely on drugs. Here, listen."

muffled shouting "I am the Son of the Father and humanity's Lord and Savior. Heed my words before it is too late. My Father's house will not be turned into a den of thieves and greed."

"Please get someone down here to take this crack head away."

"Help is on the way."

oOo

It had been 2000 years since I had set my eyes upon the tiny blue dot in the sea of blackness. A planet that could sustain life as my Father had intended. I hadn't checked in on humanity since my Father had told me that I would be returning one day. My first visit had been eventful to say the least. My Father said it was time to witness their progress again, to see for myself if they had heeded the lessons from my first trip.

I decided to visit a place called the United States first. It was, my Father told me, a place that claimed to be a nation based upon my teachings. It has been disappointing. This is a place that had selected a leader who is so vile and reprehensive that it angered me simply listening to him speak. He spouted lies with every incoherent sentence he muttered and the crowds still cheered him on. The people of the United States had created their own Golden Calf.

I had hoped that the first time I had shared my teachings that humanity would learn. But they had not.

Something had to be done before mankind destroyed itself, but I needed to see with my own eyes. To bear witness to the acts of the children to the Father.

As before, I fellowshipped with those who were most in need. I visited those who were without homes and saw them cast apart from society. I visited those who were hungry and without food and they were shamed and blamed for all the wrong in the world. I visited those who were desperate and sold their bodies for money and took drugs to forget the things that had been done to them and they were called whores and junkies. The people who needed me most were given labels. They were called illegal, rapists, and treated as criminals because of their birth. I saw them reviled and spit upon simply because of the color of their skin and the clothing they wore.

So I remade myself in their image. I dressed as they dressed and lived where they lived. I spoke to them about my teachings and though many had heard them before, most had never experienced them in their lives. One of the gifts my Father had given me was to see the experiences of all humans' memories and souls.

I wept for them.

I then visited the wealthy and affluent. I entered gated neighborhoods—gilded and protected by men with weapons and high walls. I entered these places and was myself cast out.

Slowly, but with surety, anger inside of me was growing. I had expected some humans to be wicked in their hearts. For that is the nature of things.

But to see an empire claiming to be ruling in my name and claiming to heed my teachings while casting aside those with the most desperate need? I was seething by the time that I visited one of the Churches that had been established in my name.

Opulence and extravagance rose about me when I entered the supposed house of my Father. Power had corrupted their hearts, minds, and souls with greed and the lust for money. The leaders of these Churches were using the Father's name and MY name to live in ways that would have shamed a Pharisee. They exploited their flocks turning my teachings into gospels of wealth and prosperity for themselves.

In the temple of the Father which was adorned with my name I found men and women selling their wares. Instead of animals as it had been before, it was now clothing and jewelry, adorned with my visage and symbols of the cross.

Food and drink were being sold by merchants, instead of being freely given to the hungry and thirsty.

I arrived as I had when I made myself in the image of the homeless, hungry, and downtrodden. I sought help but was given none.

I did what my heart told me was right.

oOo

This is unit 73 reporting in, I've arrived at the location of the 1015, and it is still in progress.

Copy that 73, backup is in route, do you require additional assistance?

Affirmative dispatch, I can see him, and he's not armed except for a charging cable, he's stripped off most of his clothes though and is shouting at anyone who will listen. The area is mostly clear, but we'll need some units for crowd control.

Copy that 73, backup should be there in less than 10.

"You ready Jenkins?"

"Ready as I'll ever be. Confronting crazy people is my favorite. Hey, does this guy look familiar to you at all? I swear I've seen him before."

"He does look familiar, I think we just kicked him out of that gated community over on 4th Street. Stay sharp, keep a watch out for weapons and have your Taser ready, if we have to take this guy down it may not do much if he's on a bunch of drugs."

"My name is Yeshua, I am the Lamb of God, follow me and I will show you the true mercy of the Father."

"Sir, yeah Sir we're talking to you. Keep your hands in the air for me. Don't make any sudden movements, Sir."

"Ah, young Peter and John have finally arrived. I shall obey your commands and you shall be the first to follow me."

"Sir, please put your hands behind your back. No one cares about your Twitter, no one will be following you today. You have the right to remain silent. You have the right to. . . wait, how did you know our names?"

"I know a great many things Peter, how is your brother Andrew?"

"He's. . . he's good, just got back from fishing in Alaska."

"I'll need to speak with him as well. Come take my hand I will show you the way."

Yeshua reaches out and takes the hands of both young police officers and a bright light engulfs them.

"Jesus? Is that really you? I'll. . . I'll make sure that Andrew comes to you."

"MARY! NO! STAY AWAY FROM THAT MAN."

The young girl rushes to Yeshua and hugs his legs refusing to let go.

"You can't hurt him, you can't take him away. He's the Lamb of God, leave him alone!"

Yeshua kneels down and picks the young girl up in his arms, she buries her face in his neck and begins to cry as he gently cradles her.

"It's okay child, no one will hurt me, or you. Peter, John, the time has come to gather the others."

Unit 73, what's your status?

Sirens sound and a woman wails

"Leave your weapons you will not need them."

The officers take their badges and guns over to their vehicle and place them inside.

"Yes, my Lord. But where are we going, what are we going to do?"

"We're going to gather the others."

Were You Good Stewards?

Joyce Frohn

"Where are my treasures?
The dodo was right there.
I was proud of that one.
A pigeon turned
top-of-the-food chain carnivore.

"How could you destroy it?
Do you know how long that took to evolve?
And here. My pandas.
They're almost gone.
They were another of my triumphs.

"A carnivore turned
super-specialized vegetarian.
I liked their thumbs best.

"Here, the thylacines, were here.
A marsupial carnivore.
I suppose you killed them so fast
you never saw them hunt.

"The platypus.
It is such a fine joke.
Do you know how hard it was to get those
Poison glands?

"So few left.

"What is the use of making marvels
if you are more interested in destroying
Than admiring?"

Joyce Frohn

Righteous Spirits

Lillian Csernica

A muffled sob split the silence, then a long, shuddering inhale. Tanya stared into the darkness, every muscle rigid with fright. The pain, the sorrow... it didn't sound like Mother or Baba. It didn't sound like anything human. She listened, sudden sweat gluing her nightgown to her skin. Moment after moment passed. She forced her fists to pull back the covers, then swung her legs over the edge of the mattress.

Another wail shook the night. Tanya flinched, heart thumping. She had to do something. Had to—had to find Baba. Baba would know what to do. Tanya launched herself at the door. The shadowy rectangle stood miles away through the noisy darkness. Her fingers closed on the cold brass of the doorknob. She turned it, whispered a vague prayer, then yanked the door open. A hulking shape blocked the hallway.

"Baba! *Baba!*"

Familiar arms crushed her against a lumpy bosom. The smells of stuffed cabbage, borscht, and incense surrounded her. Tanya clung to her grandmother's thick waist, shuddering against her shoulder.

"Sh, Tanya. Do not be afraid." Baba gently pushed Tanya back through the doorway, then stepped in and shut the door.

"Baba, did you hear it? That horrible sound—"

"To bed, Tanya. You should not be up at this hour."

Tanya huddled under the covers. Baba sat beside her and smoothed Tanya's long dark hair back from her cheeks.

"I had hoped you would not hear it."

"What, Baba? What is 'it'?"

"The *domovoi*."

"Oh Baba, come on! You think there's some little man living under our stove? That's just a fairy tale."

"Ah, you know all about it. *Horosho*." Baba patted Tanya's side and stood up.

"Baba!" Tanya caught Baba's hand. "I'm sorry. I'll listen."

Baba sat down again. "There is trouble in this house, Tanya. The *domovoi* weeps because of it. He wants to live in a happy house, not one torn by anger and grief."

Tanya's mouth set. "I'm fine, Baba. Mother's fine. We're all fine."

"Then why does the *domovoi* weep?"

"Maybe he misses Daddy."

The sudden depth of Baba's silence made Tanya blush.

"I'm sorry, Baba. I wish Daddy was here." She sighed, thinking of his booming laugh. "Mother made him go. They had to have more amber for the shop. Amber and Palekh boxes and eggs. People buy a lot of that stuff around Pascha."

"That is not enough to make the *domovoi* weep."

"Then what's wrong?"

"Can you try to make your mother happy, Tanya? There must be some young man in the parish you could like."

Tanya thumped her head against the pillow. "Baba, all I did was go to church with Enrique to see the Stations of the Cross. We could have been doing worse things, especially during Great Lent."

"But he is not Orthodox. There is a difference."

Tanya sighed. Mother she could ignore, but not Baba. "You really think a *domovoi* made that noise? You never said we had one before now."

"There was no reason to tell you. The *domovoi* was content. Now..." Baba shrugged, then patted Tanya's side again and rose. "Goodnight, little dove. God Bless."

"But—Baba—"

The door closed.

Tanya lay there, staring at the ceiling. She couldn't see it, but she knew it was there. Twenty years of church, of praying, of sacraments and icons and Great Lent. Twenty years of being a Russian Orthodox Christian, and she still believed in a ceiling more than she believed in God.

Tanya burrowed down into the pillow, her stomach a sick knot of worry. Baba still held on to old country superstitions? Baba believed in God, and Tanya believed in Baba. If Baba didn't really believe, not all the way, where did that leave Tanya?

oOo

Tanya sipped her Coke, wishing the sunny day and the laughter of the other students in the cafeteria could lighten her worries. Enrique sat beside her, looking over the growth charts Brenna kept for their Biology project. They'd chosen a frog, experimenting each week with new types of food to see which helped Kermit grow the fastest.

Tanya picked at her French fries. Only three weeks into Great Lent, and already she hated the taste of potatoes—no meat during the fasting ritual. She bit into one, then dropped it with a sigh.

"You okay?" Enrique asked.

"I'm going crazy. Every year it's the same thing. Forty days of Great Lent, then Holy Week and Pascha. Pray harder, take care of the poor, think about your sins and clean up your act."

"It's not so bad," Enrique said. "That's what we're supposed to do all the time, right?" He flashed her that confident smile, bright against his olive skin. He always looked so happy with his black hair falling into his eyes like a puppy dog's floppy ear.

"Sin is such an outdated concept." Brenna took a dramatic drag on her clove cigarette. "Like God has nothing better to do all day than keep track of all the rotten things people do to each other." She shook her head, making the six earrings in her left ear jingle. "Believe in yourself. The only constant thing in your life is you."

Tanya nodded. That made a lot of sense. She turned to Enrique. "Do you really believe what the priest says every Sunday?"

Enrique shrugged. "I guess so. You know how it is. When *Abuela* makes you go, you go."

Brenna scowled. "Why are you two so afraid of those old ladies?"

"I don't know if I believe in God," Tanya said, "but I definitely believe in Baba." She hesitated. "Last night this horrible noise woke me up. Somebody crying, wailing even. Baba said it's a *domovoi*, a house spirit."

Brenna perked up. "What, like some kind of Russian poltergeist?"

"It's this little old man who lives under our stove and cleans the house while we're asleep."

"In San Jose?" Brenna smirked. "I believe it. You better make sure his sleeping bag doesn't catch fire."

"It's not funny." The bigger problem loomed up before Tanya, filling her heart with a cold, sickening dread. "I always thought Baba believed in God and only God. Now she's telling me this Russian fairy tale like she'd talk about the mailman."

"You want me to ask *Abuela* to say a novena for you?" Enrique took Tanya's hand between his. "Maybe talk to Fr. Antonio?"

"Thanks." Tanya squeezed his hand. "If things get that bad I'm sure Baba will call Fr. Vasili."

"So is this thing real or not?" Brenna asked.

"I don't know. I tried to catch it last night, but I ran into Baba first. She made me go back to bed."

Brenna shook her head. "That old lady is running your life. The sooner you move out, the sooner you'll start finding some real answers."

"Like what?"

"Like the fact that those icons and holy water and all that stuff can't be doing you much good if you've still got this little Russian spook screaming at you all night."

Tanya stared at Brenna, too horrified to speak. This runaway Catholic just came right out and said what Tanya hadn't even dared think. Brenna grinned.

"See? It's all just brainwashing." She stood up and slung her backpack over her shoulder. "If any of that really worked, your house wouldn't be haunted." She walked away, her spiky heels clicking on the pavement.

"Hey." Enrique put his arm around Tanya's shoulders. "Don't listen to her. Ain't nothing as nasty as a bad Catholic girl. She just likes to upset everybody."

Tanya laid her head on Enrique's shoulder. What if Brenna was right? It made Tanya feel cold and sick all over.

oOo

Tanya sat on a stool by the kitchen counter drinking tea. Baba pulled the mushroom *pirog* out of the oven and set it on the range to cool. The *pirog* looked perfect, the crust golden brown over the mushrooms and glass noodles inside. Baba sliced it into neat squares.

"Baba, how do we make the *domovoi* stop crying?"

"Make peace. Forgive and ask forgiveness. That is why God gave us Great Lent."

It wasn't that easy. Not with Mother. "Enrique says his grandmother is just like you. She prays all the time and collects food and blankets for the poor. She makes him go to church every Sunday."

"How does she make a full-grown boy go to church?"

"She—just looks at him. You know. The way you look at me sometimes."

"Do I make you go to church, Tanya?"

"No, Baba. Not lately."

"On Clean Monday your mother told me you are a grown woman now. You know what the Church requires of you. If you want to go to Divine Liturgy, you will." Baba shrugged.

Tanya opened a cabinet and took down three plates, moving around the table in a daze as she set the plates down and fetched the cloth napkins from the sideboard. No mild hints about going to Confession. No reminders about reading the Three Canons in Preparation for Holy Communion. No gentle nagging about anything. Tanya had started to wonder if Baba just didn't care anymore. All because Mother told Baba to leave her alone. Tanya's shock hardened into something hot and sharp.

"So," Baba said. "Enrique was there. Who else?"

"Just Brenna. She's our lab partner."

"Bre-nah?" Baba frowned. "What kind of name is that?"

"She says it's Celtic. It means 'raven maid'. Her real name is Cecelia."

"Her parents let her do this?"

"They don't care. Her father ran off with his best friend's wife about three years ago. Her mother works at an insurance company where all they talk about is when people are going to die."

Baba shook her head. "Poor child. You should be friends with her, Tanya." Baba carried the *pirog* to the table. "Bring her home for dinner."

"Mother wouldn't like her. Brenna dresses all in black, dyes her hair black, even wears black lipstick."

"*Gospodi pomelui!* Lord have mercy. She's one of those?" Baba crossed herself. "This is what happens when children do not get what they need from the Church. The demons fill their heads with evil."

"Oh come on, Baba. Brenna's not possessed."

"No? You say those 'Goths' like to pretend they are dead. They want to be vampires. Tell me they are not possessed!"

Before Tanya could reply, the kitchen door opened. Mother dropped her purse on the counter and shut the door with her elbow, untying the scarf that protected her fresh perm.

"I can't wait for Grigory to come back. He insists that computer is a blessing, but I can never find the records I need."

Tanya sighed. Another typical entrance from Mother, no greeting, just a complaint.

"It smells delicious." Mother kissed Baba's cheek. "What would I do without you?"

"Get up even earlier."

Baba set the soup bowls next to the stove where the big pot of borscht bubbled, then carried a basket of French bread slices to the table. She recited the blessing in Russian. Tanya crossed herself, then sank down into her chair. Cold sickness and hot anger tied her stomach in knots, killing her appetite. She wanted to go lay down, to get away from Mother before the inevitable fight began. She picked at a slice of *pirog*.

"Tanya," Mother said. "You look pale. Are you sick?"

"I didn't get much sleep last night."

"Why not? You went to bed early."

Tanya shrugged. "Bad dreams."

"Demons." Mother took a delicate bite of *pirog*. "If you went to church more often, they couldn't bother you so much."

"Wouldn't they bother me even more? I thought they ignored you as long as you weren't trying to be righteous."

"Sometimes God will let them attack people because of their sins."

"That's merciful."

"Tatiana."

Tanya bit into her bread. She tried to think of something pleasant, or at least neutral, to say.

"Baba wants me to bring one of my friends to dinner."

"Which one?"

"Brenna."

"What kind of name is that?"

"She's a baptized Roman Catholic, okay?"

"Another one? Don't you have any Orthodox friends?"

"This is serious, Sophia," Baba said. "She's one of those 'Goths'."

"And you want her here? In all that makeup and leather?"

"She needs a grandmother."

Mother fussed with her piece of bread, ripping it into tiny pieces. Tanya could see the words gathering in Mother's mind, each chosen with her usual fanatic attention to detail. Mother dropped the last pieces of bread and wiped her hands on her napkin.

"We have enough trouble in this house without bringing in some stray who looks like a—a hooker from a Dracula movie!"

"Mother!" A hot flush burned Tanya's cheeks. "Aren't we supposed to be charitable? Aren't we supposed to help people, especially during Great Lent?"

"Charity begins at home. You want to help someone, help yourself. When was the last time you said your evening prayers? When was the last time you even thought about going to Confession?"

"You want me to be charitable, Mother? Watch me." Tanya pushed back from the table. "I won't say any of what I'm thinking. I'll just go to my room."

"You'll stay here and eat. Don't you dare waste Baba's cooking."

"Why can't you just back off? You told Baba to leave me alone. Shouldn't you follow your own advice?"

Mother glanced from her to Baba and back again, her mouth tightening into a thin line. Now Tanya had done it. Baba was in trouble too. Tanya ran down the hall and threw herself across her bed. Great Lent made everything worse. What kind of religion was it that put people through this kind of torture year after year? Tanya felt all torn up inside, just like the bread Mother had ripped apart.

oOo

A long, low noise woke Tanya. Her eyes snapped open. The dim light from the big *lampada* in the living room flickered around the edge of her door. A moan of intense grief made her shiver all over with fright. Tanya slipped out of bed and tiptoed to the doorway, then put her eye to the crack between the door and the jamb. The hallway was empty. She eased the door open. A loud sob tore the silence. A sudden rustling of cloth in the living room made her dash forward. Baba stood in front of the icon corner, her *tchotki* whispering through her fingers as she said a prayer for each of its hundred knots. A shadow slid toward the closet in the foyer. Tanya lunged forward. Baba's hand closed on her elbow.

"Baba, no! Let me go! I saw the *domovoi!*"

"Tatiana. Be still."

That tone froze Tanya where she stood.

"Leave the *domovoi* alone. Would you want someone to chase you while you were crying?"

"Baba, how can the *domovoi* be here while you're praying? Why don't the angels make it go away?"

"I am tired, Tanya. Will you read the Canon to the Theotokos? My old eyes will not let me see the words."

Baba did sound tired. That frightened Tanya more than the *domovoi*. On the bookshelf next to the icon corner sat Tanya's prayer book, along with the service books and lives of the saints and the writings of the Holy Fathers. The dust on the top of the books made her wince.

"Through the prayers of our holy fathers, Lord Jesus Christ have mercy on us and save us. Amen."

"*Amin.*"

"Glory to Thee, O God, Glory to Thee. O Heavenly King, the Comforter, the Spirit of Truth, Who art everywhere and fillest all things—" Tanya faltered.

"Treasury of blessings," Baba murmured.

"Treasury of blessings and giver of life, Come and abide in us and—and—"

"Cleanse us..."

"Cleanse us of every impurity, and save our souls, O Good One." Tanya read through the Supplicatory Canon, struggling to put her heart into the words. The Mother of God had to help her. Her own mother certainly wouldn't. After the final Trisagion, Tanya closed the book and set it back on the shelf. She turned to kiss Baba goodnight.

"Tanya, your book."

There, wedged in among the service books, was her commemoration book. It was dusty too, filled with names, some written in little-girl printing. At least four of the names under the Living should have been moved to the list of the Dead. Tanya wiped the dust off on her skirt, then read the prayers for both lists.

"I remember when you read those names every night," Baba said. "Have you forgotten those people, Tanya? Perhaps that is why the *domovoi* weeps."

oOo

Tanya stood inside the school cafeteria, gripping her tray of French fries so tightly her knuckles ached. Enrique sat at their usual table. Brenna slouched across from him. Tanya hesitated, torn between the need for Enrique's cheerfulness and the sure knowledge of Brenna's snide remarks. Tanya sighed. If nothing else, hanging out with Brenna would infuriate Mother. She hurried over. Enrique smiled and made room so she could sit beside him.

"How's the little Russian spook?" Brenna asked. "Still howling at the moon?"

Tanya ripped open a packet of ketchup and slathered it all over her fries. "It's a *domovoi*, and yes, he's still crying."

"Lent's enough to drive anybody crazy." Brenna picked up her cheeseburger and bit into it. The meat was so rare reddish juice ran down her chin, bringing Baba's comments to mind. Brenna did look like a demon crouched over her prey. She looked away, one hand pressed to her mouth.

"What's with you?" Brenna asked, still chewing.

"Nothing. It's just—Friday. During Lent." Tanya couldn't help glancing at the dripping cheeseburger.

Brenna grinned. "Just call me Captain Ahab."

Brenna's shameless posing tempted Tanya. "Baba wants to meet you. She told me to bring you over for dinner."

Brenna stopped chewing. She swallowed, gulped some Coke, then eyed Tanya with suspicion. "Why would Baba want to meet me?"

"You better watch it." Enrique laughed. "Those old ladies, they're sneaky. Mexican, Russian, Chinese even. Doesn't matter. They're all sneaky."

"That's what I thought." Brenna wiped her mouth on a napkin, leaving a smear of black lipstick and blood. "I'm nobody's charity project, understand?"

"Would you relax? Baba just wants somebody else to feed." Tanya studied Brenna, trying to imagine what she looked like before she went Goth. Cecelia must have been on the gawky side, with a long nose, long neck, and a crooked smile. In the Goth outfits, "Brenna" looked strange and exotic. Someone to be noticed, if not admired.

"Tell me something," Tanya said. "What do you get out of all this? All the vampire stuff, the black clothes, the weird music. It's not really a religion, right?"

"It's my religion now. My church, my altar, my gods."

"But why? Do you pray? Do you get answers?"

Brenna looked away.

"Enrique? What do you really do?" Tanya asked. "Do you ever sit down for a minute and just talk to God?"

"Sometimes." Enrique tugged his big gold crucifix out from under his white tee shirt and looked at it. "It's pretty cool to think God came down and actually lived, like we have to. Hungry, cold, getting chased from one place to another." He grinned. "Sounds like my Uncle Pablo. And then, when all those guys who thought they were so smart decided no way could Christ be God because he wasn't all big and important like they wanted him to be, they killed him. But that didn't stop Christ." He kissed the feet of the corpus and dropped the crucifix back inside his collar. "Nothing stops Christ."

His smile was so brilliant Tanya hugged him, holding on tight. Maybe some of his certainty would rub off.

"Bullshit!" Brenna snapped. "In one of my history classes I heard how the Pharisees were sure the Apostles stole the body just so they could go around saying God rose from the dead. It's all just bullshit!"

"Hey!" Enrique stood up, glaring down at Brenna. "We don't laugh at you for wearing those stupid fake fangs. Don't you go talking like that about Christ."

"Oh please!" Brenna sneered. "You only believe in God because you've been taught to be afraid of Him. Just like my mother. If you don't go to church on Sunday, God will punish you. If you don't tithe, God will punish you. If you don't spend every minute of your life on your knees begging Him to forgive you, you're going straight to hell."

Brenna thrust her hand into her jacket and fished out a small box. She jammed her fangs into her mouth, then picked up her cheeseburger and took a huge bite, pulling her upper lip back into a snarl that bared her falsely elongated teeth. She chewed messily, making the blood run down her chin.

"The difference between you and me is you're afraid and I'm not!" Brenna spun around, bellowing so loud everyone around them turned to stare. "I'm not afraid!"

Enrique shook his head and crossed himself, muttering in Spanish. He held out his hand to Tanya. "Come on."

Tanya grabbed her book bag and followed him outside.

"She better watch her mouth," Enrique said.

"It's not her fault," Tanya said. "Her father ran away. She just hurts, Enrique. All the time. God must understand that, right?"

"Maybe. But she has to ask for help. *Abuela* says all you have to do is ask."

oOo

When Tanya walked in the door, the house smelled like Heaven. Fresh *kulich*, some baking, some cooling. The warm sweetness of the egg bread lifted her spirits. She dropped her purse and book bag inside the front door and hurried to the kitchen. The sight of Mother standing beside Baba made her stop short.

"Oh," Tanya said. "Hi. I didn't know you'd be home early."

"Someone has to help Baba," Mother said. "The bake sale is this Sunday, remember?"

Baba beckoned Tanya, handed her the little cardboard box of colored sugar, and pointed to the bowl of frosting on the counter. "Finish the *kulich*."

Tanya spread the thin white frosting over the top of the first *kulich*, letting it dribble down the sides, then sprinkled a large pinch of colored sugar all over the top. Now the *kulich* looked like a mushroom from fairyland. When Tanya had finished all six, Baba stuck silk rosebuds into the tops of the frosted *kulich*.

"Did you talk with your friends today?" Baba asked.

Tanya bit her lip. "We had a fight."

"Really?" Mother said. "Why doesn't that surprise me?"

"Did you make up?" Baba asked.

"It wasn't the kind of fight you can apologize for. It went too far."

Baba clucked her tongue. "Tanya, you know better. You can always say I'm sorry."

"Not this time, Baba. Brenna was making fun of Christ. Enrique got really mad at her."

"And what did you do?"

"I—" She'd done nothing. Enrique told Brenna off.

"Well?" Mother prompted. "You're never at a loss for words around here. What did you say to her?"

"I didn't say anything. I just walked away."

Baba patted her shoulder. "That's the best way."

"Mama, don't tell her that." Mother gave Tanya a long look. "Well? Why didn't you say something?"

Tanya let the spoon hit the frosting bowl with a clatter. "I suppose it's because I don't have the courage of my convictions. And that's because I don't *have* any convictions! There! Are you satisfied?"

Mother's glare impaled Tanya, drove her backward until she bumped into Baba.

"Sophia—"

"Mama. Please." Mother picked up a dish towel and very carefully wiped her hands. "I tried to let you be a grown-up,

Tatiana. I can see that was a mistake." She threw the towel aside. "From now on, as long as you live under my roof, you will go to church, you will say your prayers in the evening, and you will not associate with anyone foolish enough to mock Christ. Is that clear?"

"Are you saying you want me to fake it? To go through the motions whether or not I really believe?"

"Tatiana, I warn you—"

"I'm just trying to make sure I don't commit even bigger sins until I figure out what I can really put my faith in! Do you want me to be like those Pharisees and just put on a good show in public?"

The color drained from Mother's face, leaving her so pale Tanya feared she might faint. Mother pushed past Tanya and rushed out of the kitchen. Her bedroom door slammed so hard the whole house shook.

Baba suddenly looked much older and very tired. "Now maybe you can guess why the *domovoi* is weeping."

oOo

"You want me to come in with you?" Enrique asked.

"No. That will only make it worse."

It was after midnight. Tanya sat beside Enrique in his brother's Mustang, half a block down from her house. Bad enough she'd upset Mother so much. Now she'd stayed out way too late without even telling Baba where she'd be. Enrique's house was so warm and noisy and happy. Tanya could hardly bear the thought of the cold silence waiting for her at home.

"Here." Enrique pulled a chain off over his head and dropped it around her neck. A holy medal hung on it. "The *Madre de Dios* will take care of you."

"Thanks."

Tanya tiptoed up the front walk. The light from the big *lampada* shone into the foyer, making a faint glow inside the glass panel next to the front door. Tanya put her ear to the door. The *domovoi* wailed so loud Tanya stumbled backward, stunned by the raw agony in its voice. The *domovoi* had been noisy before, but now it sounded like someone was killing it. Tanya crept around the side of the house to the kitchen door. Tonight she'd catch the *domovoi* and force the little monster to get out.

She eased the door open and slipped inside. More messy sobs disturbed the silence. Tanya inched her way toward the dining room doorway. She'd have a clear view into the living room of whoever or whatever it was. She peeked around the door jamb. Her mouth fell open, her eyes opening so wide they hurt. Mother was on her knees before the icon corner. Huge wracking sobs poured out of her. Baba stood to one side, near the front door. Of course. Now Tanya understood. Baba was standing guard, waiting to intercept Tanya when she finally came home. Just like she'd caught Tanya in the hallway that first night.

Shame nagged at Tanya, making her cheeks sting with a painful blush. She stayed where she was, hoping to catch some hint of what made Mother cry like that. Mother reached out her hands to the icon of the Most Holy Theotokos, begging her in broken Russian, repeating one word over and over again. Tanya's name. Why would Mother pray for her so hard, with such tears?

With sudden perfect clarity Tanya realized it didn't matter. That was between Mother and God. What mattered was the way Mother poured her heart out, praying as hard as she could. Mother had never been good at showing her feelings. Maybe she only had two speeds, uptight and hostile during the day, then showing all that hidden feeling in her prayers. Tanya had needed proof before she could believe. She couldn't ask for better proof that Mother and Baba loved her.

Tanya tiptoed out the back door to the sidewalk. She gave Enrique a thumbs-up, then kicked the trash cans as she walked back to the front door. She had to give the *domovoi* enough time to get away.

Last Words

Paula Hammond

"So it's a test?"

"Think of it more as an assessment of character."

"What happens if I don't take it?"

"Nothing."

"Nothing?"

"Absolutely Nothing. Of course, to some, Nothing is infinitely more terrifying than Something."

"You mean I'll just—well—die?"

"You are already dead."

"Well, yeah. I guess. But I'm here. Talking to you, right? So I'm not totally dead."

"Technically, you are a suspended possibility. A moment in time. You are a fraction of a second between your last breath and oblivion."

"But they could bring me back?"

"It is possible."

"Then I could just wait? Rather than take the test, I could just wait. Maybe they'll bring out the paddles. Shock me back to life."

"It is. . . complicated."

"Explain. Go on. I've got time."

"Have you heard of Schrödinger's Cat?"

"The cat in the box thing?"

"Indeed."

"To be totally honest, I never really got that."

"In 1935, a German scientist called Erwin Schrödinger postulated a thought experiment to explain a fundamental principle of quantum mechanics called quantum superposition. In this experiment, a cat in a box is linked to a random subatomic event that may or may not occur. The result is that the cat may be simultaneously alive and dead."

"What are you saying here? That I'm dead and alive?"

"In this moment, yes. You are both. And for as long as this moment lasts—for as long as I can stretch the possibility, hold back the entropy—those two realities will co-exist."

"You make it sound like time is like some huge, over-stretched elastic-band. What happens when you let go?"

"Whatever will happen, will happen. Time continues. Fate unfolds. The wave function collapses and you will be revealed to be either dead or alive."

"So, they could bring me back?"

"It has happened. Yes. It is possible."

"Then why are you here now? I mean, why not wait? Wait to see what happens. Then if I really die—once I'm 100 percent dead—offer me the test."

"Because you need to make an informed choice."

"Let me get this right? I can talk to you now, when I'm one second dead, but not later when I'm dead-dead?"

"Yes. That is correct."

"You're not really one for in-depth explanations are you? Come on. Humor me."

"Medically speaking, death happens in several stages. Clinical death happens between four to six minutes after your heart stops beating. During this time, your organs continue working. Your brain experiences a surge in activity, flooding the body with signals as it tries desperately to save your life. Ironically this will do irrevocable damage to your heart: the chances of being successfully revived at this point are minimal. However, for a short time, a rise in gamma oscillations increases the coupling between lower-frequency brain waves and higher. The resultant perceptions are realer-than-real: sensations of intense pleasure, elation, and audio and visual hallucinations. These are often referred to as near-death experiences. To put it simply: you get high."

"And you don't want me making important decisions while I'm stoned?"

"Precisely so."

"Hold on. Hold on. If what you said is true, then maybe none of this is real. My brain could just be playing tricks on me."

"If that were the case, then you would be playing tricks on yourself. Your brain is merely an organ, not an independent consciousness."

"Are you screwing with me?"

"That is not my intention."

"Oh, come on! This is getting silly. Are you real or not?"

"I am Death. In many cultures I am considered to be about as 'real' as you can get. Indeed, one of your favorite sermons was entitled 'What to do when Death comes a-calling'. I understand I featured prominently."

"Well, yeah. Sure. Nothing gets people putting their hand in their wallets like a reminder of their own mortality. But I could just be lying on an operating table, dreaming you up. How do I know that I'm not just talking to my own subconscious?"

"You don't. Does it matter?"

"Well, no, I suppose not. But let's say you're the real deal. Death come-a-calling: waving offers of salvation and damnation under my nose. . ."

"I made no mention of salvation or damnation."

"No, but it was pretty clear what was implied wasn't it? You said, 'an assessment of character'. You're not assessing me for membership of the Shriners."

"That is true."

"Great! Now we're getting somewhere. So, I'm about to take the most important test of my life. Well, my afterlife. Whatever."

"Just so."

"And if I don't take the test, then nothing happens."

"Nothing. Your muscles relax. You soil yourself. Bacteria in your gut begins to consume your stomach walls. Calcium in your bones leaches into your muscles causing rigor mortis to set in. Your skin loses its color. Blood pools at the lowest point of the body forming red and purple bruises. Nothing. Nothing of significance."

"Look, I know the scriptures. For unbelievers: death, corruption, oblivion. An eternity in the grave, never waking even when God's trumpet rings. For the righteous the resurrection of life, just rewards, angelic choirs. For sinners, the resurrection of condemnation, hell, fiery pits. Now you're saying that if I don't take this stupid test I get thrown in the spiritual trash? Even sinners get a better deal than that! I'm righteous, I'm a believer, how's this even fair?

"If I may quote you: 'A god who offers love, grace, and mercy, without judgement and wrath is no god. He's a hippy. It is not God's job to be fair.'"

"Wow. You've really been paying attention, huh? But you said that I'd get to make an informed choice. Things clearly aren't exactly how I thought they'd be. So throw me a bone: before I make my mind up, what can I expect?"

"That is not in my purview."

"And I'm talking to a seven-foot skeleton, dressed in black velvet, and carrying a scythe. That's not in my purview either."

"Mmm."

"What? What's so 'Mmm'?"

"I merely found your perception of me interesting."

"My perception? Doesn't everyone see you in the same way?"

"No. It seems to be determined by your own. . . expectations. Yours is surprisingly traditional."

"I'm a very traditional guy. What do other people see?"

"Family, friends, loved ones, religious figures. Lately film stars and comic book characters have become popular."

"Seriously? I mean, I get why people might see their parents, but who wants to be carted off to the Here-After by Batman?"

"Captain Haddock."

"Sorry?"

"I believe Captain Haddock is the most common form of avatar. No one has ever visualized me as Batman."

"Captain Haddock. You mean the drunk sea captain from TinTin?"

"I believe so."

"No. Now you really are screwing with me."

"There is also a mouse. . ."

"Right. Forget I even asked. Clearly the world is way more messed up than I ever imagined. So what about What Comes After? Is that determined by my expectations too?"

"I have no data to answer that. What Comes After is not in my. . ."

"Let me guess. It's not in your purview."

"Exactly."

"But you can guess. Come on, you're an intelligent man. You can tell me."

"Mmm."

"Mmm, again? What now?"

"Nephthys, Ereshkigal, Badb, Hel, Śmierć, Giltinė, Santa Muerte. These are just some of the names by which history has chosen to remember me. It is true that things have changed recently—since the fall of Rome. The old goddesses have been replaced by a more phallic pantheon. However. . ."

"You're a woman?"

"Indeed."

"Shit. Sorry, no offense. It's just, I wouldn't have thought that they'd give an important job like this to a woman."

"And yet here I am."

"Great. Just great."

"Is there a problem?"

"No. Sure. Death's a woman. I can roll with that. Ok, Sweetheart, all those centuries. All those discussions. All those souls shuffled off. You must have seen something. Heard something. Know something."

"I do not. It is not. . ."

"Not in your purview."

"Correct. But I believe you have some quite definite ideas on the subject. Did you not call yourself part of the 'elite'? Did you not say that God himself would appear to welcome you into Paradise?"

"It's all there in the book, Honey: 'In My Father's house are many mansions. . . And if I go and prepare a place for you, I will come again and receive you to Myself'"

"If that is what you believe, then you should have no concerns about judgement or the hereafter."

"Well, truth be told, I'm starting to think I might have been a bit over-confident."

"About. . .?"

"Quite a lot of things. I mean, I'm a good person. Mostly. I've done some bad stuff, but haven't we all? It's not like I broke any Commandments. Well, maybe a few. Just the small ones. But you know how it is. And if you'd seen my show you'd know that I've done a lot of good for the cause. Raised a lot of money. You should see that church I built out West. Well—the church I was going to build because I've had a few problems with my finances. The whole parsonage exclusion is incredibly complex. Sure there's a lot of land and a couple of condos in my name, but that's Church property. . ."

"I shall take your word for it."

"There's no need to sound so damn snarky."

"That was not my intention."

"Sure, but I'm definitely getting a vibe. . ."

"Perhaps it is your own conscience speaking?"

"Hey, wealth is a sign of God's favor. If I—the Church— is prosperous, then we can be all the more effective in spreading the Word. At least that's what I thought—but then you came along. Damn it! Everything was so simple when I was making the rules. If I don't take the test, then I die. I lie in the grave and rot. What if that's a better way to spend eternity than failing the test? What if I'm headed— you know—Down There? How do I know?"

"The story of your life was crafted by you and you alone. Do you not know if it is sound? If it will stand to be tested?"

"Come on! I'm human. I'm fallible. I'm stupid. I think one thing and I say another. I'm mean, and petty, and generous, and loving, and angry. And religion? I know I sound confident standing in the pulpit but shit's just got real here. I'm not the only one who thinks I've got a direct line to The Almighty. What if I got it wrong? Maybe what'll get me damned are the pork chops I cook when the guys come 'round on Arbor Day. Am I a good man? Maybe that's not even important. Maybe it's all about bacon."

"I suspect that it is about more than bacon."

"Easy for you to say. How am I supposed to judge my own life? Balance out all those days when I did the right thing against the days I didn't? How can any human? I mean, there's an experiment where they offer a chimpanzee one treat now or lots of treats if it can wait until a bell rings. And no matter how many times it's shown the trick, it can't help itself. It grabs that one treat. Slaps itself on the forehead. Then does exactly the same thing the next time. Chickens can wait. Can you believe that? Chickens."

"So, you do not want to take the test?"

"Look, I stand up in front of millions every day and tell them what they want to hear. I think I believed it, once, but being here, right now, has made me realize something. At the end of the day, it doesn't matter how much I dress it up, I'm just like that chimp. A sensation-seeking ape in a designer suit. I tried to do right—I really did. But when you're on TV, and you're a big name, and the money is rolling in, you grab whatever's offered and worry about the consequences later. And I've grabbed A Lot. Oh, you try to justify it to yourself. Hell, I'm standing here trying to justify it to you. But I haven't been my brother's keeper for a long, long time. I've been casting stones left, right, and center. Peddling indignation and judgement. Boy does that sell. And my camel? I don't have a camel, I have a big-ass $1,456,584-a-year Learjet. What hope do I have? But you must know. You're Death."

"With your permission, I merely open the book. Another will read it. Weigh its contents."

"What Other? God? The Devil? Osiris? Yama? Galactus? Who?"

"I cannot say. I am a lacuna. A gap in the final page of the manuscript. A pause before The End."

"Or The Happy Ever After?"

"Again, I cannot say. This is your story."

"Ok, nothing ventured, nothing gained. So how does it work? Do I get the whole life flashing before my eyes thing? Or is it more of a Vulcan Mind Probe?"

". . ."

"Hey, don't quit on me now? Come on. I'm ready. Hit me."

"Apologies. I was. . . distracted."

"Death can get distracted? By what?"

"It seems that your time is not now."

"I'm going back?"

"Indeed."

Oh, thank God! I mean, thank You. And I'm sorry about the things I said. Did. That's not who I am, I swear. Been keeping bad company recently. The Church, you know? Somehow things got twisted. I got twisted. I swear, I'll do better."

"That is your choice. Use what time remains well. We will meet again."

The Good Mexican

Melvin Charles

Bori Diaz limped along the dimly lit sidewalk. The day had been long, and the walk to where bus service was still available this time of night was almost a half mile. Each step sent a twinge of pain through her knee. She paused to rub it every ten steps or so. She knew it wasn't serious, but it still hurt.

She hadn't seen the edge in the uneven sidewalk and the trip had slammed her into the steps coming down from one of the many landings that opened to the sidewalk. Her knee cap took the brunt of the impact with the concrete. Her expert probing had told her that nothing was truly wrong, there would be a bruise and more pain. She would ice it when she got home.

The steel railings embedded in the steps had weathered well, but the doors, with their faded numbers looking down on the street, were worn. The windows at street level were uniformly shielded with small iron bars that sheltered the curtains, blinds, or sometimes taped fragments of newspaper that shielded the tiny apartments from the prying eyes of the street.

It was this way every night when she took the extra shift. Higgins would come into the shift room with his clip board and announce that somebody needed to stay. Bori would look around the room at the ducked heads. Cody had a family. Emily, cheerful bright Emily with dreams of that big house, would be looking again for that perfect man.

Bori had only herself. Malcom had passed, was it almost five years now? She smiled and agreed to take the shift. You couldn't leave the old people to a short-staffed shift in an already short-staffed home. Who would make sure Wanda took her medicine? Who would take the time to stop by Jenny's room when Jeopardy came on, and listen, as if it were a new story, of the time Jenny had been on Jeopardy and won two shows in a row. She had spent the money on a trip to Paris. Among her few possessions was a small tourist image of the Eifel tower.

And the others. All the other lives crammed into rooms on the long hallways. Tiny pockets, spiraling towards becoming one of the forgotten. Forgotten by lovers, friends, family, and, for many, themselves.

It was her life to care for them. Soothe them, listen to them. Already she was well on her way to becoming one. She still got the phone call on Mother's Day and on her Birthday, Maquito. No. Malcom now. She always had to remember that, he had ceased being Maquito on his first day of Junior High. He would make the trek across town to take her to a meal. During those brief visits, she could still see her little Maquito instead of Malcom. But since his father's funeral, it seemed he needed more and more of a reason.

The hour was late, and she wanted to get to the bus stop. Morning would come soon, and the walk was long. Ahead of her the lights were brighter. There, the sign across the ornate doors read Southpoint Community Outreach Center. It seemed far out of place, but, she thought, it lit the sidewalks around the doorway better, and it was said if you were willing to sit through a nightly service, you could get a sandwich and a bottled water. She hadn't been that hungry yet, but who was she to care. Everyone served God in their own way. The church front housed a "missionary" family and had a small tabernacle formed by ripping the walls out and putting up chairs. They were an urban renewal mission of the big mega church down in Atlanta.

She wasn't alone on the street. Across from her a man walked in hurried steps. His manner betrayed his nervousness. His backpack bulged with what could have been everything he owned, or just a trip to the store. You never knew. This wasn't the best of neighborhoods, it wasn't the worst. She had walked these streets dozens of times when the shift demanded it. She carried no illusions, but fear was for the timid and maybe the wise. She considered herself neither. She was simply Bori.

She barely caught the motion as the pack of youths came out from between the buildings. It took seconds. A shout. The sound of the scuffle. The man was on the ground. The swings, the kicks.

For the first time on these walks she did know fear. She had little on her to steal, but there was a difference between little and nothing. She froze as the man held a brief frantic grip on the strap to his backpack before a kick to his face snapped his head back. It was that sound that pulled her mind free.

"Stop it," she screamed—loudly and with authority. The same voice she used when she had caught Mr. Wright groping for Cindi's breasts at the Care Center. Five faces suddenly looked in her direction. Already they were stripping the man of his wallet, or cell phone or whatever could be had. Clothing ripped. A smaller member of the pack even held one of the man's shoes, black and gleaming in his hands. The glances shifted from her to the near empty street.

She scurried off the sidewalk towards the group. Another look at the streets by the feral pack.

"Fuck it," she heard, as the man's second shoe was pulled off and the youths loped into the dim streets. One turned and flipped her off.

She held back the urge to return the gesture.

A light flickered on in a window above where the man lay.

She continued across the street, the pain in her knee forgotten until she knelt by the man. The light from the Outreach Center allowed her to see the man's face was bloody, his nose smashed, and teeth had cut through his lips. His arm was bent in a way that she knew meant broken.

He moaned.

She reached into her bra and pulled out her cell phone. It took precious seconds to enter the passcode. There was no signal. She turned on the light function to closer inspect the man.

A door opened and yellow light flooded over her. She could see the man better for a second until a shadow obstructed the light. She looked up and drew back instinctively at the profile. The figure stood on his stoop. The slim barrel of the AR in his hands was backlit in profile as he looked up and down the street for threats.

"Call an ambulance," she said. "This man needs help."

"Those bastards would eat lead if they tried that with me."

"Please, call," she insisted.

"The cops? And let them take Sally away?" He raised his gun in a defiant and loving gesture. "Ain't my problem. I'd have killed the thugs."

He stepped back into the light and the door shut.

She slipped her purse from around her neck and slid it under the man's head. He only moaned. Across the street the lights from the Outreach Center beckoned. Taking one last look at the man, she rose to her feet with a grunt and crossed the street to the ornately decorated doors.

The doors were locked. She pounded on them until she saw the call button. She intermittently pressed the button and pounded on the doors.

She didn't see the cruiser until the spotlight caught her peripheral vision. Relief flooded through her. She turned and leaned against the doors. She let herself feel the pain in her knee as she watched the cruiser slow and the light play across the fallen form. Then, with an abrupt squeal of tires, it accelerated. She took two steps towards the street, her hand raised in supplication as she watched the red tail lights disappear around the next corner. Then she saw what they saw. A tattered figure laying against a stoop, an object under his head. Just another drunk. Not enough for the police to worry about.

She leaned again against the door. Hopelessness threatened her. She felt each of her sixty-two years. There were lights in the Outreach Center now. She resumed her pounding on the door.

"Please," she wailed. There was motion. The shadow of the window blinds separated and the outline of a person peering out could be seen. She waved frantically and the slit closed. And as quickly the outside lights for the Southpoint Community Outreach Center went dark. She gave the door one last pound and then slumped against it.

Across the street the figure lay unmoving.

She looked back from the direction she had come. She knew that she could get a signal five blocks in that direction. The man would get no faster care if she delayed so she broke into a hurried walk. She clutched her cell phone looking for the bars that would end this. She had gone two blocks when she stopped and looked back. This wasn't her business. She leaned down and rubbed the knee again as the man's shattered face flashed before her and she pushed forward. Only three blocks. A thin sweat was chilling her in the night air.

A single bar.

And then two.

She made the call. Assured that help was on the way she leaned against the lamp post, its steel more ornate than any that might have been installed in the last fifty years. The colorless paint worn bare by the weather.

Her purse was gone when she got back. She some how knew it would be. She sat heavily on the gritty sidewalk next to the man and waited, her back against the stoop. She could feel the knee beginning to stiffen.

Lights from the cruiser startled her as they lit the street. The officer nodded curtly as he exited the cruiser. He spoke into his radio. Voices answered. She heard the word ambulance and slowly rose to her feet and found herself looking up at an officer.

"I need to see some ID," he said.

She gestured towards the man and shook her head in frustration. "I—"

"Do you have any ID ma'am?" His tone was more pointed.

"I-"

Again, he cut her off.

"Are you a legal resident?"

"Yes." She snapped out the words. For the first time in years becoming aware of her own accent.

He turned and spoke into his microphone.

She was tired and not a little worried.

"I'm going home now," she said.

"I can't let you leave ma'am."

The radio squawked again.

He answered.

She took a step and felt his hand on her arm. "Please," he said. "Don't make this harder than it has to be."

She was still standing in the chilly night, the man unmoving on the sidewalk, with the red and blue light reflecting off the darkened front of the Southpoint Community Outreach Center, when the immigration van arrived.

Christian Nation

David Gerrold

If there is one thing that is true about the internet, it's that a little ignorance can go a long way.

There are online "experts" who mistakenly assert that the United States is a Christian Nation. This particular bit of revisionism requires one to ignore the entire history of the colonies and the myriad factors that eventually brought about the American Revolution.

The non-historians who assert this belief are usually religious figures attempting to assert an undeserved authority over the political process. Their "evidence" is the belief that the original thirteen colonies were founded by people fleeing religious persecution in England and Europe.

This is a convenient assertion. Yes, the pilgrims arrived on these shores with the intention of setting up their own religious communities where they—and not the other guys—would be the ones who established the state religion, often creating their own specific persecutions. Puritans anyone?

But by 1789, when the Continental Congress convened to write a Constitution for the new nation, the argument that the colonists were fleeing religious persecution, was no longer a valid one. Most of the colonies had their own dominant faiths, but the commerce between the colonies required a necessary tolerance.

So, the American revolution wasn't about religion. It was about taxes. It was about commerce. It was about the local residents demanding control of their own resources. It was about the removal of foreign ownership.

But. . . nowhere in the ensuing revolution was there a commitment to establish the new nation as a Christian one. It just didn't happen that way.

The first official document of the United States of America, the founding document of the nation, was the Declaration of Independence—it said, very simply, "We are no longer subjects of the crown. We are a new nation, based on the idea that a well-educated, well-informed population can govern itself. We will be the authors of our own destiny."

The only mention of God in the Declaration of Independence is in this single assertion: "We hold these Truths to be self-evident, that all Men are created equal, that they are endowed *by their Creator* with certain unalienable Rights, that among these are Life, Liberty, and the Pursuit of Happiness. . . "

But the interesting thing about that statement is that the first draft of the Declaration did not contain the words "by their Creator".

Those words were inserted by the fuddy-duddies in the Congress who believed that rights had to have a divine origin. Okay—but notice, the phrase "by their Creator" does not specify the nature of that creator, and the reasoning behind that omission is precisely why the United States is *not* a Christian Nation.

The charter for this nation is the Constitution. It is the foundation of all law. There is no higher authority than those seven articles and 27 amendments. It is in this document that essential nature of the United States is distinguished. Without the Constitution, we're just a bunch of ornery people surviving on the North American continent, but we're not America.

To put it simply, the Constitution *defines* America.

Our mission statement is the preamble: *"We the People of the United States, in Order to form a more perfect Union, establish Justice, insure domestic Tranquility, provide for the common defence, promote the general Welfare, and secure the Blessings of Liberty to ourselves and our Posterity, do ordain and establish this Constitution for the United States of America."*

Nowhere in that statement of purpose is there any mention of God, nowhere is there acknowledgment of or submission to any supernatural authority. Very simply: "We the people are establishing this government to provide these services for ourselves."

The Constitution of the United States is the sole authority for the existence of the American government. And the authority for that government comes solely from the will of the people.

And in the entire text of the Constitution, all the articles that describe how the government will work, and all 27 of the amendments that adapt that government to the circumstances of time and history, there remains no mention of God.

No mention at all. Nothing. Nada. Zilch.

Because the Constitution is not a god-inspired document. It's a contract, an agreement between men, acting as representatives of their respective states, on how they will govern themselves.

And *this* is why there is no mention of God in any of our founding documents:

The thirteen colonies represented different religious faiths. All of them were skeptical of the others—but it wasn't just resistance to religious tyranny, the states were equally resistant to economic tyranny. The south was especially skeptical of the north's resistance to slavery as an unacceptable economic threat. To forge a single nation out of thirteen colonies, the northern states had to accept the southern states as slave-holders.

The prolonged negotiations that eventually resulted in the Declaration of Independence were only a foretaste of the much more difficult negotiations that produced the Constitution. No colony wanted any of the other colonies' specific religious beliefs written into law or established as a state religion.

The idea expressed in the Declaration of Independence—that all people have certain inalienable rights—is a founding principle of the Constitution. It is understood throughout, but especially referenced in the ninth and tenth amendments, that all rights not specifically affirmed in the Constitution still belong to the people. Indeed, those first ten amendments, often called "The Bill of Rights" is not about the government granting rights—those amendments limit the power of government to infringe on the rights of the people.

Any government strong enough to grant rights is also strong enough to take them away, and by that standard, those wouldn't be rights. They would be privileges. This is why the Constitution specifically prevents the Congress from having any authority at all over the rights of the people. That includes establishing a state religion or preventing the free expression of ideas. The first amendment specifically states that Congress shall make no law respecting the establishment of religion. This is an affirmation that church and state must remain separate.

Nevertheless, today, we have people who have not studied history, who apparently did not have any kind of Civics class in high school, who feel comfortable asserting that not only is this a Christian Nation, but that such was the intention of the founding fathers. Some have even gone so far as to state that "freedom of religion only applies to Christians."

Oh, good grief.

The assertion that this is a Christian Nation is an offensive statement. It is ignorant, it is ugly, it is bigoted. We are not a Christian Nation—not in our laws, and certainly not in our behavior.

Yes, a majority of Americans identify themselves as "Christian", but which branch is really Christian? Presbyterian? Protestant? Lutheran? Methodist? Catholic? Anglican? Baptist? Episcopalian? Evangelical? Mormon? Greek Orthodox? Russian Orthodox? Dominionist?

Westboro Baptist? Or any of the other thousand schisms and interpretations?

You cannot fault non-Christians for being bemused—the Prince of Peace sure has a lot of people explaining what he really meant. And if you ask any of them about any of the others, they'll all claim that the others are misguided. Based on that evidence alone, we are most definitely *not* a Christian nation—we're a nation of a thousand different religions that all claim to be Christian.

What we are, what we are supposed to be, what we are promised to be, is a nation where you are free to practice your specific faith without interference or restriction from the government. Not just Christian, but Jewish, Hindu, Buddhist, Muslim, Jain, or even no faith at all. But if you must insist on Christianity—well, then please practice it.

I've read the bible. The important parts are the words written in red. These are the things that Jesus (allegedly) said.

For example, Jesus told us, "By your deeds you will be known."

If we look at the deeds of this so-called Christian nation, it's not a pretty picture. That same bible that tells us to "love one another" has also been used to justify the enslavement of Africans, the genocide of indigenous peoples, the oppression of women, the segregation of races, child labor, the exclusion of minorities, the denial of rights to LGBT+ people, and a continuing misinterpretation, disapproval, and oppression of joyous human sexuality that defies rationality.

Where is Jesus in any of that?

Jesus fed the poor, he healed the sick. If we were truly a Christian nation, that's what we would be doing—providing shelters for the homeless, making health care affordable or even free. We would insist on our government providing those services. (In the long-run, it's cheaper to have the government take on the responsibility, set standards, and maintain those programs as a publicly-monitored utility than to abandon them to a haphazard quilt of state and local communities.)

But no. Instead we punish the poor and bankrupt the sick. We hold health care hostage for profit. Instead of helping the poor and the sick, instead of reaching out to help them, we judge them as moochers, unworthy of help.

We have forgotten that Jesus told us not to judge one another. "Let him without sin cast the first stone." So we judge immigrants as being both lazy and job-stealers. We judge people from rural states, we judge people from urban states. We judge the rich, we judge the poor, we judge the educated, we judge the ignorant, we judge the famous, we judge the infamous. We have self-appointed ourselves the judges of everything despite the fact that Jesus told us not to be self-righteous.

We are one of the most self-righteous cultures on the planet. We talk about American exceptionalism, how we're number one—while our infant mortality rate approaches that of a third world banana republic.

Prayer? Jesus told us not to parade our faith loudly in the streets, but to pray quietly and privately, God will hear us. Nope. Instead, we build multi-million-dollar cathedrals and hold stadium events in his name. We send our wealth to televangelists and online preachers, ignoring the evidence that they are charlatans, frauds, and phonies.

And then those same fraudsters engage in aggressive politics—despite the fact that Jesus openly argued for separation of church and state. He said, "Render unto Caesar the things that are Caesar's, and unto God the things that are God's."

Jesus told us not to be hypocrites, And yet, we send hypocrites to Washington DC and we overlook their lies, their adulteries, their thefts, their corruption, their sins against us, because we want to believe that they are on our side. We're the hypocrites for enabling them—the evidence is clearly visible in so many social media comment threads, cesspools of ugly self-righteousness.

We have seen elected representatives—and even those who claim to be speaking for Jesus—using his name to justify the most corrupt behaviors. They use his name to justify sending young people off to war. They use their "Christianity" as a justification for doing the very things Jesus spoke out most angrily against. So, if we're truly a Christian nation, I see no evidence of it in the behavior of this nation. And certainly not in the behaviors of some of those who call themselves Christian.

Jesus said this as well: "I give you two new commandments. The first is love God, the second is love one another."

I see no love for either God or our fellow human beings in any of the behaviors of those who insist that this is a "Christian Nation". No. What I see is the perversion of Jesus' teachings as a claim to an unearned and undeserved moral authority.

The real question isn't whether or not we're a Christian Nation—we're not. The real question is where one can still find real Christians? The ones who still follow the teachings of Jesus?

It's the little acts of kindness and courage that demonstrate that human beings can be both rational and compassionate.

Teaching a child, caring for an elder, providing aid to the poor and the sick—look there for starters. Look to the teachers, the caregivers, the doctors, and those who create opportunities for others to become generous and giving.

It is when our reason and our empathy are congruent that we most approach that level of humanity that defines the heart and soul of what Christianity is supposed to be. We don't need a Christian Nation for that—we don't even need to be Christian.

We simply need to be human beings—the best kind of human beings: rational, compassionate, thoughtful, and caring. And beyond that, we need to be a nation that lives up to its promises of liberty and justice for all—we do that with partnership and commitment. That's where it starts.

David Gerrold

A Parable About the 8th Day

Jane Yolen

On the day God
turned his name around
and made dog,
and dog's tongue
sloppy and slippery,
licked God's hand,
God laughed.

Then God flung a stick
He'd so recently created,
and dog—with a memory
that worked forward
as well as backward—
remembered fetching
and ran off, returning
with the stick in his
satisfied mouth.
And God laughed again.

Then God walked
around His garden
dog following
at His heels
without ever being
instructed to do so.
So God knelt down
and dog sat down,
It was the eighth day,
And God saw that it was good.

What cat saw was something else.
But then cat always had
a bit of the devil in him.

The Forsaken Wall

Tom Barlow

"How are you tonight?" Micah, the assistant minister, asked Shannon as he extended a welcoming hand. Although it was only choir practice, he still met everyone at the door.

"I've been better," she said as she picked up the scores for tonight's pieces.

"Peyton?"

"I tried to have a heart-to-heart with him. I don't know what to do with Eric's life insurance. It's a lot of money, and while Eric was my husband, he was the boy's father, too, so I'd hoped he'd express some interest on how we spend it."

"The two of you have been through a lot," Micah said. "If you'd like me to speak with him. . ."

"Thanks, but he won't talk about it—at all. He's angry and I think he blames me for letting Eric compromise his health. The weight. The long hours at work. The beers, the pizzas." She shook her head. "That was Eric. Every time I suggested he visit a doctor or join a gym he accused me of harping at him."

Micah nodded. "He was a stubborn man."

"I think the manner of his death is haunting Peyton. The two of them were watching a Browns game and Peyton had his nose buried in his phone. He didn't even realize Eric had passed away until halftime. He's had anger issues ever since."

"And the insurance settlement brings it all back to him. How are you fixed financially?"

Shannon gave a dry laugh. "We don't even need the insurance money, after the sale of Eric's company."

"Maybe Peyton would feel better if you donated it to some charity that your husband supported."

"Don't even go there." Her husband had sworn off charities after once working for months to raise funds for a local food bank, only to have it stolen by the treasurer.

The idea of a tribute resonated with her, though, and a few nights later, as she thumbed through photos from their Mediterranean cruise honeymoon, she hit upon the perfect way to commemorate him.

SIX MONTHS LATER

Anger is underrated, Shannon thought as she inspected the structure, built on the property of the All Souls Church atop a bank of the Whetstone River. She had settled for calling it The Forsaken Wall. And now she stood, one last time before the Wallunteers wrapped it in tarps for the unveiling, still wondering if this had been a good idea after all.

Anger had seen her through the project, the same way anger had fueled her husband in his daily battles with contractors and clients. *Maybe Peyton comes by it honestly.*

The first television crew arrived shortly thereafter to set up for the grand unveiling at noon. Micah pulled in at the same time, carrying a very welcome tray of coffees and a bag of doughnuts.

"Busy night?" he asked as he handed Shannon a cup.

"Not a peep." She twisted her neck, stiff from spending the night in a lawn chair guarding the wall from vandalism.

"That's a relief. I see the press has arrived."

"Eric and I used to make fun of them every evening, but now they show up for the unveiling and I'm pleased. Does that make me a hypocrite?"

"It makes you human." He gave her arm a friendly squeeze before heading toward the church 100 paces away. The TV reporter, a white, middle-aged man with a high hairline and sideburns, limped across the asphalt to the open front of what had been dubbed The Grievance Tent. Shannon stood and greeted him with her best perky smile.

"Mrs. Baxter? He extended his right hand, a notebook clasped in the other. "Chad O'Conner. Mind if I ask you some questions?"

She swiped a sweaty palm against her thigh before shaking his hand. "Call me Shannon. Please—ask away."

Chad pointed his pen at the tarp-covered wall perched atop the bank overlooking the Scioto River and said, "You were responsible for this, is that right?"

And so it begins. "Yes. As a tribute to my late husband Eric. The church was kind enough to provide the land."

"You call it The Forsaken Wall. What's that about?"

"Well, it's a wall, obviously. It's made of 720 Corning, wide-bevel glass blocks, a single course 40 feet long, and 8 feet high. Eric owned a glass block installation company, you see."

"And you built it yourself?"

She held up her hands in response. She hadn't yet buffed out the pits and scratches on her nails, and the blisters were only now beginning to heal. "With the help of the Wallunteers."

"Where does 'forsaken' come in?"

"When we toured Jerusalem on our honeymoon, we saw worshipers jamming written prayers into the joints of the Western Wall. Eric said that what the world needed was a complaining wall, where all the forsaken could tell God, if there is one, what he'd done wrong." None of this was new. The building of the wall had already inspired a degree of controversy, especially in the church. But now that it was real, the story had spread beyond page five.

"So the idea is that people who have a bone to pick with God write down their grievances on those pieces of paper," he pointed to tablets of palm-sized paper on the card table in the tent, "roll them up and stick them in your wall?"

She'd braced herself for the typical reporter's faux incredulence, but Chad seemed dulled, or perhaps tired. "Exactly," she said. "We set small glass pipes in the grout between each glass block to hold the grievances."

"You realize you'll tick off a lot of people, right?" Flip. Scrawl.

"I get ticked off every time I drive past a graveyard full of crosses. Fair is fair."

Chad flipped his notebook closed. "Could you use those same words when we're taping?"

Shannon wondered how Peyton would react to seeing his mother on the news. He probably wouldn't react; since his father's death, he barely spoke to her at all. If anything, the wall had driven them further apart.

"Just don't blame the church, OK?" she said. "They just let me use the land. The wall is all on me."

"You're kidding, right? A little persecution is great for the offertory."

"You're rather cynical, aren't you?"

"Me? Lady, you're the one with the Forsaken Wall."

oOo

When Chad wandered away to call his producer, Shannon took the opportunity to dash home to change clothes for the unveiling.

She found Peyton in the kitchen, toasting a piece of the peasant bread she'd brought home the night before. "Hi, Sweetie," she said as she poured a glass of orange juice.

Peyton grunted. His wiry hair was flattened on one side and uneven. Shannon had been trying to wheedle him to the barbershop for the past three weeks, but when he was in one of his slumps, he was as hard to push as a rope.

"How'd work go?" she asked, hiding her peevishness that he hadn't told her about his job at Café Ray. She'd had to figure it out from the aroma of coffee in his laundry.

He slid two more slices into the toaster oven, flipped the door closed and twisted the dial to dark, ignoring her question.

"I hope you're going to come to the unveiling?"

The motion of his head told her she'd been subjected to an eye roll.

Same to you, buddy, Shannon thought, and left him alone in the kitchen. She needed a shower.

She arrived back at the wall shortly before noon to find four more television crews clearing sight lines for their cameras. A hundred or so spectators had gathered for the unveiling, claiming spots on the grass apron in front of the wall. Micah stood at the podium, fiddling with the microphone.

Shannon took a deep breath before exiting the car and crossing the lot to the podium, at the south end of the tarp-covered wall. The crowd turned to watch her approach, and, suddenly self-conscious, she lost her gait and almost fell.

This isn't so bad, she told herself when she finally reached the podium. Micah winked and yielded the microphone. She licked her lips once, then turned to face the crowd and the cameras.

The crowd hushed as she read her dedication. The television light glare directly in her face made it impossible for her to gauge the expressions of the onlookers. As she described the purpose of the wall, though, the words she'd so carefully crafted struck her as glib and simplistic.

She could only hope the reality of the wall would make her point more clearly. Picking up one end of the ceremonial red braided cord that ran like a waistband around the wall, she waited for Micah's nod, then said, "I give you—Eric's Forsaken Wall." She tugged the cord free as the Wallunteers pulled the tarps aside.

The sun, directly overhead in a cloudless sky, brought the undulating glass block wall alive; translucent, pale green, geometric, reflective. As applause reverberated from the wall, Shannon closed her eyes to savor the moment, the relief. In that darkness, she glimpsed, for the first time since Eric's passing, life beyond grief. With it came a bone-weariness.

Then several people at the other end of the wall began to boo loudly. The cameras immediately swung to the northern edge of the crowd, searching for the source. There, a gangly teenager in baggy shorts and a *Jesus Pwns Spiderman* t-shirt pulled several eggs from his pocket and lobbed them toward the wall. Two reached their target, the splats lost in the sudden surge of crowd noise. A clump of resolute-looking youngsters quickly surrounded the egger, facing out as though to protect him from a lynch mob.

Several uniformed cops—*where had they come from?* Shannon wondered—rushed forward, cutting the kids out of the crowd. A short, pie-faced man wearing a suit, BluBlockers and a broad-brimmed straw hat stepped from behind the group of youths and said something to the officer in charge, who in turn spoke to the other cops. They relaxed noticeably as the man pulled the boy aside for a short, mostly one-sided conversation.

The press pounced on the man when he stepped away from the boy. He identified himself as J. David Matthews, pastor of the Hayden Falls United Methodist Church. Yes, he said, the teens were members of his church. No, the church did not support the egg attack. The boy had already agreed to do community service to show his repentance.

He doesn't look repentant, Shannon thought.

"At the same time," Matthews continued, "I can't help but feel that this wall sends the wrong message to those who are suffering. Blame doesn't heal wounds; forgiveness does."

While the pastor continued to usurp the press attention, Shannon, biting her tongue lest she spoil the day with a shouting match, returned to the tent to find that the rest of the crowd, presuming the conflict over, had set to the writing of grievances. A human chain twenty people long quickly formed behind the table, each person using the back of the person in front of him as a writing desk. As one finished, he would roll up his grievance, select a pipe in the wall, and slide the paper in. One scant-haired elderly woman held a fist full of grievances.

"Sweetie, I wish you could see this," Shannon whispered to her dead husband.

oOo

The Wallunteers, fearing further assaults on the wall, organized a 24/7 vigil. After the reporters departed, they ordered a grateful Shannon home to rest.

There, she found Peyton horizontal on the couch, watching *The Walking Dead.*

"I thought you worked tonight," she said.

"I took a sick day. My feet hurt." He muted the TV. "How much of Dad's insurance money did you waste on that piece of crap wall?"

"All of it. I thought you'd be happy to see your father honored."

"You call that honor? A picture of the wall is up on Wikipedia already."

She had learned to wait before responding. Her son had developed a malicious gift for timing.

"Under the entry for *futile gesture.*"

Shannon kicked off her heels and reached down to rub her feet. She couldn't help but remember Peyton as a curious, adventurous child. In fact, her written grievance read, "*What have you done to my son?*" She had loved him so. Now she didn't even like him, and, since Eric's death, he appeared to despise her.

oOo

By mid-morning the next day a steady stream of gawkers was cruising through the parking lot, most stopping long enough to take snapshots of the wall. A few posed for a photo in front of it, and one in ten took the opportunity to write and insert a grievance. Shannon was disappointed by the visitors' flippancy, turning properly somber only when they caught her glare.

She and the Wallunteers were sharing a lunch pizza when one of them, mouth full, pointed his wedge toward the road. There a line of fifty or so marchers, led by Pastor Matthews, still in his straw hat and BluBlockers, had come into view trudging single file south along the eastern edge of the church property on the berm of River Road. Matthews was carrying a large white cross over his shoulder like a squirrel gun. Several others carried signs; "God Forgives," read one; another read "None who repent are forsaken."

Shannon was relieved to see the marchers were mostly gray-hairs with shambling strides. Not people likely to launch an assault.

She expected them to turn into the driveway and approach the wall, but they stuck to the road, passing by a hundred feet from the wall with no sound except the scuffing of their shoes on gravel.

Shannon turned to follow their progress. When they reached the southern boundary of the church property, Matthews, still in the lead, turned west and crossed the lawn of the church's neighbors, an asthmatic family who rarely left their air-conditioned home in the summer. The line of marchers followed as Matthews picked his way down to the river and turned north, following the fisherman's footpath along the river's edge. Only the bank, about twelve feet high, separated the marchers, at river level, from the wall atop the bank.

"I don't like them that close, with all those river rocks nearby," one of the Wallunteers said.

When Matthews reached the northern boundary of the church grounds, he turned east and climbed a set of old cement stairs provided by the city for river access. At River Road he turned south again, completing the rectangle. He immediately began another circuit. The rest of the marchers followed.

Micah stepped to Shannon's side. "If they block traffic, you want us to call the cops?"

"Better them than a lynch mob. Let's wait and see what they do."

To her relief, when the first car of sightseers made to turn into the drive, the marchers yielded.

She dragged her chair into the shade of the three-sided Grievance Tent and half-closed her eyes. Eric would have relished such a protest, not at all bothered by confrontation. Shannon, however, found the slow, stately march of grim-faced, unremarkable people uncomfortably powerful. And the wall? As Peyton would no doubt point out, it was just a wall, and could respond to Matthew's protest only by enduring.

oOo

At 2:00 p.m., a truck pulled into the neighbor's driveway and a frenetic group of youths quickly set up a large canopy, tables, chairs, and grills within. Several portable toilets arrived moments later. The marchers began taking turns stopping for rest, food, and drink.

Two of the Wallunteers continued to debate the intent of the marchers, one certain it was a prelude to an assault on the wall, another equally convinced that they wanted to see themselves on the network news. Shannon put up with an hour of their meandering debate before she had to walk away, exasperated that the protesters had gained a place in the story of the wall. When she spotted Pastor Matthews climbing the cement steps yet again, she marched down the drive to intercept him.

"May I talk to you?" she asked when she caught his eye.

Matthews stepped out of line and waved those behind to continue. Tossing her a soft smile, he set down his cross, removed his wide-brimmed straw hat and swiped his sweaty forehead with a shirtsleeve. "You're the woman that built the wall, right?" He extended his hand. "I'm J. David Matthews."

She took his hand, exchanging sweat. "Shannon. Yes, I built it," she said, terse but polite. "I'm curious about your intentions."

"Mind if I sit for a bit?" Without waiting for her answer, he sank to the grass and kicked off his shoes. "Boy, that feels good."

Shannon had chosen white slacks that morning, so she grudgingly dropped into a gardener's squat.

They watched the protesters pass for a moment before he said, "There are a lot of angry people in the world, and some of them go to church every Sunday. You all meet on Sunday?" He nodded to the church.

"Usually."

He waved hello to a passing marcher. "When I first heard about your project, I figured the odds were 50/50 that it would draw a violent response. Walking the border is a way for people to express their opposition without anyone getting hurt."

She was taken aback at the thought that he, that these people, thought they were protecting The Forsaken Wall from harm. "But you don't agree with the wall, right?"

"I suppose I don't," he said. "But we're not as far apart as you might suppose. God invites skepticism. Without doubt, there would be no faith. I doubt you'll find any grievances in your wall more poignant than Psalms 88." Matthews leaned back on his elbows and closed his eyes. "It ends, 'You,' referring to God, 'have taken my companions and loved ones from me; the darkness is my closest friend.' I suspect you're familiar with that darkness."

The son of a bitch is trying to minister to me. "So you're all just here to protect the peace?"

"The wall is going to draw wounded people like road kill draws crows, and that's right where Jesus wants us to be. The fact is, though, that most of my people operate on a much simpler level; you're either for them or against them, and most have no doubt which side of the wall you're on. I'd say the long-term outlook for your wall is grim."

"The long-term outlook for everything is grim," Shannon replied.

"That's a matter of perspective. Maybe the view will change for you, in time."

"In five billion years the sun's supposed to explode. Is that time enough?"

He grinned, put on his shoes, stood, and brushed the grass from his rear. "You be careful, Shannon. Feel free to seek me out if you want to talk again."

As Matthews rejoined the marchers, Shannon returned to her post. She wanted to dislike the man but couldn't. His *wounded people* comment, however, rankled her for the rest of the afternoon.

oOo

That afternoon, to her surprise, Peyton swung into the parking lot aboard the Vespa scooter Eric had bought shortly before his heart attack.

Her son deftly wove his way through the bystanders and came to a stop a few feet from the table, where he dismounted and tugged off his helmet. His hair slowly decompressed.

"I'm glad you came," she said, not daring a step in his direction.

Peyton nodded and slowly took in the wall, up and down, left and right, with an expression of bereavement. Shannon steeled herself.

"It's not as hideous as it looks on television," he finally said. "You have a lot of empty pipes, though. Maybe people aren't as unhappy as you'd hoped."

"Come on—I don't *want* people to be miserable." They just are. Why aren't you at work, by the way?" she said.

"We had a philosophical parting of the ways."

"You quit? Were you fired? Peyton, how do you expect to support yourself if you can't hold on to a job? Do you want to live in the basement for the rest of your life?"

"No, just the rest of yours," he replied. Before she could react, he hurriedly added, a stricken look on his face, "That was a joke."

Shannon was at a loss for a reply, and Peyton, after waiting for a moment, returned to his scooter and departed. For the rest of the afternoon, she was haunted by the memory of Peyton's face as he studied the wall. He had never looked more like his father than at that moment.

oOo

That evening the wall received fifteen seconds leading into the second break of *NBC Nightly News*, including shots of Shannon, the protesters, and a demented-looking woman jamming a grievance into a pipe. The anchor promised that the network would stay on top of the story.

oOo

All three networks were now dunning her for on-air interviews, and *Ellen*'s scheduling intern called the next morning, just to introduce herself, while Shannon was lingering over a bowl of oat flakes and praying that the thunderstorms forecast would arrive to quell the media frenzy. She even entertained the thought of covering the wall with tarps again, to give everyone time to rest and regroup.

When she could delay the inevitable no longer, Shannon carefully primped for her network news interviews. She chose the best casual summer outfit in her closet, a dandelion-yellow Oscar De La Renta she'd bought for their 20th anniversary dinner. She wondered what the devout would make of the color.

Shannon arrived at the wall to find the number of marchers taking part in Matthew's protest had quadrupled overnight. Like the Wallunteers and the fifty or so visitors milling about the wall, they were sweating profusely in the dense, dead air. Cars in the lot sported license plates from as far away as Missouri and Ontario. Three-quarters of the pipes now held grievances.

Micah sat in the tent.

One look and she asked, "have you been home at all since yesterday?"

He shook his head. "I figured somebody should watch the church building. Peyton and some of his friends were here all night, though, so I was able to catch some ZZZs."

"My Peyton? Friends?"

"The Deists, they called themselves. Or maybe that was their band; I wasn't sure."

What was her son playing at? Could his actions be some kind of sarcasm she didn't recognize?

Rain overnight had caused the level of the river to rise onto the path the protesters had been taking on their northern leg. Micah told her that, for their safety, he had given them permission to walk along the top of the bank on church property, a scant 10 feet from the wall.

By noon, grievers were streaming into the parking lot, parking, and congregating at the wall. The nature of these visitors seemed different, not downcast and forlorn but angry and fervent, much like the change in the weather.

"Look." Micah pointed toward a television truck. "Tonight is the payoff—a live report on the national news."

"I built the wall for Eric, not NBC," she said half-heartedly. *And Peyton.*

Shortly before news time, as she and the network reps were setting up a schedule that would give each a few minutes of her time during the evening news half-hour, she saw Peyton and a small group of people his own age congregating near the Grievance Tent. She tried to catch his eye, but he kept his back to her. She did note that the marchers in Matthews' group seemed younger and more boisterous than on previous days.

The CBS producer grabbed Shannon by the bicep a few minutes before 6:30 p.m. and marched her to a spot at the south end of the wall. She was introduced to the reporter, who shook her hand warmly and assured her that he would treat her with respect. Chad the reporter was standing behind the camera operator; he caught her eye and gave her the thumbs up.

Then the producer was giving them a finger countdown; ten, to one, and she made herself smile and breathe as the reporter briefly described the scene to the evening anchor.

As the reporter posed his first question to Shannon, though, loud cheers drowned him out. The camera abruptly swung away to focus on the other end of the wall, where chaos had broken out.

The marchers northbound on the bank had rushed the wall. Through the thick glass, Shannon could see them cramming papers into the grievance pipes as fast as they could. More protesters were racing to join them.

A girl's head appeared between the tent and the wall, perched on the shoulders of the boy who had thrown eggs. She yelled to the reporter, "We're stuffing the wall with blessings!" All the cameras convened on her face. The reporter hurried off in the girl's direction.

Shannon was bumped from behind but caught herself, looking up in time to witness Peyton lead a charge of Wallunteers and other supportive bystanders to the church side of the wall. Wallunteers raced down the line of supporters, picking the fallen grievances.

Shannon stood open-mouthed as the bedlam quickly evolved into a set battle—Matthews' people packing one pipe after another from the river side of the wall with blessings, until old grievances were forced out the other end. The forsaken responded in kind, reinserting the fallen grievances. Micah brought a box of felt-tipped marking pens from the church office, which the grievers used to dislodge the blessing in the pipes. The marchers responded in kind, with sticks.

Matthews appeared unexpectedly at Shannon's side, but she ignored him and the ecstatic television crews flying back and forth in search of footage of the enraptured and enraged. She barely noticed when Matthews put a comforting hand on her shoulder.

She was too entranced by her son. She had never, never seen such determination on his face, as he directed his friends, pointing out pipes, passing out encouraging slaps on the back. He looked in her direction once, and she took an involuntary half-step back, expecting disdain, but he just winked at her, turned around, and attacked the wall again.

The animal noise of battle kept rising, and Shannon took several more steps back, groping behind her for the support of a tent post.

She was watching the road for sign of a police cruiser when a sudden, thunderous rending sound brought everyone to a halt. She turned in time to see a crack race down the length of the 40-foot wall, following the joint between the lowermost two rows of blocks.

Shannon held her breath as the whole wall undulated, once, twice, grinding, growling. The protesters and defenders retreated at full speed. All except Peyton, who squatted a hands-span from the church side of the wall, calmly studying the crack.

Shannon screamed his name, but her voice was drowned by a staccato series of snaps, then a squeal, then a slow roar, like a glacier calving. Peyton stepped back as the wall slowly, majestically, canted toward the river, twisting like a ribbon as it fell and landing, almost gently, on the lip of the riverbank. There it hung for a moment, as every soul stared in silence, before sliding down the bank into the wildly rushing river.

The protesters and the grievers, Shannon, Matthews, Peyton, the press, all crossed to the lip of the bank to watch the wall torn apart under the assault of logs caught in the flood.

Shannon, numb, retreated to the remains of her wall, now only an ankle-high row of blocks like broken teeth, strewn with dislodged grievances and blessings. At her feet, one unrolled grievance caught her eye. She recognized the handwriting, as distinctive now as it had been when it first appeared on her refrigerator door.

She picked up the paper, smoothed it against the back of her hand, and read, *My mom blames me for my dad's death. Thanks for nothing.*

She balled the grievance in her hand and angrily began kicking down what remained of the wall. Some of the crowd turned to watch her, puzzlement on their faces.

With each kick, the pressure in her chest lessened. Peyton appeared at her side, caught her eye, and raised an eyebrow. When she nodded, he took her hand and began to methodically kick down blocks too.

When they were finished, Shannon, spent, walked to the lip of the bank and tossed the grievance into the river. Then, taking Peyton by the arm, she pulled him aside to beg his forgiveness.

An American Christian at the Pearly Gates

Larry Hodges

Caleb Isiah Noah Oldfield was a Christian, a conservative, and a rich man, in that order. And now, he was a dead man in a spirit body that felt exactly like his normal one. And as a result of his lifetime support for family values, he was here, standing in line, at the Pearly Gates—which greatly irritated him, as virtuous people shouldn't have to stand in line at the Pearly Gates, no more than they should have to wait for a table at Chick-fil-A.

Death wasn't what he had expected. He still had a beating heart. His chest rose as he breathed in the perfumed air that leaked from Heaven itself. He even felt a bit hungry. He was still in the somewhat overweight body he had died in. Where was the perfect body he had expected? The one he'd had as a youth. Wasn't that the promise? He patted his gut—too much sacramental bread, he'd convinced himself, though French food (oh, how he loved his beef bourguignon!) and fine wines may have had something to do with it.

He did feel lucky that he'd died in his best Armani suit and red power tie, with an American flag pin on one lapel, his initials monogrammed on the other, and a cross around his neck. Dying at the National Prayer Breakfast, instead of the bathroom, definitely added dignity.

Heaven was just as he'd always thought—all puffy white clouds and a gate made of white pearl, guarded by Saint Peter himself. A little short for a saint, was his first thought, only about 5'5", with a Santa Claus-like white beard and a white robe that nearly blended into the clouds and pearl background. Floating just over his head was a hazy white halo. Caleb stared at the rather large wart on the saint's left cheek, the only thing breaking up the eye-straining whiteness. Didn't they have wart removal services in heaven?

Ahead of Caleb in line were two groups and a lone child. First was a group of seventeen, fourteen of whom looked like high school kids, plus three adults. Second was a group of ten ragged bronzed-skinned Middle Easterners, mostly kids. Then there was the single fair-haired child in Spider-man pajamas, about eight. The child turned to stare at Caleb with big brown eyes. Caleb nodded at the boy, then averted his eyes.

"Hi mister!" exclaimed the child. "I'm feeling so much better now!"

"What happened to you?" Caleb asked.

"I had new-mone-ya," said the child, sounding it out carefully.

"Did you go to the doctor?"

The child shook his head vigorously. "Mommy said we couldn't afford it, but she gave me chicken soup. When I did go, I was on a bed in a big car with a siren and flashing lights. Am I dead?"

They were interrupted by the *ding-ding-ding* of a bell. The gate to Heaven opened and the 17 went through. Then the gate closed, and Saint Peter called out, "*Next!*" The ten Middle Easterners stepped forward.

"I'm afraid we're both dead," said Caleb to the child. "I had a heart attack. Nothing healthcare can do about that."

"What's helfcare?"

"It's like an expensive toy that everybody wants, but they want *me* to pay for it."

"Nobody should pay for 'spensive toys and helfcare, they should save their money for important stuff. I wish someone would have paid for my new-mone-ya medicine, but I guess they bought toys and helfcare instead."

They were interrupted by another *ding-ding-ding*. Once again the gate to Heaven opened, and the ten Middle

Easterners went through. The gate closed, and Saint Peter called out, "*Next!*"

"That's me!" exclaimed the child. He turned to Saint Peter and said, "Hi, I'm Billy. What's your name?"

"Hi Billy! I'm Saint Peter, and welcome to Heaven!" The saint giggled to himself, his halo bobbing back and forth in what Caleb found a very unsaintlike fashion.

Billy tilted his head and frowned. "Is your first name Saint or Peter?"

"You can call me Peter."

"Hi Peter! I like your wart."

Caleb didn't agree. Now that he was closer he could see hairs coming out of it. Yuck. Was there anything in the Bible about Saint Peter having a wart? Maybe that's why it took so long for Christianity to spread that first century—who could pay attention to the Sermon on the Mount when they were staring at that ugly wart?

"I see you died of pneumonia," Saint Peter said, "and were living in the streets with your parents, so of course had no health insurance. But that's just an expensive toy, right?" Saint Peter glanced over at Caleb, who bit his lip. "But guess what? I see that you liked playing soccer. We've got a whole soccer stadium just for kids your age! Want to see it?"

"Yes!"

"Then come on in!" There was another *ding-ding-ding* and the gate to heaven opened.

Billy turned to Caleb. "Goodbye, mister, see you in a few minutes!" Then he went through, staring about as he entered and gasping in excitement. "Wow!"

Then the gate closed, and Saint Peter said, "*Next!*"

"Hi there," Caleb said, nervous at meeting the great Saint Peter. "Sorry about the healthcare-toy analogy—I was just joking." He fingered the cross around his neck, hoping Saint Peter would notice.

"No problem, everyone likes a good joke. And nice monogram! Now, I see that you were a devout Christian."

"I tried my best!" said Caleb, beaming. He wondered if they had hot tubs in Heaven. How could one live without one?

"I see that you were a solid conservative,"—his fingers seemed to be ticking down a list—"says here you were pro-life, only believed in traditional marriage, anti-immigration. You pretty much hit the biggies there. And wow, you really supported the NRA, gave them quite a pile of money. Was that a part of your Christianity?"

"No, of course not. But it takes a good guy with a gun to stop a bad guy with a gun, just like in the movies, so shouldn't we Christians have guns since we're the good guys? I hate it when there's a shooting and kids die, but we gotta respect the Second Amendment. But I always send my thoughts and prayers."

Saint Peter suddenly grew eight feet tall, his skin turned fiery red, the halo turned into a circle of flames, and his voice became a roar as he leaned over Caleb. "So it was a tradeoff, dead kids in return for Christian values? Like those fourteen kids and three teachers who just entered Heaven?"

Caleb dropped to his knees, his world ablur. "I only—"

"You sent thoughts and prayers to those who died because of policies you supported! *How dare you!*" boomed Saint Peter.

"But—" He stopped, knowing this was it, a lifetime of avoiding the truths he'd always known deep down but avoided had come to an end, that he would now pay for his sins, oh God *No No No!!!*

"Just kidding!" said a suddenly giggling Saint Peter, his appearance and voice returning to normal. "I understand. Of course you had to go along with the other conservatives, even the ones who weren't as smart or as Christian as you, and of course the Second Amendment should have been one of the Ten Commandments—God really dropped the ball there. Wouldn't want the atheists or liberals running things!"

"No way!" said a relieved Caleb, rising to his feet again, his heart still racing. "You had me going there!"

"Even a saint has to have fun sometimes. Now, I see that you were against letting any of those six million Syrian refugees into the U.S., correct? Were you scared of them?"

"Of course I was scared of them! Everyone was. If just one of them got through with an AR-15, who knows what might have happened. The best way to fear no evil is to keep it out of your country."

"The ten who were ahead of you died in a sinking boat in the Mediterranean, trying to find refuge. Most were kids. Were you afraid of them? How many times did you recite at prayer, 'Yea, though I walk through the valley of the shadow of death, I will fear no evil: for thou art with me; thy rod and thy staff they comfort me.' As a Christian, do those words mean anything to you?"

"Of course they mean something to me! I'm a devout Christian! But—"

"Then you know the words of Jesus." Once again Saint Peter grew to eight feet and turned red, the halo turned to flames, his voice a roar. "Depart from me, you, who are cursed, into the eternal fire, prepared for the devil and his angels. For I was hungry and you gave me nothing to eat, I was thirsty and you gave me nothing to drink, I was a stranger and you did not invite me in, I needed clothes and you did not clothe me, I was sick and in prison and you did not look after me. Truly I tell you, whatever you did not do for one of the least of these, you did not do for me."

"I'm sorry! I made a mistake!" Caleb covered his face with his hands, cringing. Was he going to the eternal fire? What had he done! Please, God, *don't do this!!!*

"I'm just kidding again!" said Saint Peter, once again giggling. Caleb peeked through his hands, and the saint was back to normal, a big grin on this face.

"God, you got me again!"

"Taking the Lord's name in vain?" Saint Peter, raising his eyebrows.

"No, I didn't mean—"

"Jesus, you are too easy! Relax, you were a good American Christian, so you'll no doubt find the doorway to Heaven. Now, let's move on to one more thing. You were against universal healthcare, even for the poor and needy?"

"That was always a tough one," admitted Caleb, once again trying to calm his racing heart. "But do we really owe it to others to give them what is ours? That's not fair. It'll just lead to others having to rely on us hard workers to take care of them. I worked hard to get what I had, and I expect others to do the same."

"So, you see no problem with little Billy living in the streets and dying of pneumonia that could have been prevented with a ten-dollar bottle of pills?"

"That's his parents' fault, not mine! Healthcare isn't a right. How can it be a right when all it does is take something away from someone and give it to someone else? It's welfare! It's socialism! It's *communism!*" He was feeling the old words coming easy, but now? They sounded. . . defensive. But what did he have to defend for? He tried to stay calm. Saint Peter was on his side, despite that terrible sense of humor. "I tithed my 10%, what more could you want?"

"So, you got yours, so forget others? When given the choice on healthcare to either help the poor or not help the poor, you chose to *not* help the poor? Despite the words of Jesus?"

For the third time Saint Peter grew to eight feet tall, turned red, his halo turned to flames, and his voice boomed. "*Blessed is the one who is kind to the needy. Those who give to the poor will lack nothing, but those who close their eyes to them receive many curses. Speak up for those who cannot speak for themselves, for the rights of all who are destitute.*"

Saint Peter leaned over Caleb, his fiery halo shooting sparks that singed Caleb's face. "Shall I go on? There are more, did you notice there's nothing from Jesus about being anti-gay, anti-abortion, or all the others you tried to pass off as Christian values while ignoring Jesus's primary message of helping the poor and needy? Did you think wearing a cross and making sure everyone saw you tithe would blind us and get you favor? *Beware of practicing your righteousness before other people in order to be seen by them, for then you will have no reward from your Father who is in heaven.*"

Saint Peter's eyes were now like supernovas as they bore into the cringing Caleb. "Can you explain why you should not be cast into the eternal flames of Hell?"

"No, I'm sorry, I'm sorry!" Caleb cried. He could already feel the burning touch of those flames, and they'd go on and On and ON, for all eternity, pain, Pain, nothing but *PAIN!!!*

"Gotcha again!" giggled Saint Peter, returning to normal again. "As you said, you tithed; what more do those liberal moochers want from you?"

"Do you do this to everyone?" Caleb's heart was racing, and he felt out of breath; having your guts squeezed out and eternity in flames flashed before your eyes by an eight-foot red monster with a flaming halo had a way of getting the adrenaline running. Oops, he'd also peed himself. He grinned, hoping that would draw attention away.

"No, just the deserving few." Saint Peter giggled again. "You earned everything you got. No, you and I see eye to eye, and you are welcome to Heaven. In fact, there is a special doorway to the third level of Heaven for truly godlike people like you. But getting there means you have to go through a small room on the edge of Hell."

"Why would the entrance to the higher levels of Heaven be from Hell?"

"The Lord works in mysterious ways." He giggled as Caleb ground his teeth in irritation at this charlatan. What a letdown from the stern, holy figure portrayed by the church.

"So you're sending me to Hell before showing me my entrance to Heaven? Is this another joke?"

"Thrice I have seemingly denied you entrance to Heaven; only once before have I denied one such, and you are obviously worthy of him. I promise, no joke this time!" Saint Peter stopped on the verge of another set of giggles.

This was the great Saint Peter? Caleb shook his head in disgust. What had Jesus seen in this Bozo? Finally, the saint regained control of himself.

"This gateway here," and Saint Peter pointed at the pearly one behind him, "only goes to the first two levels of Heaven for regular folk, and you get to go to the third level. Now, don't be alarmed, you're about to drop really fast, but it's all for the good, trust me."

Why would he trust someone with such an ugly wart? Wasn't that a sign of witchcraft or something? He wanted to yank it out. Or maybe—

The cloudy ground beneath Caleb suddenly disappeared, and he began to fall. "*What the hell!*" he cried out.

"*TRUST ME!*" came the again booming voice of Saint Peter, followed by giggling, which quickly receded into the distance.

Caleb screamed, but after about twenty seconds he stopped. He seemed to be falling through. . . nothing. All was whiteness in all directions.

Then something blood-red appeared below him. He screamed again as he fell into it. For a moment he felt the scorching flames, and then he slowed almost to a stop as he went through a hole in the burning ground, gagging on the brimstone air.

He floated to the floor of. . . his own living room? Everything was there—the original Picassos on the wall, the black leather sofa and chairs, Persian carpets, the hot tub with bubbling hot water, cherry blossom incense, and the fireplace with a mirror over it so he could study himself while basking in the warm flames. Home, with only a touch of that brimstone smell.

"Welcome!" Caleb whirled about. An extremely old woman stood before him, a hag with dirty gray hair and endless wrinkles, no more than four and a half feet tall and stooped, leaning on a red three-pronged pitchfork, wearing a shapeless and worn black dress that dragged on the floor. Her eyes were just black penny-sized holes. "Hope you don't mind my stopping by to welcome you personally. I'm told you'll only be here for a short visit, is that so?" She leaned forward and peered at the initials on the lapel of his suit. "Nice monogram!"

"Saint Peter sent me here so I could go through the door to the third level of Heaven. Are you the Devil?" So the Devil was a woman? That explained a lot!

"Guilty! What, were you expecting me to be red, with horns, and a forked tail? I wouldn't want to scare you. But it is kind of itchy keeping these things in—do you mind?" A pair of horns sprouted from her head. "Ah, much better. Now, I thought I'd make your short stay here more comfortable by matching your home. You had a pretty nice house, didn't you?"

"The best that money could buy!" Caleb wouldn't have said that to Saint Peter, but the Devil would understand. "So where's the door?"

"It's right over there, on the mantel above the fireplace, by the mirror."

Caleb walked over but didn't see anything. "Where is it?"

"Oh, there's one thing first," the Devil said, "just a small formality." She pointed the pitchfork at Caleb.

Agony shot through him as if his insides were trying to escape him. His back arched outwards, his feet enlarged, his legs expanded, his mouth pushed forward. He fell over on all fours, and continued to grow. Hair sprouted out from all parts of him. He screamed in pain and terror as he got larger and his body continued to transform.

"What have you done to me?"

"Why don't you take a look?"

On all fours he clopped over to the mirror on the brick mantel over the fireplace and looked into it. The face that looked back was that of a camel, with a huge hump coming out of his back, orange-tan fur, and a god-awful smell like a compost heap on a sunny day.

Then he noticed the tiny needle taped to the brick wall above the mantel next to the mirror. "No. . . *it can't be!*" For even he knew that passage.

"And that is your doorway to the Kingdom of God," said the Devil. "Now all you need to do is just go through the eye of that needle, and you will spend eternity in Heaven!"

Caleb put one eye against the eye of the needle. He could barely make out people on a beach, laughing and playing, splashing in the water, tanning on the side. Then the face of Saint Peter came into view, his wart so close Caleb could make out each gross hair.

"Well, Caleb, what are you waiting for?" the saint exclaimed, giggling. "There's a hot tub right here on the beach. Come join us!" He stepped back, and he saw little Billy standing next to him, holding a beach ball, a white halo over his head that matched Saint Peter's.

"Hi mister!" the boy cried out. Then he turned and ran off into the beach.

"Better hurry," said the Devil behind him. "You don't have a lot of time."

Caleb butted his camel head against the eye, frantically trying to squeeze through, then smashed it against the needle, knocking out both front teeth against the brick wall. Dust and broken mortar flew through the air. He barely noticed his transformation back to human form as the walls on all sides came tumbling down, the flames came in, and he screamed. . . forever.

Alternative Beatitudes for the New Right

Janka Hobbs

Blessed be the warmongers, for they shall become rich.
Blessed be the rich, for they shall control the flow of information.
Blessed be the businessmen, for they have measurable worth.
Blessed be the lucky, for they know their God loves them.

Blessed be wealthy white men, for they have created a God in their own image.
Blessed be those who lack imagination, for they shall believe what they are told.
Blessed be those who mock science, for reality is in the eye of the beholder.
Blessed be the ignorant, for they shall not know any better.

Blessed be the self-righteous, for they shall persecute others.

Blessed be those who persecute others, for they shall feel vindicated.
Blessed be those who lack empathy, for they are not troubled by guilt.
Blessed be the polluters, for they shall bring on the end of the Earth.

Woe unto the abused, because they must have brought it upon themselves.

Woe unto the poor, because they must
occasionally sleep.
Woe unto women, because they do not
produce sperm.
Woe unto the suffering, because everything
happens for a reason.

Lilith's Daughters

Liam Hogan

"And on the sixth day, God created Lilith and Adam—"

"Adam and *Eve*, Mummy!" my darling little one corrected.

I gave her a stern look and she shrank beneath the cartoon dinosaur bedspread. "Eve came later."

"That's not what Sister Rose says." Amy's voice was a little squeaky, a little unsure.

"Genesis is murky," I observed, eyebrow raised. "If you actually read it, that is, rather than what they teach at St Stephens."

Her uncertainty lingered. It had been a bit of a shock when Amy asked to go to Sunday School. I'd been secretly thanking the first amendment for keeping religion out of the state school system. I should have been paying more attention to her friends, to her first-grade class mates. To who was being invited, or more importantly *not* invited, to sleepovers and birthday parties.

Peer pressure trumps parental atheism, every time.

"I *like* what Sister Rose teaches. . ."

A less appropriate name would be hard to come by. No 'Sister', that was certain. When she wasn't meddling with the minds of innocents on Sunday mornings she till-checked at the hardware store out on the Interstate. As for 'Rose', this one didn't smell so sweet; more stale tobacco and moth balls than floral. But, since Amy had to find her own way, I could hardly tell my cherub what I really thought of the Sunday School spinster.

I was damned, however, if I'd let all the nonsense my daughter came home with go unchallenged.

I leaned in and we rubbed noses, her eyes widening and struggling to focus, going cross-eyed with the effort. Lowering my voice to a hushed whisper I asked: "Do you want to know the rest of the story?"

Amy nodded, her hand sneaking out from beneath the covers to find mine, her features reanimated with an easy smile.

"Ok then. What the Sunday School version doesn't tell you is that God created man twice."

"Twice?"

"Yup. The first was shortly after creating the animals he didn't have time for on day five. I quote: 'So God created mankind in his own image, in the image of God he created them, male and female he created them.'"

I felt her grip loosen in confusion. "Excuse the mangled syntax, blame Genesis 1:27, not me. So: unnamed male and *female* humans, number unspecified, created together."

"What's a sin-tax, mummy?"

"That's for another time. When you're older."

The pout was almost as endearing as her smile. "I *am* older," she said, "I'm six!"

I shook my head and plowed on.

"The second time—and this is after a day's rest, over in Genesis 2—he creates Adam and from him, or from a part of him, Eve. Sticks them in the garden of Eden with a tree full of temptation and a serpent."

"I know *that* story."

"Well, ignore it. It's hooey."

"Hooey?" Amy's eyes widened.

"Hooey," I repeated. "Listen up, this here is the *real* story."

She settled back on her stegosaurus-shaped pillow. Amy was a smart little six-year-old. She'd already been through the shock of discovering the shoes in the written version of *Wizard of Oz* weren't ruby red, and she still hadn't forgiven me for suggesting Cinderella's slipper was probably squirrel fur, not glass. She knew that stories were made up and made up things changed. The 'real' story was simply the version someone else thought was fixed, unalterable. "Gospel".

"So before Eve, there were Adam and Lilith, Lilith and Adam. Debate rages over which of them was created first; some saying it must be Lilith, as God is a woman—"

"He is? *She* is?" Her mouth round in astonishment.

"Hush, little one, otherwise I'll never get to the end. Some say it must be Adam, as God is a man. I say he-she created them at the same time, because God is, must be, *both*. Which explains the confusion of what I read out a moment ago, 'And God created male *and* female in His/Her own image.'"

Amy looked doubtful. There was a very real danger of getting lost in the details. "Hmm. Since tonight storyteller and listener are female—that's you and I, kiddo—I'm going to be using 'She' as shorthand for 'God' going forward. Is that OK?"

Amy nodded solemnly.

"Lilith was Adam's equal. Equal in intelligence, in courage, in morals, and in number of ribs. In pretty much every way except for one: *she* didn't get in a huff when Adam tried to get it on. She simply said "No". Politely, even, which is sensible when you're the only two people around."

Amy squirmed. The trick, I'd decided early on once it was clear I would be raising my daughter on my own, was not to gloss things over. Words and expressions could and would be discovered in a whole host of different places and trying to avoid them or worse, lie about their meaning, was plainly foolish even at such a tender age.

What they *meant* to Amy evolved. Right now, 'getting it on' was a mysteriously icky thing adults did, which was just about fine.

"Adam, however, was mightily put out. The story goes— the one written by men—that Adam complained to God and God made Eve as a replacement. And Lilith got forgotten.

"If you go to your books and look for her, you're not going to get a whole lot of joy," I told Amy. "She's not in the

King James Bible at all, so don't go asking your Sunday School teachers about her, all right?"

Amy looked like she was about to argue the point until I held out my little finger for a pinky promise, hoping it was one she'd keep. The problem with those Sunday School stories was that they're *powerful*. While I myself had a penchant for Roald Dahl's *Matilda*, it's hard to argue with the bible's "Greatest Story Ever Told" tagline. And that's for the marginally less fantastical New Testament, when God calmed down a bit.

The only way to counteract such ammunition was with other stories. And not just things I could make up; I needed stories that had history, that could *compete*.

Fortunately, there were more of them out there than most people knew about. You just had to look a little harder.

"Lilith was mostly written out. No bible stories at all. Just some old tales that call her all sort of bad names." I spared Amy the full explanation; the ancient stories closer to myth than religion, the Babylonian Talmud, for example. Stories that paint Lilith as the most wicked of wicked people; a witch, a child snatcher, a temptress, a demon, a vampire. Even her name translates as "night terror".

"That's not fair," my little darling insisted. "What did Lilith do wrong?"

"Nothing, hon. Nothing at all. She's punished for not bending to Adam's desires. For being his equal. For wanting control over her own body. For wanting to be on top."

Amy giggled and I winced. I'd gotten carried away, she was only six after all. "Ah, never mind that last bit. Here's the take home message, kiddo. It's *Eve* that's the myth. There was and is no such creature. She's what men wanted, not what God made. Man's invention, because some men are afraid of strong women. Eve is what men call Lilith—what they call you and I—when they're trying to con us."

Amy's eyelids were fluttering. Bless. I'd rambled on too long. Time to wrap things up.

"Do you know what 'con' is short for, Amy? It's 'Confidence'. Eve is a confidence trick. A way of suggesting women are secondary, weak and inferior. Are obligated to men. And are somehow solely responsible for the fall from Paradise, for all the sin in the world, taxed or otherwise.

"It's not true; not if you don't let it be."

I kissed my daughter's forehead, inhaling innocence.

"So, Amy Spencer, light of my life, love of my heart. Next time Billy Hutton says you can't do something just because you're a girl, what are you going to do?"

Called upon to answer from the fringes of sleep Amy frowned for a moment. "Be like Lilith," she said, a soft smile transforming her adorable little face.

I tucked her in, dimmed the bedside light, eyes adjusting beneath a constellation of glow-in-the-dark stars. "Atta-girl, Amy. Atta-girl."

Believing

Jane Yolen

". . . she brisked out, plump with Jesus."
Ursula K. Le Guin, from "Religious Connections"

Your beliefs should be held close
but not close to me who chooses a
different route.
Don't crowd my path, please, and I'll keep
my size nine and a half boots off yours.
You're pregnant with your message, I get
it,
and want to be delivered of it.
I'm neither your midwife nor your birthing
coach.
I don't want to swaddle your beliefs
in a blanket of my choosing.
This inn is closed from now till—well—
eternity or the infinite dark, whichever
comes.
I don't expect to be around to do wheelies
in wings
or burn in some everlasting vengeance fire
by an easily-slighted god.
I hope neither one of us is disappointed.
But then hope has always been one of my
curses,
not certainty—which is yours.

Angelica

Jill Zeller

"Did you hear that they're increasing our caseloads again?"

"That's a baseless rumor, Armiel."

"No. Fact. Starmiel told me, and she's like *this* with the Boss. They walk to the Terminal Bar every day after work, did you know that? You're oblivious to everything, Juriel."

"I choose to be. It makes life simpler."

"Anyway, she said a 25 % increase in cases. By the end of the year. And we won't even see an improvement in our metrics until the third quarter."

Sound of stringed instrument falling to the ground with a twang.

"Be careful!"

"Sorry, Juriel, but your office is a disaster zone. A Red Cross sniffer dog couldn't even find you in here. And why you chose the banjo as your stringed instrument doesn't make sense to any of us, unless you're just a poser after all, being all anarchic. I suppose you thought it was funny."

"Nothing's funny about this job."

"You know what I just realized about you? You're an idealist. A romantic, and now you're bitter. No wonder no one likes you. You complain all the time. 'No one tells me anything.' You bitch and moan."

An email ping in the background.

"No one does tell me anything."

"See? Point made. I'm telling you something, because I think you're probably the smartest Agent in the entire office. Something is wrong upstairs."

"You're just figuring this out now?"

"Hear me out."

Rustling papers, clink of coffee mugs being pushed aside.

"Now. Juriel. Listen. We've had a hiring freeze for the last 50 or so *anno dominis*, right? Ever since the Movement, what-do-you-call-it, and all that big ruckus. The biggest since the Reformation, remember?"

"The Secularity."

"Right. That. I mean, we're big all around the world—Latin America, the European Diaspora, Africa and all, but it's been tough ever since the Secularity. The Thrones Congress made that decision to freeze hiring because invocations dropped way down."

"I think it was more complicated than that—"

"Whatever. Hiring freeze was the outcome. But now—"

More shifting papers. The sound of papers hitting the floor.

"Oh, sorry. Anyway. Now, Juriel, what's your caseload?"

"126.5."

"Is that million or billion?"

A moment of silence.

"Don't look at me like that. Ok, your caseload is 126.5 million, rounded up, right? And how many more cases are filling up your roster? Right now. Show me."

Sound of wheels on a tile floor. Tapping computer keys. Silence.

"Wow. Juriel. That's crazy. Look there's another one. The numbers keep—another one! It's worse than I thought."

"Maybe they've increased the workload four months early."

"I'd better go check my numbers."

Sound of someone kicking a waste can.

"Hey, be careful. I keep my consecrated wine in there."

"Is that how you keep your plants looking so good? Oops."

"Oh, Armiel, you just broke off the new shoot of my Wandering Jew."

"What are we going to do, Juriel? How can we possibly keep up with all the pain and suffering? How can we answer all the requests, the prayers, the *milagos,* and the candles? I get fifty or more candles an hour."

"They send all the apostolic stuff to you, because you're good at that. But me, I get everything else. I even have sworn, died-in-the-wool atheists sneaking prayer notes into the slots whenever they tour a cathedral. And it's worse than ever. You can't tell me different. Prayers from children separated from their parents by unfair laws. LGBTQ folks begging for relief from discrimination. Requests for enough money to feed families until the end of the month, prayers for jobs, for enough money to go to school, for young men of color murdered by police. For the police who shoot them, too. It never stops, Armiel and it has gotten a lot worse. A lot. People are suffering more than ever, fleeing persecution, even in the so called 'civilized' nations. There's so much hatred. Anger. The Boss's name being taken in vain over and over."

Silence. Sound of a quiet sob.

"Oh, Armiel. I didn't mean to make you cry. I cry too. Every day at 1:45pm I close my door and weep. It's a thing, now, a movement, a historical shift. In the eons of creation, it's just a blip. I only wish we could do more. I do wish that."

"So do I, Juriel. So do I. You really are the best of us. Really the best. You should ask for a promotion. The Boss could use you upstairs. You'd keep a harness on the Thrones."

"Thanks, Armiel. But I belong here, on the lowest tier where I can do the most good. There needs to be more good in the world."

"Right-o. Say, would you play me that song? The one you learned from that folk singer a while ago."

"He sure is a nice guy. Be happy to."

Sound of banjo tuning. Then strumming, and a celestial voice.

"This land is your land. . . "

Whose Good News?

Joanna Hoyt

An open letter to my brothers and sisters on the Christian right

Dear Brothers and Sisters in Christ,

I'm finding it difficult to be openly Christian in America today. I've heard some of you say that this is hard because Christians are being persecuted. I haven't experienced persecution. I'm just struggling with the ways in which I hear my faith being used to hurt the very people in whom we're told we'll meet Jesus.

Can we talk about that?

You and I worship Jesus. We strive to serve him, imitate him, and draw people to him. I've seen the love, zeal, courage and self-discipline you bring to this. I've volunteered beside you in soup kitchens, sung with you on Sundays, prayed for you and been grateful for your prayers. I know we're members one of another (Romans 12:5). Sometimes when we talk about vital political questions we seem to be strangers and adversaries. I hope we can look at the things that divide us without forgetting the things that unite us.

oOo

We all want to encourage people to encounter Jesus. But how do we speak in Jesus' name? Do our words draw people in?

I'm a Christian. When I hear some of my fellow progressives describe Christians as ignorant superstitious cruel hypocritical bigots, I feel shamed and furious. Sometimes I remember that I am supposed to pray for people in those moments, and to try to understand the hurt that may lie behind their words. Too often I just resent them.

I'm also a progressive and a Medicaid recipient. When I hear some of you describing Medicaid recipients as lazy welfare leeches, or progressives as enemies of our country and our God, I respond with the same blend of shame and fury, the same struggle to pray and listen rather than striking back. I suspect that non-Christian progressives have a similar response—and some may generalize that response to all Christians, whom they associate with the angriest speakers they've heard.

It's not just bad tactics to revile other living souls made in God's image; it's also bad Christianity. Jesus tells us to bless people who curse us (Luke 6:28). James says, "With the tongue we praise our Lord and Father, and with it we curse human beings, who have been made in God's likeness. . . This should not be," (James 3:9-10) and warns, "Human anger does not produce the righteousness that God desires. . . Those who consider themselves religious and yet do not keep a tight rein on their tongues deceive themselves, and their religion is worthless." (James 1:20, 26) Jesus also warns us against judging and suggests strongly that we remove the planks from our own eyes before picking specks out of the eyes of our neighbors. (Matthew 7:2-5) What would happen if Christians took that seriously? If we confessed the harm done by our people and tried to make restitution? If we acknowledged the good as well as the evil in people who disagree with us?

oOo

We all want to serve and obey Jesus. How does our treatment of other people reflect that?

In Mark 12:29-31 Jesus says the most important commandments are to love God wholeheartedly and to love our neighbors as ourselves. In Matthew 25 he shows that these two commandments are really one. Christ is God. Christ promises that he will come to us in "the least of these," in our neighbors who need our help. What we do for—or to—those neighbors is what we do for—or to—God.

I know you know this. When a neighbor's kid is sick, when a friend is injured at work, when a fellow parishioner's house burns down, you help out, raise money, offer comfort. But I've heard some of you deny that same neighborly care to people who are less familiar to you. I've heard some of you say we should turn away refugees and imprison asylum seekers, quoting Pat Buchanan or Franklin Graham about how Muslim immigrants will undermine "our Christian nation". Sometimes you say that we have to help our own people first, and can't take any thought for others' needs so long as there are still suffering white native-born Christians.

But that's not what Jesus taught. In Luke 10, when Jesus laid out the central commandment to love our neighbors, a listener asked, "Who is my neighbor?" Jesus told the story of a Samaritan—one of those people whom Jesus' people sometimes saw as invaders, racially and religiously foreign and wrong—who showed mercy to one of Jesus' people. Jesus said we're all supposed to follow that Samaritan's example; that the Other who needs our mercy is the neighbor whom we must love as ourselves.

Jesus had said such things before. Luke 4 describes how Jesus told his home congregation that God's prophets are sent to people from outside their in-groups—that in the great famine Elijah helped and was helped by a Sidonian widow, not an Israelite, and brought a cure for leprosy to a Syrian, not an Israelite. At this the worshippers became enraged and tried to kill Jesus.

Jesus himself was a refugee child; when he was a baby his parents fled with him into Egypt to escape Herod's death squads. As an adult Jesus was killed by the government, which was trying to protect national security; his death was approved by religious leaders who wanted to preserve the purity of their tradition and also the comfortable relationship they had worked out with the State.

Jesus said in Matthew 25 that he will come to us as a stranger, and that we will not recognize him. What would our churches look like, what would our world look like, if we remembered that what we do to aliens and strangers is what we do to Jesus? If we stopped condemning Jesus and turning him away to die in Jesus' name?

oOo

I also hear some of you condemning, not helping, people whose suffering is caused by the actions of our government—saying that we must punish undocumented immigrants and take away their children because God means us to follow the law, condemning Black Lives Matter protestors as unpatriotic while ignoring the injustices they are protesting, reposting Franklin Graham's remarks about how police shootings could be prevented if people obeyed orders unquestioningly, saying that the Bible tells people to submit to the authorities. I know that Paul said in Romans 13, "Whoever rebels against the authority is rebelling against what God has instituted. . ." But let's consider what the rest of the Bible says about resistance and obedience to the authorities. The Roman authorities killed Paul. They killed Jesus too. Shiphrah, Puah and Moses disobeyed Pharaoh's unjust commands. Shadrach, Meshach, Abednego and Daniel defied the edicts of Babylon's ruler. Elijah, Jeremiah, and many other prophets challenged the rulers of their own Hebrew people who had turned away from God and exploited the poor. Paul wrote in Hebrews 13:3 "Remember those in prison as if you were together with them in prison, and those who are mistreated as if you yourselves were suffering." Jesus told us in Matthew 25 that he would be in prison and that we would not recognize him. What would our churches look like if we cared for prisoners and people at risk from the authorities as we care for ourselves, or as we would wish to care for Jesus? What would our country and our world look like?

oOo

Following Jesus more closely, and looking more closely for Jesus in the suffering people around us, is not a recipe for the success or security or prestige that some people say Christians deserve. But I don't believe that Jesus' good news promised us any of those things. The devil offered all those things to Jesus at the beginning of his ministry (Matthew 4 / Luke 4), and Jesus turned them down. Jesus calls us to let go of our possessions and privileges. To give freely. To see Christ in neighbors and strangers. To acknowledge and remedy our own harmdoing before we chastise others. To love and forgive enemies. To die to ourselves. God loves us and God remains in us and with us, always. Jesus lives, suffers and dies in every person hurt by our injustices. Jesus lives in us, bringing strength and compassion in our sufferings, bringing the chance of repentance and forgiveness in our wrongdoing, bringing joy and abundance of life.

I still call myself a Christian, despite all the harm that's been done in Christianity's name, because I believe in that Good News. Can we work together to claim that Good News in our own lives and share it with the world?

Your sister in Christ,
Joanna Michal Hoyt

Contributors

Sara Codair, the cover designer, is also a writer. They live with a cat, Goose, who "edits" their work by deleting entire pages. They teach and tutor at a community college, write when they should be sleeping, and read every speculative novel they can get their hands on. Sara's debut novel, *Power Surge*, will be published by NineStar Press on October 1, 2018. Find Sara online at https:saracodair.com/ or @shatteredsmooth.

Gwyndyn T. Alexander is a feminist, activist poet. She lives in New Orleans with her husband Jonathan. They are owned by Scout, who is a cat. She is a dick, but they love her.

When not writing, Gwyndyn creates fabulous feathered barrettes and headpieces. Her motto is "Be the parade you want to see in the world!"

Tom Barlow is an Ohio writer whose works straddle the literary, crime and science fiction markets. Over 80 stories of his may be found in anthologies including *Best American Mystery Stories 2013, Best of Ohio Short Stories #2,* and *Best New Writing 2011,* and many periodicals including *Hobart, Temenos, Redivider, The Intergalactic Medicine Show, Crossed Genres, Mystery Weekly, Red Room,* and *Switchblade.* He is also author of the science fiction novel *I'll Meet You Yesterday.*

More information may be found at his web site, www.tjbarlow.com.

David Brin is an astrophysicist whose international best-selling novels include *The Postman, Earth,* and recently *Existence.* Dr. Brin serves on advisory boards (e.g. NASA's Innovative and Advanced Concepts program or NIAC) and speaks or consults on a wide range of topics. His nonfiction book about the information age—*The Transparent Society*—

won the Freedom of Speech Award of the American Library Association.

(http://www.davidbrin.com)

Anton Cancre daylights as a herder of teenagers and has oozed symbolic word-farms onto the pages of *Jamais Vu, D.O.A. II*, and the *Quick Shivers* series while vomiting malformed literary opinions at *Cemetery Dance* as well as editing *Recompose Magazine*. His mommy is quite proud of her vicious little boy.

Adam-Troy Castro made his first non-fiction sale to SPY magazine in 1987. Among his books to date include four Spider-Man novels, 3 novels about his profoundly damaged far-future murder investigator Andrea Cort, and 6 middle-grade novels about the dimension-spanning adventures of that very strange but very heroic young boy, Gustav Gloom. Adam's darker short fiction for grownups is highlighted by his collection, *Her Husband's Hands And Other Stories* (Prime Books). Adam's works have won the Philip K. Dick Award and the Seiun (Japan), and have been nominated for eight Nebulas, three Stokers, two Hugos, and, internationally, the Ignotus (Spain), the Grand Prix de l'Imaginaire (France), and the Kurd-Laßwitz Preis (Germany). He lives in Florida with his wife Judi and either three or four cats, depending on what day you're counting and whether Gilbert's escaped this week.

Melvin Charles grew up virtually alone in the basement of a house in Kansas where books were his escape. In the cranny's of that basement he found old clothbound books with slick pages and woodprints that told him of Horatio at the Bridge and other epic work. Plutarch guided him through history and the Greek and Roman gods lived alongside Jesus in his pantheon. Librarians would nod as he stood in the musty aisles, scanning the books for his next meal. He lives quietly in seclusion with his computer and dog.

C. A. Chesse is an evangelical turned skeptic who lives in Portland, Oregon. Formerly a resident of Houston, Texas, her entry explores the messages she grew up with, both stated and implied. She attended elementary at Second Baptist School, which also produced Ted Cruz. You can visit her at cmtaylor.dreamwidth.org.

J. W. Cook is an avid reader who loves everything that has to do with science fiction and fantasy. He has three college degrees (none of which are in English or Writing) and works in emergency preparedness in the nuclear waste cleanup field. When he is not working, reading or writing, he likes to hang out with his wife and his five—yes, five—dogs, play video games and occasionally leave his house. Joe is currently working on completing his YA fantasy series, The Harbingers of Magic.

Lillian Csernica's fiction has appeared in *Weird Tales*, *Fantastic Stories*, and *Killing it Softly Vol. 1* and *Vol. 2*. Her pirate novel *Ship of Dreams* is available from Digital Fiction Publishing. Born in San Diego, Lillian is a genuine California native. She currently resides in the Santa Cruz mountains with her husband, two sons, and three cats. Visit her at lillian888.wordpress.com.

James Dorr Indiana (USA) writer James Dorr's The Tears Of Isis was a 2013 Bram Stoker Award® nominee for Superior Achievement in a Fiction Collection. Other books include *Strange Mistresses: Tales Of Wonder And Romance*, *Darker Loves: Tales Of Mystery And Regret*, and his all-poetry *Vamps (A Retrospective)*. His latest, out in June 2017 from Elder Signs Press, is a novel-in-stories, *Tombs: A Chronicle Of Latter-Day Times Of Earth*.

An Active Member of HWA and SFWA with more than 500 individual appearances from *Alfred Hitchcock's Mystery Magazine* to *Xenophilia*, Dorr invites readers to visit his blog at http://jamesdorrwriter.wordpress.com/

Colin Patrick Ennen writes from the high-altitude desert of Albuquerque, New Mexico, amid frequent interruptions from his dog, Shylock. (Yes, he's a pretentious Shakespeare nerd.) This is his second appearance in a B-cubed title, having also been seen in *Writers Resist* and *The*

Coil. Someday he may actually finish a novel he starts. Find him on Twitter @cpennen

Joyce Frohn became a writer after her beloved slimemolds couldn't pay her. She has been published professionally over two hundred times. She is married and has a teen-aged daughter. She has two cats, a lizard and too many dust bunnies. She would like to thank the monsters under her bed for having such interesting lives.

David Gerrold was a runner up for this year's one-line biography award, coming in only six votes behind Vonda N. McIntyre's one-line bio.

Debora Godfrey was previously published in *More Alternative Truths: Stories from the Resistance.* She lives in a modern-day commune (cohousing) on Bainbridge Island, Washington, with one husband (part-time), two dogs, two birds, and a variable number of lawyers.

Philip Brian Hall is a Yorkshireman and a graduate of Oxford University. A former diplomat and teacher, at one time or another he's stood for parliament, sung solos in amateur operettas, rowed at Henley Royal Regatta, completed a 40 mile cross-country walk in under 12 hours and ridden in over one hundred steeplechase horse races. He now lives on a very small farm in Scotland.

Philip's had short stories published in the USA and Canada as well as the UK. His novel, *The Prophets of Baal* is available as an e-book and in paperback.

He blogs at *sliabhmannan.blogspot.co.uk/*

Paula Hammond has been in love with stories since she was old enough to read them for herself. When not hunkered over a keyboard, she can be found prowling London's crusty underbelly in search of random weirdness.

Larry Hodges is an active member of SFWA with over 90 short story sales, including 26 "pro" sales—14 to Galaxy's Edge and 12 others, including a recent one to Analog. His third novel, *Campaign 2100: Game of Scorpions,* came out in March, 2016, from World Weaver Press. He also co-wrote a novel with Mike Resnick and Lezli Robyn, *When Parallel Lines Meet,* which came out in spring, 2017. He's a graduate of the six-week 2006 Odyssey Writers Workshop, the 2007 Orson Scott Card Literary Boot Camp, and the two-week 2008 Taos Toolbox Writers Workshop. In the world of non-fiction, he's a full-time writer with thirteen books and over 1800 published articles in over 150 different publications.

Liam Hogan is an Oxford Physics graduate and award winning London based writer. His short story "Ana", appears in *Best of British Science Fiction 2016* (NewCon Press) and his twisted fantasy collection, "Happy Ending Not Guaranteed", is published by Arachne Press. Http://happyendingnotguaranteed.blogspot.co.uk/ or tweet @LiamJHogan

M. J. Holt's stories and poems appear in the poetry anthology *300K, Short-Story.me, Gutter Eloquence, Big Beautiful Woman, Timeless Love*, and other fiction and non-fiction publications. She abandoned consulting and the city to live on a certified organic farm with her husband and many animals on a peninsula in Puget Sound where she writes full-time. She is a member of SFWA and MWA.

Janka Hobbs lives in the Puget Sound lowlands, where she studies Aikido and Botany when she's not playing with words. Visit her blog at http://jankahobbs.com

Joanna Michal Hoyt is a Quaker who lives and works with her family at St. Francis Farm, a Catholic Worker community in upstate NY which seeks to live a sustainable life based on the Gospels and on Catholic Worker principles as an alternative to the consumer culture.

Joanna grew up among people whose faith shaped their lives—and led them to very different practices and party orientations. She's worked and worshipped with people whose lives are shaped by different faith traditions. She's seeking open-minded and open-hearted conversations about how faith shapes our lives, and if you disagree with what she's written here she'd be glad to hear from you: write to joannahoyt@yahoo.com

Her essays have appeared in publications including Uisio, *Friends Journal: Quaker Thought and Life* Today, and The Christian Shakespeare; her short stories have appeared in venues including *Factor Four Fiction, Crossed Genres*, and *Mysterion: Rediscovering the Mysteries of the Christian Faith.* For more information see http://joannamichalhoyt.com

E.E. King is a painter, performer, writer, and biologist—she'll do anything that won't pay the bills, especially if it involves animals.

Ray Bradbury calls her stories "marvelously inventive, wildly funny and deeply thought-provoking. I cannot recommend them highly enough."

Her books include *Dirk Quigby's Guide to the Afterlife, Electric Detective, Pandora's Card Game, The Truth of Fiction* and *Blood Prism.*

King has won awards and fellowships for art, writing, and environmental research, most recently the Whodunit 2018 award.

She was the founding Director of the Esperanza Community Housing's Art & Science Program, worked as an artist-in-residence in Los Angeles, San Francisco, Sarajevo and the J. Paul Getty Museum's and Science Center's Arts & Science Development Program.

Her landmark mural, A Meeting of the Minds (121' x 33') can be seen on Mercado La Paloma in Los Angeles. King has also painted murals for Escuelas Para La Vida in Cuneca, Spain and in Tuscany, Italy.

She's worked with children in Bosnia, crocodiles in Mexico, frogs in Puerto Rico, egrets in Bali, mushrooms in Montana, archaeologists in Spain, butterflies in South Central Los Angeles, lectured on island evolution and marine biology on cruise ships in the South Pacific and the Caribbean, and has been published widely.

Check out paintings, writing and musings at www.elizabetheveking.com

Rebecca McFarland Kyle Born on Friday 13, Rebecca developed an early love for the unusual. Dragons, vampires and all manner of magical beings haunt her thoughts and stir her to the keyboard. She currently lives between the Smoky and Cumberland mountains with her husband and three cats. Her first YA novel, *Fanny & Dice*, was released on Halloween 2015. In 2017, she will be editing a charity anthology and releasing works in young adult, urban fantasy and dark fantasy. She's working on both short and long fiction on her own and with co-conspirators.

Louise Milton is a writer, social worker, mother of four grown daughters, and a wife with a wife. She has lived and worked in Northern BC for the last twenty odd years. Previous writing credits for fiction are *The Home Team* which aired on CBC Radio Alberta Anthology in February 1989 and *The Birth Circle* in *Voices and Echoes: Canadian Women's Spirituality,* eds. Jo-Anne Elder & Colin O'Connell, 1997.

During her hiatus from writing fiction she established a career in geriatric social work, earned a Master's Degree in social work, and took on the arduous but amply rewarding journey of guiding four daughters from infancy to adulthood. Currently she works as a manager in Health Care and lives in the tiny rural community of Salmon Valley, ten kilometers north of Prince George. She lives contentedly in a barn-like country home with her wife and three cats including the fierce and semi-feral Samuel Levi who guards the household against the visiting bears. Many times she has thought that this home has been waiting for her all her life and now that she has arrived she can be at peace.

Kara Race-Moore studied history at Simmons College as an excuse to read about the soap opera lives of British royals. She worked in educational publishing, casting the molds for future generations' minds, but has since moved into the more civilized world of litigation. Ms. Race-Moore first came to science fiction through Anne McCaffrey and is still grateful to her for showing an impressible teenager that women can be in and write science fiction too.

P. James Norris is working on three novels, one of which, *The Order of the Brotherhood*, is a work of dystopian fiction set in a prison that investigates the value of democracy in an America that has largely forgotten it. In 2018 he started getting short stories published by the likes of *Moon Magazine, Fantasia Divinity, Tigershark Publishing* and *Rhetoric Askew*. He's written several spec teleplays, including an original TV pilot *Project Ωmega*. He lives in Idaho with his wife and a dog and two cats, where he is pursuing his PhD in Physics. He can be reached at https://www.linkedin.com/in/pjamesnorris/

Irene Radford has been writing stories ever since she figured out what a pencil was for. A member of an endangered species—a native Oregonian who lives in Oregon—she and her husband make their home in Welches, Oregon. The will often look out on the woods from their back deck, where deer, bears, coyotes, hawks, owls, woodpeckers, and cougars feed regularly.

Want to be the first to see new covers, new releases, and updates on public appearances? Sign up for the newsletter at: www.phyllisames.com/newsletters She promises no spam. Just an occasional notification. Or check out all of her titles at www.ireneradford.net

Mike Resnick is the author of 77 novels, more than 280 stories, and 3 screenplays. He has edited 42 anthologies, and currently edits Galaxy's Edge Magazine and Stellar Guild Books. According to Locus, Mike is the all-time leading award winner for short fiction. He has won 5 Hugos (from a record 37 nominations), a Nebula, and other major awards in the USA, France, Japan, Spain, Catalonia, Croatia, Poland, and China. He was Guest of Honor at the 2012 Worldcon. His daughter, Laura, is also a science fiction writer, and won the 1993 Campbell Award as Best Newcomer.

Heather Truett is a writer, a mother, and a somewhat heretical pastor's wife. Her credits include: *The Mom Egg, Vine Leaves Literary, Tipton Poetry Journal, Drunk Monkeys, Panoply Zine,* and the *Young Adult Review Network*.

Charles Walbridge is retired from working as an environmental biologist. Follows algae news the way some people follow sports news. Apparently incapable of writing dystopian fiction. Currently tracking the co-evolution of human and artificial intelligence.

Jill Zeller is the author of numerous short stories and novels. She lives near Seattle, Washington with her patient husband, two self-absorbed cats and their thralls, two adult English Mastiffs. Her works explore the geography of reality. Some may call it fantasy but there are rarely swords and never elves.

For more go to https://jillzeller.com or visit her Facebook page https://www.facebook.com/scribblerjmz/

Jane Yolen who has been politically active most of her life (including being a delegate to the 1972 Democratic Convention pledged to McGovern) is often called "the Hans Christian Andersen of America." She has over 370 published books including *Owl Moon*, *The Devil's Arithmetic*, *How Do Dinosaurs Say Goodnight* and two books of political poems—*The Bloody Tide* and *Before/The Vote/After*.

Her works, which range from very young rhymed picture books to novels and poetry for adults and every genre in between, have won an assortment of awards including two Nebulas, a World Fantasy Award, a Caldecott, the Golden Kite, three Mythopoeic awards, two Christopher Medals, a nomination for the National Book Award, the Jewish Book Award, the Kerlan Award, and the Catholic Library's Regina Medal, as well as six honorary doctorates. One of her awards set her good coat on fire. She lives in Massachusetts most of the year, but Scotland in the summer. She writes a poem a day.

Meg Bee is from a small town in Southern Utah, where she has always been a true fish out of water. Whether she's rocking blue tights with combat boots, or fishnets under ripped jeans, Megan does the electric boogaloo to the beat of her own drum. She is a writer, voracious reader, lover of red lipstick and all things vintage.

The recipient of several awards, including the Lorenzo

Snow award and a Utah Press Association award for her work as a journalist, Megan's two collections of poetry, *Mermaid in the Valley*, and *Junkyard Princess*, explore the themes of grief, love and discovering what happens when you stop being nice, and start getting real.

Christopher Nadeau is the author of the novels *Dreamers of Infinity's Core* and Kaiju as well as over three dozen short stories in various anthologies and magazines. He received positive mention from Ramsey Campbell for his short story "Always Say Treat," which was compared to the work of Ray Bradbury and has received positive reviews from SFRevue and zombiecoffeepress. Chris has also served as special editor for Voluted Magazine's 'The Darkness Internal' which he created.

He resides in Southeastern Michigan and works for two libraries.

Jim Wright is a retired US Navy Chief Warrant Officer and freelance writer. He lives in Florida where he watches American politics in a perpetual state of amused disgust. He's been called the Tool of Satan, but he prefers the title: Satan's Designated Driver. He is the mind behind Stonekettle Station. You can email him at jim@stonekettle.com. You can follow him on Twitter @stonekettle or you can join the boisterous bunch he hosts on Facebook at Facebook/Stonekettle. Remember to bring brownies and mind the white cat, he bites. Hard.

Thanks Phyl,
it's been a hoot.
Bob B

Made in the USA
Middletown, DE
21 January 2019